MW00648001

BURNED AND SCARRED

BRENDA POPPY

First published by Glass Fish Publishing 2021

Copyright © 2021 by Brenda Poppy

All rights reserved. No part of this publication may be reproduced, stored or transmitted in any form or by any means, electronic, mechanical, photocopying, recording, scanning, or otherwise without written permission from the publisher. It is illegal to copy this book, post it to a website, or distribute it by any other means without permission.

This novel is entirely a work of fiction. The names, characters and incidents portrayed in it are the work of the author's imagination. Any resemblance to actual persons, living or dead, events or localities is entirely coincidental.

First edition
ISBN: 978-1-7356181-2-8

www.glassfishpublishing.com

To all the damsels who
can save themselves from distress.

And to all those willing to take a chance on
indie books and their eccentric authors.

Prologue

Auburn stared down into the depths of the Pit, contemplating death. Seeing as she was bound, gagged, and surrounded by armed Peace Officers, it was a rather imminent concern.

She took a moment to glance at the soldiers gathered around her and counted eight guns pointed in her direction. They sure had rolled out the cavalry for her. Well, technically for her and Hale. But since the strongman was currently lying unconscious on the ground, the soldiers were focusing the majority of their attention on her.

When she'd asked why so many officers needed to be on hand to watch her jump to her death, she'd been told they were there for "encouragement." As in they were there to encourage her to throw herself down the large hole that led to oblivion.

No one knew for certain what was down there. Some believed that the bottom was covered with large spikes that would impale a person the moment they reached the ground. Others thought the hole might go directly to the center of the planet, where the jumper would be burned alive in an instant. Still more believed that it was just a big hole, and anyone who went down it would simply go *splat*.

Burn, as she was commonly called, didn't know what she believed. All of those options seemed like a gruesome way to go. If she had been given a choice in the manner of her death, she would have chosen none of the above.

Still, curiosity tugged at her, so she sent her senses into the depths in search of answers. That was her gift after all.

Due to some combination of Kasis' pollution and the planet's inherently toxic atmosphere, over the last few generations some of the citizens had started to develop differences, changes in their genetic makeup that allowed them to do things that normal people couldn't. For Burn, that meant the ability to detect even the smallest sounds – the hints of a whisper or the faintest rustle of movement.

Yet right now she couldn't hear a thing. As she listened to the Pit, it stayed silent, giving no hints of the secrets that lay inside. The quiet was disconcerting, and Burn didn't know what to make of it. Was there truly nothing down there? Or was it such a long drop that even she couldn't penetrate the depths? Both scenarios gave her chills, and she tore her attention away from the edge.

Looking up, she noticed that her guards had started inching closer, closing their ranks around her in a less than subtle form of encouragement. *Jump or we'll push you,* they seemed to say, and she took an involuntary step closer to the mouth of the Pit. Glancing down at her feet, she saw that she was perilously close to the drop-off, with only a few inches standing between her and the deep, dark hole.

Her mind raced for a way out, a way to avoid this seemingly inevitable conclusion, but she came up empty. She had used up all of her time and all of her favors. She had no more tricks up her sleeve.

This was it. This was the end.

She spared one last look at Kasis and its tiers, filling her sights with the familiar polluted landscape. It was dirty and damaged, full of ghosts and pain, but it was home, and she was going to miss it.

Her final thought before the end was of her sister, Scarlett. A desperate longing came over her, a desire to say goodbye – or to say anything at all. Burn couldn't imagine how this would affect her, but she had to believe that her sister was strong enough to make it through. Burn couldn't protect her any longer. Or, rather, they could no longer protect each other.

Pushing the pain and sadness to the back of her mind, she took a deep breath, her lungs filling with the city's smog, and jumped into the Pit.

Needless to say, this was not how she had expected her week to go.

Chapter 1

Burn's week had started off rather well. Or as well as could be expected when you're part of a rebel alliance that's been labeled an enemy of the state. All in all, though, that hadn't really affected her.

It did help that her allegiance to the Lunaria wasn't common knowledge amongst the government's Peace Force. If it had been, it was probable that things like "a sudden and violent arrest" and "torture" would have been in her near future.

As it was, she was safe – at least as safe as anyone else in Kasis. With a government that was run by the military and laughed in the face of due process, the concept of safety was always a bit tenuous. And ever since the Lunaria had foiled the Peace Force's plans to murder its poorest and weakest citizens, those that resided on the bottommost levels of the tiered city, the government had been on high alert.

Burn still didn't understand how their leaders could have done it, deeming an entire class as unworthy of life, as if their presence were a stain on the city. Their hatred wasn't new, but it had been growing over the decades, seething under the surface like a creature in its den. It was ever-present, ever-felt, a constant oppression, a bitter injustice. It seeped into the government's decisions, their actions, their treatment of the mutated *freaks*. It lurked behind every disappearance, every unsolved crime, every wrongful arrest.

Yet the ManniK Battles had been different, active, a purposeful show of hatred. The Peace Force had plotted and planned, conscious of their goal. They'd abducted citizens and tested them, searching for their weakness. They'd armed their officers and taught them to kill. It had been strategic, calculated, deliberate. They'd stirred up unrest, turned the citizens on themselves, and used it as an excuse to go in shooting. And when it hadn't worked, when the Lunaria came in to foil their plot, the Peace Force had thrust the blame on them, staining the rebels with guilt to make their hands look clean.

In the aftermath, they'd put in place a slew of new security measures designed to "protect the peace" – like PeaceBot droids equipped with full-body scanners and mandatory curfews enforced by armed patrols. They had also increased their random searches, targeting houses on the lower and middle tiers several times a week. But besides causing Burn some mild annoyance, the government's new security procedures hadn't inconvenienced her too greatly.

Which was a relief, seeing as how she had recently killed the de facto head of the Peace Force, General Illex Cross, during the battle that he himself had orchestrated. She had been expecting some backlash from that. However, just like her allegiance to the Lunaria, the truth about that particular incident seemed to be buried in secrecy.

That hadn't been her finest moment: shooting Cross dead with a bullet between the eyes. Although, in her defense, she had been driven mad by ManniK, the drugged gas that Cross had released onto the tier as part of his plot to kill its residents, so he kind of had it coming. Still, murder wasn't something she took lightly.

The event weighed on her, as did the battle that had led up to it, and both made frequent appearances in her nightmares. More than once she had awoken screaming, certain that she was back in that place, surrounded by bodies and smoke and gunfire. Yet Scarlett would always come to reassure her that it was over, that they were safe.

Scarlett herself had nearly died in the onslaught. She had taken a bullet to the heart, and in the end, she had only survived thanks to her gift. Not only did her sister have an intrinsic understanding of machines and electronics, but she was almost a machine herself, with large swaths of metal in place of skin and wires intermixed with her curly red hair. So, instead of piercing her chest with a fatal blow, the bullet had met metal and ricocheted off, leaving only a dent in its place.

Still, Scar, as she was known to those closest to her, had suffered other wounds that weren't as easy to shake off. She had lost someone, someone dear to her, and she still hadn't fully recovered. Instead, she had thrown herself into her work, replacing feelings with faulty machinery and heartache with hacked systems.

Burn was afraid that Scar would retreat completely into the world of electronics and gadgets, succumbing to the unfeeling, metallic part of herself and leaving behind all traces of humanity. So she pushed her sister, encouraging her to go out, to talk to people, to find something other than cold steel and programmable chips to fill her life.

Burn had even dragged her along to the Lunaria's meetings, knowing that if she could find a way to instill a purpose into Scar's life, a way to revenge Symphandra's death while making a difference in the city, then maybe she could bring the light back into Scar's eyes. It wasn't an easy feat, but it seemed to be working, drawing Scar out of her shell and giving her a reason to keep going, keep trying.

The Lunaria's meetings had become more frequent since the battle, taking place several times a week in safe houses across Kasis. For the first time, it felt like they had gained traction in the city. People were unhappy. Not all of them believed the lies that the Peace Force had spread following the attacks: that the Lunaria had caused the chaos as part of a terrorist plot. Many people suspected the truth: that it was all a cover-up to disguise the force's botched plan to rid themselves of the poor and mutated citizens on the lowest levels.

People wanted to join the Lunaria, to stand with their neighbors and fight. The Lunaria's ranks had been depleted after the battle, cut almost in half from casualties and the loss of those who could no longer stomach the fight. Now their numbers were rising again as people began to realize the true corruption behind the slick veneer of their government.

Burn had long been one of the leaders of the movement, a driving force behind the Lunaria and its actions. Yet ever since the battle – and her defeat of Illex Cross – she had been placed in a position of honor, seen almost as a savior to the people, like a beacon of hope. She understood their urge to look to her for answers, but the truth was that she didn't have them.

Burn didn't know how to free these people, how to topple a government that had been in place for centuries. But try telling that to a room full of eager new recruits who were chomping at the bit to make a difference. Most of them took her desire to shun the spotlight as modesty, a trait which made her even more appealing as a leader. All she could do now was continue on as she always had, making decisions as they came and hoping they were the right ones.

"Burn!" Scar yelled across the house, either unable or unwilling to march the few feet into her bedroom. "If you're not out here in two minutes, I'm leaving without you."

Burn knew she wasn't lying. In fact, Scar had left her behind on more than one occasion, sometimes not even bothering to issue a warning beforehand. Burn hastily finished her business, sending one final piece of blackmail out into the ether before folding up her tab and stowing it in her pocket.

"I'm coming," she shouted back, donning her cloak and grabbing her mask and goggles.

The world outside their door was highly polluted, with an ever-present haze lingering in the air. Their tier, which was a little more than halfway up in the vertical city, possessed only a light smog that hardly impaired visibility. The lower you went, though, the worse it got, until the endless blanket of gray obscured nearly everything in your wake.

The goggles and masks helped, allowing people to see and breathe through the dense clouds, but prolonged exposure could still be deadly. Burn's own mother had perished because of it when she was only 4, the toxic substance poisoning her lungs until she began to cough up hideous globs of blackness.

Thankfully, they wouldn't be descending too far on this particular excursion. The Lunaria had been gathering in different locations for each meeting, varying their modus operandi to avoid drawing unwanted attention. This evening's event would take place only a few tiers down, in the home of one of Burn's longtime friends, Meera. Equipped with its own secret entrance, it was a convenient place for clandestine assemblies.

You see, what they were doing was incredibly illegal. When the Peace Force had established their new rules following the ManniK Battles, they'd made sure to spell out these forbidden activities in no uncertain terms.

It was now considered a criminal offense to meet in groups larger than six, to organize meetings without a permit, to fraternize with known members of a terrorist group, and to plot in any way, shape, or form against the Peace Force or any of its members. Tonight, they'd be breaking all of those rules. But at least they were adhering to the curfew, so they had one mark in their favor.

Burn shuffled out of her room just as Scar closed the front door behind her. She silently cursed her sister's promptness, yanking on her mask and goggles as she jogged after Scar. She caught up with her several blocks down the road, impeded somewhat by her sister's long strides.

Burn was an average height, taking after their mother in looks and build. Scar, however, resembled their father, Arvense, whose red hair and gangly stature had made him stand out in a crowd.

Of course, Scar's semi-metal exterior also made her stand out. On this particular occasion, though, she had taken measures to obscure her peculiar appearance, tucking her wiry curls under the hood of her cloak and wearing modest garments to cover her slashes of silver skin.

Being a "mutant," as the Peace Force called them, wasn't illegal. It wasn't socially acceptable, either. They were more or less outcasts, looked down on by "polite" society – and outwardly shunned by the not-so-polite. Burn's gift was easy to hide, but Scar's made her a target. She didn't like going out in public, much preferring the safety of her workshop, but when she did venture out, she made sure to conceal her differences and stick to the shadows.

The sisters walked cautiously through the city, taking a circuitous route to shake any possible tails. They remained quiet, not wanting to draw attention as they merged with the early evening traffic. Everyone they passed was similarly subdued, cowed down by the threat of violence from the armed patrolmen and the PeaceBots they used to enforce their control.

The sisters were stopped just once during their journey, forced to submit to a PeaceBot scan before they could continue, but their trek was otherwise unimpeded. They arrived in good time, finding themselves outside of the blue-doored house earlier than they had expected.

Before entering, Burn scanned the area – and the house

– listening for anything out of place. No matter how much she trusted Meera and the others, there was always the chance that they had been caught or turned – or blackmailed into something they would never have dreamed of doing. She would know that better than anyone, having curried her fair share of favors through such unethical means. As she examined the tier, though, she heard nothing out of the ordinary.

Turning to the door, Burn gave a few light taps, administering a coded knock that had been agreed upon during their last meeting. At her touch, a notch in the blue wood slid open. They just glimpsed a pair of eyes, no doubt confirming their identities, before the door opened a crack and they were able to slip inside.

Burn gave Meera a quick hug before finding a seat next to Scar in the small living room. The house was cozy, with a modest kitchen across from them and a bedroom and bathroom off the back. It was the perfect size for Meera, who had lived alone since her husband died, but it was going to be a squeeze for the Lunaria, who'd have nearly 30 members in attendance.

Right now, there were only a few individuals present, meaning there were still seats available. If they'd arrived any later, they would almost certainly have been relegated to the floor. As it was, they settled themselves on a small sofa just big enough for two.

Despite the risks of their meeting, the mood was light and energetic. As more people wandered in, both from the front door and the secret entrance at the back, discreet conversations arose, filling the space with whispers as people shared their progress and ideas. Burn, however, remained quiet, content to listen to the room and absorb the energy as others spoke.

Eventually, the room filled to capacity, with people flowing into the kitchen and hallway, seated on the counters and floors and any other surfaces they could find. Burn no longer knew everyone there by name, with so many of their old members lost to the battle and so many new ones joining their ranks. It was a strange feeling, Burn thought, as if the old guard was slowly being replaced by the new.

Hale, who always seemed to lead the meetings despite them having no official "leader," got up and made his way to the center of the gathering. It was a slow process, and he had to climb over several seated figures as he went, but he managed it, and he stood for a moment considering the group. The group considered him in return. His large stature, paired with his gift of strength, made him an imposing figure, and the room promptly quieted for his address.

"Thank you for joining us once again," came his deep voice, commanding their attention. "We've made some incredible progress over the past few days, and I know that some of you have ideas that will take us even further. Later on, we'll open up the floor so you can share your suggestions with the group. But now I'd like to invite Raqa to the floor to discuss his PeaceBot project."

Raqa stood up from his spot on the kitchen floor, looking around tentatively in search of a path toward the room's center. Apparently deeming the journey impossible, he quickly gave up and remained where he was, standing awkwardly against the kitchen table. Seeing this, Hale sighed and settled himself down.

Raqa was one of their newer members, a twitchy man who always seemed to be glancing over his shoulder. His gift was similar to Scar's in that he had a certain aptitude for robotics, although his powers did not include a mastery of all machines like hers did. Nonetheless, they'd been paired together on this particular project – much to Scar's chagrin. She preferred to work alone and tended to view anyone else's "help" as interference.

"Scarlett and I have been working on a way to override the PeaceBots' essential programming," he said, practically tripping over his words. "Our aim was to hack into their systems and reprogram them to work for us. Scarlett's previous work with PeaceBots was a critical component to our mission. With the key she provided, I was able to find a backdoor into their system and rework their code."

He stopped there, as if he had adequately explained their operation. Yet everyone else continued staring at him, waiting for more.

After a few awkward beats of silence, Hale spoke up. "Raqa, what will your changes mean for us and our mission? What will the PeaceBots do now that you've changed their code?" He spoke gently, as if addressing a toddler.

"Ah, yes," Raqa said, pushing up his glasses on his nose. "We now have two PeaceBots that will relay intel to us instead of to the Peace Force. They'll still appear to be online and active in the Peace Force systems and will still accept commands, but they won't act on them. That means we can see what the Peace Force is searching for – and if they find it. We'll also be able to observe the bots' cam data and obtain information on all the people they're currently seeking." With that, Raqa promptly sat down, thereby ending his report.

Scar sighed and shook her head. Even without words, Burn could tell that her sister was annoyed with Raqa and his presentation. No doubt she thought she could have done better.

"Uh, thank you, Raqa," said Hale haltingly, as if he wasn't entirely certain what he was thanking the man for. "I'm sure that will come in handy. Now, is there anyone who would like to propose a new idea or course of action? If so, I invite you to come forward now."

A few seconds of silence followed, with no one wanting to be the first to speak. Hale looked to Burn, hoping she'd have an idea to present, but she merely shrugged, not sure what the next step forward would entail.

Then a timid voice came from a corner of the living room, and all heads swung around to locate the source. A small woman stood up and addressed the crowd, clutching her hands in front of her and visibly shaking.

"Uh, hi. My name is Cali. I'm new." She gave a small smile as she introduced herself, bowing her head to the crowd. Burn remembered the woman, having been part of the group that had vetted her prior to her admission, and she smiled at Cali's sense of initiative. It was always heartening when new recruits did more than merely stand by and watch.

"I work in the ventilation and airflow field," Cali continued. "We handle all of the piping and air circulation throughout the city." She said it almost like a question, as if she were uncertain of her own occupation. She paused, looking around the room, and made eye contact with Burn, who nodded in encouragement.

"Well, I sort of had an idea. You see, I know the locations of all the air intake points along the top levels. That's where the pollution that's generated on the top of the city gets collected and piped down to the lowest tiers. It's one of the main reasons that the topmost sectors have such clean air. Well, that and the lack of factories." She paused, taking a second to organize her thoughts.

"If we were to sabotage the air intake valves in some way, then they would no longer be able to siphon the toxic air down to the lowest tiers. Meaning the bottom of the city would get a reprieve from pollution while the rich would finally feel what it's like to live like the rest of us do."

The room silenced for a moment as the other members took in her suggestion. It was a risky idea, to be sure, but Burn trusted that Cali knew what she was doing. She'd learned a lot about the woman during her initiation, and Cali had quickly proven herself to be exceptionally clever. This plan was no different.

Hale apparently agreed. "Hmm," he rumbled from his seat on the floor. "That's definitely an intriguing idea. If the decision-makers of the city, the rich and powerful, were forced to experience the realities of the city's pollution, they might finally take action and address it. But the air systems would need to be effectively taken offline, something they can't just fix in a day."

"I have access to all the locations," Cali said, her confidence growing from Hale's words of approval. "I could take them offline, then change the access codes."

Hale thought for a moment, his brows furrowing. "No," he said slowly, "they'll automatically assume someone on the airflow team is responsible. I don't want you to be their primary suspect for this. You should be in plain sight during the entire process. If you give us the locations and access codes, we can send someone in to dismantle them."

"There are patrols in that area," Cali said, a hint of warning coloring her voice. "Both armed Peace Officers and PeaceBots. You'll need at least two people – someone to work on the systems and someone to keep watch."

Hale's eyes immediately fell on Burn. With her gift to detect any hint of movement, she was a natural lookout. It wasn't something she was happy about. No matter how promising the plan, she didn't relish the idea of enacting it. She furrowed her own brows in response, giving Hale a look that clearly said, "Don't make me do this." He raised one eyebrow in return, as if to respond, "You're our only option."

Damn it, Burn thought, resigning herself to the inevitable.

"I can act as lookout for Hale," she said, roping him into the operation whether he liked it or not. Although based on the look of triumph on his face, he did, in fact, seem to like it.

"Good. Then it's settled," Hale responded, once again playing the leader. "We'll get the details from you before you leave tonight, then schedule the operation for later this week. If all goes according to plan, this should make quite the impact."

Quite the impact indeed – assuming they didn't get caught in the process, Burn thought, mulling over the plan. It was entirely possible they could disrupt Kasis' entire ecosystem in a single strike. Or they could just as easily doom themselves and the whole of the Lunaria.

Chapter 2

Two days later, Burn received the message she'd been waiting for – and simultaneously dreading.

"Everything's set. Meet me at noon in the Saffron Quarter."

A pang of nervous energy shot through her as she read Hale's words. She knew that if anything went wrong, their heads would be on the chopping block. Or, more likely, falling down the Pit.

Scar wasn't keen on the idea, either. The plan itself was fine; the issue was Burn being paired up with Hale. Scar was even less of a fan of the lumbering man than Burn was, and she automatically assumed he would do something to jeopardize the mission. He had, after all, nearly cost Burn her life several months ago when he had spread the rumor that she was a turncoat who had joined up with the Peace Force. That one act had led directly to her getting captured by Cross and nearly used as a lab rat in a fatal experiment. Scar did not forgive that kind of thing easily.

Yet, despite her reserves, Scar did equip her with some killer gadgets – literally. Exploding coins, her trusty stun gun pen, and a wickedly sharp knife disguised as a belt buckled. All of which were perfectly inconspicuous and imperceptible by the PeaceBots' scanners, and all things Burn prayed she would never have to use.

"If Hale gets himself into trouble, just leave him behind," Scar said as Burn donned her gear for the mission. Scar was not one for tact.

"I'm serious," she continued as Burn laughed quietly. "He's going to do something stupid. And when he does, run. I'd rather have you here than have the mission be a success."

It was an oddly emotional statement for Scar. Without thinking, Burn walked over and hugged her sister. Scar's body stayed rigid as she endured the embrace, and Burn soon let go to continue her preparations.

"Everything's going to be fine," Burn reassured her. "I'll be back for dinner. Cook us something nice, will you?"

Both of the women chuckled lightly at that, easing the tension in the room. Neither of them was the domestic type, and they relied more on canned goods and food vendors than any actual cooking. The idea of Scar in the kitchen was ridiculous, and it was enough to make Scar forget her worries – at least for the moment.

Burn seized the opportunity and made her way outside, pulling on her goggles and mask. Before she could shut the door, though, Scar's voice came floating out.

"Be careful," she said softly, inaudible to anyone but Burn.

Looking back, Burn gave a small nod before closing the door behind her. She took a deep breath to steady herself and stepped out into the street, losing herself in the faceless crowd.

Clothed in a neutral tunic and dark pants, paired with a rust-colored cloak, Burn looked just like every other citizen milling about. In a city like Kasis, where it was dangerous to stand out, people had a habit of blending in – which was convenient for Burn, who knew that her success hinged on her ability to pass by unnoticed.

She took her time making her way to the Saffron Quarter, keeping her head down as she walked. Although it was nowhere near curfew, the patrols and PeaceBots still made their presence felt, studying the crowd as it ebbed and flowed, searching for an unknown threat. Searching for people like Burn.

Traveling down a tier, she watched as the world around her gradually changed from residential to mercantile, with food stalls and cut-price retailers coming to dominate the buildings. The scent of roasted meat and fresh-baked bread wafted from carts and shop windows, tempting people into the streets and alleys. Once there, the merchants could pounce, enticing customers with offers of cheap electronics, secondhand robotics, and gadgets of dubious provenance and legality.

Those offerings, in particular, made Burn a frequent visitor to the Saffron Quarter. Between there and the scrap heaps, she was able to source just about all the parts Scar needed for her harebrained builds. Burn almost felt at home there. If it weren't for the pickpockets and small-time con artists, it might actually be considered nice.

Burn weaved her way nimbly through the streets, swerving around carts and skirting salespeople. She knew instinctively where Hale would be: tucked into an alley on the far side of the quarter, lingering in the darkness. He liked to lurk, stowing himself away in shadowed corners waiting for his chance to pounce. It was an unsettling characteristic, but one that worked well when your goal was to take people by surprise.

Which is exactly what he did. Even though Burn had been expecting it, when Hale stepped out of the alley in front of her, it made her flinch. His huge form towered over her, and she automatically put her hands in front of herself in a defensive pose, her body poised for a fight.

"Why must you always do that?" she asked, the agitation clear in her voice.

A growl that Burn assumed was laughter emerged from Hale's throat. "Because I like to watch you jump. Did you know that you squeak when you're surprised? It's extremely amusing."

Burn released a growl of her own, although this one held no mirth to speak of. She gritted her teeth, biting back a tart reply. This was no time to quarrel, she reminded herself. They had a mission to complete, and the sooner they got to it, the sooner she could leave Hale behind.

"So what's the plan?" she asked, getting down to business.

"We have to get up near the top of the city without raising attention," he said, automatically changing into "plan" mode. "We don't blend in with the citizens up there. Even if we changed our clothes and our appearances, we would still stand out."

Well, *you* would stand out, Burn thought, eyeing his large stature. She had a feeling that Hale tended to get noticed wherever he went.

"So we take the other approach," he continued. "We go in as service personnel."

He reached around and grabbed the pack he'd been carrying. After rifling through it for a moment, he came out with two technicians' belts. He handed one to Burn, along with an ID card that labeled her as a member of the airflow division.

"Courtesy of Cali," he said, indicating the IDs and equipment. "If anyone questions you, flash the card and say that you're on official business. But I doubt that'll happen. As 'the help,' we should be invisible up there."

Burn took off her existing belt, making sure to switch the lethal buckle over from her old one before handing it to Hale to stow in his pouch. She fastened the tools around her waist, the unfamiliar weight surprisingly heaving on her small hips. She moved around, twisting and turning to ensure the belt was secure before looking back at Hale.

"What then? What happens when we're up there?"

"Cali gave us the locations and access codes to all the air intake points. There are five total, spread out across the level. I'll disable them one by one while you keep a lookout – or whatever you call it. If everything goes as planned, we'll be out within an hour. An hour and a half max."

"But how are you going to disable them?" Burn asked quizzically. She knew Hale wasn't a hugely technical man – and the process had to be more difficult than simply pressing a button or flipping a switch. There was something else to this, something he wasn't telling her.

His face hardened, as if he hadn't intended to tell her that bit, which only made her more curious. She stared back, unblinking, demanding an answer. After a beat, he sighed and dove into his bag, coming out with a small package.

"I plan to use these," he said, holding out the box for Burn to see.

She peered inside and automatically regretted it. No, she regretted this whole thing – agreeing to the plan, partnering with Hale, standing here at this very moment. Scar had been right: He was going to do something stupid.

"You can't bomb the ventilation system!" Burn whispered loudly, panic coloring her words as she looked down at the explosives.

"It's our only option. Even if we take them all offline and change the codes, the airflow team will be able to get them running again within a week. This is the only way we can ensure lasting damage."

Burn wanted to fight back, wanted to protest and tell him where he could shove his explosives, but she stopped herself. She forced herself to breathe and consider her options.

On the one hand, she could leave and put this whole situation behind her. Except Hale would no doubt go on without her, likely getting himself caught in the process. Or she could go with him and ensure that it all went down safely, with no one getting hurt – and no one getting caught. As much as she hated the idea, she knew that the second option would be the safest for everyone involved. Or at least she hoped it would be.

"Fine," she grumbled, shaking her head at the whole situation. Scar's words popped into her mind, and she added, "But if you do anything to jeopardize this mission, I'm leaving you behind to fend for yourself." With that, she exited the alley, leaving Hale scrambling behind her.

They traveled up in silence, neither one caring enough to attempt passive conversation. They weren't friends, after all, merely reluctant coworkers forced into the same boat. Their silent journey was a long one, taking them across tiers and up, and they kept their heads down, doing their best to blend in with their fellow downtrodden citizens.

As they rose, the air and the crowds both thinned, the former losing its viscosity and the latter petering out until they were surrounded only by the rich and their hired help.

It was a different world in the "heavens," as it was often called. The houses were larger and farther apart, and the few shops offered luxury goods designed to help the rich show off the wealth they had schemed and lied to get.

Burn was relieved to see that she and Hale were, indeed, invisible. Up here, tradespeople were seen as a necessary evil – although, in reality, they weren't seen at all. They were reluctantly granted access then promptly ignored. They were servants, downstairs staff who needed to be kept out of sight in order to be kept out of mind.

Honestly, Burn couldn't wait until these privileged few were forced to face the realities of life outside their bubble. When their perfect air began to cloud and they could no longer ignore the pollution they were causing, they'd be compelled to take a hard look at the city and the problems they'd triggered within it. It was, ultimately, their factories and their extravagant homes that were spewing the vast majority of the smut that the rest of them were forced to breathe. It was about time that they learned what that was like.

Invigorated by her own internal monologue, Burn felt a renewed clarity and sense of purpose for her mission. So when she was stopped by a PeaceBot, which demanded to know her name and reason for being there, she didn't hesitate with her lie. It came out so easily that she nearly believed it herself, and she was unsurprised when the PeaceBot accepted it and moved on.

She knew she shouldn't be enjoying this, shouldn't find the lies and espionage thrilling, but part of her did. The other part, of course, still thought the plan could fail at any moment, but she shut that part away, giving herself over to the optimism.

Soon enough, they arrived at the first air intake point. Without speaking, Burn positioned herself a few paces away from Hale, centering her mind and opening it up to the world around her. It was easier here than down below, where the noise of the crowds and the whirring of machines bit into her concentration. Here it was calm, with fewer footsteps treading the clean streets and light noises wafting unhindered through the crisp air.

Hale worked slowly and methodically, first typing a series of digits into the panel, then opening it up to reveal the ventilation system within. Burn knew nothing about airflow technologies or piping systems, so the whole thing merely looked like a jumble of fans and wires and tubes to her, but Hale seemed to know what he was doing.

Drawing one of the small explosives from his bag, he

stuck it firmly to the base of one of the larger pipes. Closing the cavity, he typed another sequence on the panel before turning to Burn with a nod.

"Aren't you going to set it off?" she asked quietly, moving closer to him so her words wouldn't be overheard.

"I'll do it once they're all set and we're clear of the area. For now, I've changed the code so no one will be able to open it. Come on. We've still got four more to do." Turning away, he took off in the opposite direction.

They walked for a few minutes before stopping and repeating the process. Once again, Burn heard no one approach, and Hale was able to place the explosive with ease.

It all felt too simple somehow, like they should have had to jump through more hoops in order to deal so much damage. Maybe these people had too much faith in their own invincibility to properly protect their assets – or maybe the hard part was still to come. Burn had a feeling it was the latter.

Her suspicions were confirmed when they reached the third intake point. Located along a busy pedestrian avenue, the site had nearly constant foot traffic – a fact which made Burn's job all the more difficult.

This time, before beginning, Burn and Hale assessed the crowd, leaning lazily against the wall and scanning the street for any sign of danger. Sensing none, they got to work. Unlike before, Burn stayed close to Hale, using her body as a shield to hide his actions. Her mind, however, combed the tier, searching for enemies.

All was quiet, calm, normal – until it wasn't. Burn froze as the sounds trickled into her consciousness. Hard soles clicking on pavement with military precision. Two pairs of boots moving in a synchronized rhythm. Loaded guns jostling merrily against hips, swaying in time to the steps. Burn knew these sounds all too well, and a warning screamed inside her mind, telling her to run.

Instead, she turned stiffly to Hale, whispering the words they had both feared: "They're coming."

Hale understood in an instant. Doubling his speed, he slammed the explosive into place with a concerning amount of force, then scrambled to fit the cover back onto its track. He just managed to close the panel and hastily type in a set of numbers before a pair of officers turned the corner onto their lane.

Not wanting to be spotted at the scene of the crime, the pair turned their backs to the men and walked briskly into the crowd.

"Are they still behind us?" Hale asked a minute later, his voice low and serious.

Burn listened to the road at their backs for a beat before responding. "They're half a block away but moving toward us. They haven't picked up their pace, though."

"Good," he declared with a bark. "We'll carry on as planned. The next stop is only a few streets away."

Burn's heart was pounding in her chest. Her mind was telling her to flee, to get out of the heavens and back to safety. Still, she knew they had to finish this. If they failed – or if they gave up now – there wouldn't be another chance. The Peace Force would make sure of it. So, against her better judgment, she remained on course, sticking to Hale's side as he wove steadily through the crowd.

They propelled themselves across the level, their pace quick and light as they veered around residents and skirted food carts. Rounding another corner, they finally caught sight of the fourth intake point – along with the two Peace Officers stationed in front of it.

Even at a glance, Burn could tell these men were on high alert, scanning the crowd for signs of a threat. At the same time, the officers at their backs were gaining ground, drawing nearer and nearer to their position.

They were surrounded.

"Got any ideas?" Burn asked, trying hard not to panic.

"One or two. Do you trust me?" Hale whispered in reply.

Burn wanted to say no. She did not, in fact, trust Hale – especially in a life-or-death situation. But with no other ideas springing to mind, he appeared to be her only option. So she nodded, handing over control to a man who considered violence a go-to solution. She knew she was going to regret that.

Without another word, Hale walked forward, sauntering toward the officers guarding the intake valve. Burn followed in his wake, uncertain of his plan and dreading the outcome.

As soon as the officers spotted them, they rose to attention, pointing then shouting in their direction.

"Hey, you two! Stop! We need to ask you some questions."

That was the last coherent thing Burn heard before Hale did something stupid. Reaching into his bag, he grabbed the two remaining explosives and chucked them toward the ventilation system. They landed lightly at the officers' feet.

He bellowed something that sounded like "run," and the

pair sprinted in the opposite direction. An instant later, a series of booms echoed through the tier as all five explosives were triggered, sending smoke and screams of fear into the air around them.

They didn't have a chance to look back and take stock of what they'd done. Their only goal now was to flee, to lose themselves in the smoke and chaos. With Hale in the lead and Burn trying to keep up, they darted through street after street, taking sharp turns and swerving through alleys in an attempt to escape. Yet several of the Peace Officers still pursued them, tracking them through the city.

That was when Hale made his final mistake. Leading them around another corner and down a secluded lane, they suddenly found themselves facing a dead end, with ugly brick walls barring any means of escape. Burn didn't even have time to reach into her bag for one of Scar's gadgets before the Peace Officers arrived, trapping them where they stood.

Hale, however, was never one to stay still. He lunged for one of the officers, no doubt hoping his brute strength would overwhelm the man, but that wasn't the case. Instead, in one graceful movement the officer reached out and stunned him, sending powerful currents of electricity coursing through his large form. His body vibrated with the energy for a moment before his limbs went limp and he passed out, landing with a thud on the hard ground.

Sensing that the jig was up, Burn raised her hands in submission and sank to her knees. Seizing on her surrender, they approached, tearing away her bag and binding her hands in front of her. With a gun trained on her in warning, they lowered her mask, gagged her, and forced her up, leading her away to her fate.

Chapter 3

Burn wasn't dead. That was the first thing she noticed. Or, if she was dead, the afterlife was dreadfully disappointing. Her ideas of heaven, although not fully fleshed out, had been brighter, livelier, and had definitely not included the smell of sweet, dusty earth.

Lying on her back, she looked up and waited for her vision to stop spinning, wiggling her fingers and toes to make sure all appendages were accounted for. Once the world had resolved around her, she raised her head to take in her surroundings, bringing herself up to a sitting position.

She appeared to be in some kind of tunnel, a long dark passageway that led in one direction. There was, in fact, a light peeking out at the end, so it was possible she was in an afterlife weigh station, just a stopping point along the road to her final destination. But Burn highly doubted that. For one thing, she was certain that any sort of limbo couldn't possibly have so much sand.

The granulated substance covered her, sticking to her hands and arms, and already clinging to her tongue. She realized that her gag had come undone, allowing the sand to infiltrate her mouth and lodge itself in the deepest corners. She spat a few times, trying to rid it from her mouth – and failing miserably.

She remembered falling. It had felt like she'd been falling for an eternity, but it had probably only been a few seconds. Just out of sight of the Pit's entrance, the tunnel had tapered and curved, turning into a pseudo slide. She had bumped along its smooth steel sides, somersaulting through the darkness before regaining equilibrium. Then she had slid – farther and farther – until she'd lost all sense of time and place. In the end, she had fallen once again, shooting from the slide onto the sand where she currently sat.

As if echoing her thoughts, a loud clunking noise abruptly issued from overhead. She scrambled out of the way just in time as a large object dropped from the ceiling and landed with a thud on the sand next to her. Surprise tinged with fear coursed through her already tense body, temporarily immobilizing her.

Within a few moments, however, her curiosity overcame her sense of caution, and she inched closer to the object. It was dim in the tunnel, but she could just make out its outlines, tracing the shape of a head, a torso, and a pair of legs.

The figure remained limp, unconscious, and crumpled into a ball. Burn crawled closer, her still-bound hands making her movements clumsy and slow. She gently reached out and rolled the figure over onto his back, revealing his face. Hale.

Of course it was Hale. The Peace Officers must have chucked him down right after she'd jumped, sending him to his "death" without even waiting for him to come back around. How nice of them, Burn thought acidly.

Burn doubted they'd be throwing anyone else down to join them, but she didn't want to take any chances. Grunting with the effort, she gradually dragged Hale's body away from the chute, placing him a few feet down the tunnel. Then she got to work on the ropes that bound his hands. It was slow going, with her own hands painfully fused together, but she ultimately managed to free him before going to work on his gag.

Honestly, she would have preferred to keep him bound and gagged, but after her near-death experience, she was feeling benevolent. She also figured that whatever was coming next, it would help to have someone by her side. Sure, Hale could be a pain, but at least he had a gift that would come in handy if they found themselves in a dicey situation. If he ever woke up, that was.

Burn gave Hale a minute to come around. Then another. By the third minute, she was actively shaking the large man in an attempt to speed his return to consciousness.

As Burn transitioned to lightly slapping Hale on the cheek, he finally began to wake, moaning groggily before opening his eyes. Then he lurched to attention, his fists held out before him as if daring the tunnel to fight. Surprised by his sudden movement, Burn teetered and fell backward, sending up a light dusting of sand as her butt hit the ground.

"Hale!" she shouted, both to get his attention and to chastise him for sending her sprawling. Hale turned around swiftly, aiming his fists in her direction. "Put the weapons down," she said gently, trying to sound calm and reassuring.

Hale squinted through the darkness. "Burn? Is that you? What happened? Where are we?"

So many questions.

"Yes, it's me," Burn sighed. "You got stunned by a bunch of armed Peace Officers and passed out before being thrown down the Pit. And I have no idea where we are. Now, could you please untie me? I'm losing feeling in my hands."

She swung herself around to her knees and crawled over to Hale, holding out her hands for his assistance. He mercifully obliged, leaning over to untie her, and Burn savored her newfound freedom, wiggling her fingers and wrists to banish the pins and needles.

"I think we're somewhere under the city," she continued, voicing her most likely theory. "That chute took us down quite a ways, but it also took us out, away from the city center." She pointed toward the small light at the end of the tunnel, directing Hale's gaze. "If I had to guess, that's beyond the reach of the dome. That's the wildlands."

Neither of them spoke, both lost in thought as they considered the light and what it meant. Kasis was an uninhabitable planet, with a harsh atmosphere and unnatural levels of radiation. That's why they'd built the dome and put the eponymous city underneath it. The dome kept them safe, and life could not exist beyond it. At least that's what they'd been told for centuries. Yet here they were – alive.

"What do you think's out there?" Hale asked, his eyes still trained on the dot of light.

"I guess there's only one way to find out." Getting to her

feet, Burn started toward the mouth of the tunnel. After a few seconds, she heard Hale leverage himself up and follow her lead.

The walk took longer than Burn had anticipated. The light grew steadily as they approached the entrance, but it didn't betray any hint of the world beyond. All they could see was sunlight, bright and merciless, as if they were walking directly into the planet's twin suns.

Burn instinctively reached up for her goggles to shield her eyes from the light. Her hands grazed worn leather, and a sharp thrill of hope buzzed through her as she realized that the Peace Officers had forgotten to remove them. With the messaging features that Scar had added to the lenses, it was possible she could contact her sister. She had no idea how Scar could help, but Burn might at least be able to tell her that she was alive.

With shaking hands, she lowered the goggles over her eyes. The suns' light dimmed – but so did any hope of making contact with the world above. A blinking error message told her in no uncertain terms that the goggles couldn't connect to the network. They were too far out, too far away from life and people – and Scar. The loss of hope was even worse than its total absence, and Burn's face crumpled in defeat.

Hale glanced over at her, the light in the tunnel now bright enough for him to make out her features, but he said nothing. Instead, he picked up his pace, putting distance between them. Burn gathered herself, stowing her emotions in the back of her mind before picking up her own pace to join him.

The farther they walked, the more difficult their

movements became. Each step was harder than the last, and Burn's brain began to feel fuzzy around the edges. Her head pounded to the beat of her steps, sending painful pulses across her temples. On the upside, she had forgotten about Scar and the Lunaria and the fact that she might now be separated from them forever. But on the downside, she couldn't quite remember where they were going – or why.

She glanced up at Hale, who was breathing heavily despite their sedate pace. His face was screwed up in concentration, like he was trying to hold onto something that was rapidly slipping away, and the sight made Burn giggle. She knew she should have been concerned, that something was clearly happening to both of them as they neared the entrance, but she could no longer muster the will to care.

With Burn on the verge of hysteria and Hale sweating from exertion, they finally reached the end of the tunnel. What they saw stopped them in their tracks.

Sand. Dunes of it climbed like mountains in the distance and clouds of it swirled in eddies around their feet. It was all they could see, stretching out until it met the blue-gray sky on the horizon. Burn was transfixed. There was nothing and no one amidst that forlorn expanse of sunbaked sea. It was only them, alone in the vast nothingness. For some reason, the thought made Burn break out into an uncontrollable fit of laughter.

"What's so funny?" Hale grunted, his face red.

"I…have...no idea," Burn wheezed in between peals of laughter.

"It's the air out here," came a voice to their left, and the pair immediately turned to see who had spoken. Burn's eyes came to rest on an incredibly freckled redhead in a golden straw hat. He was leaning against a wooden cart that had been expertly tucked around the side of the tunnel.

"Wha...what?" Hale stuttered, the effort of speaking clearly draining him.

"The air here has a different chemical makeup than in the dome," the man drawled, maintaining his position against the cart. "You'll get used to it in time. In fact, I don't even notice it anymore. But it can be a doozy those first few days. Really knocks you on your ass, if you know what I mean."

Burn giggled girlishly at his statement, but she clamped her hand over her mouth in an attempt to hide her mirth. Hale just stared, the same confused expression still plastered over his face.

"Now, I think you two had better come with me," the man said, straightening. He reached around behind him to grab something from the cart and twisted back toward them, a rifle in his hands. "I don't intend you any harm, but it is in everyone's best interest if you join me."

Hale, no longer fully in his right mind, lunged forward. Burn didn't know what his intention was – to rip the gun out of the man's hands, to flee, to tackle him to the ground – but he accomplished none of those things. Instead, he toppled over onto a heap of sand, which made Burn laugh even harder.

The freckled man sighed, taking in Hale's immobile form and Burn's deranged state. He muttered something under his breath, which Burn's sensitive ears naturally picked up: "I gotta stop volunteering for Pit duty." Slinging the rifle over his back, he began to drag Hale through the sand.

By that time, Burn's laughter had subsided, but she didn't have the presence of mind to flee. Or fight. Or do anything other than stand there and watch as the man heaved her colleague onto the cart and turned back to her.

"Are you coming, little lady?" he asked, his hand outstretched. Seeing no other options, Burn took his hand and climbed into the cart.

As they rode slowly through the rolling hills of umber and sepia, Burn took stock of her situation. Although her brain was still foggy from the noxious air, a little of her reason had returned, and she was able to take in some of their route as they traveled. She tried to imprint it on her memory in case she needed to retrace it later, but her inability to tell one sand dune from the next was making it difficult.

The cart was being led by the strangest animal Burn had ever seen. It looked like some combination of a donkey and a ram, with curled horns protruding from its long head. In theory, it shouldn't have been strong enough to pull them along by itself, but it was bearing the weight with ease, plodding methodically through the sand with hardly any guidance from the man beside her.

"Who are you?" Burn asked tentatively, eyeing the stranger.

On his own – without the gun – the man wasn't overtly threatening, with a scrawny build and no muscle mass to speak of. In different circumstances, Burn might have been inclined to get to know him, to discover his story and what had brought him to this perilous place. Yet out here, so far from everything and everyone she'd ever known, her first priority was to acquire as much information as she could.

"I'm Jez," the stranger said matter-of-factly, as if his name on its own would be enough to quell her curiosity. It wasn't. So Burn tried again.

"Where are we going?"

"Back to Videre," he said simply, as if trying to answer her query in as few words as possible.

She exhaled heavily, a sliver of frustration breaking through the haze of her mind. "And what is Videre?"

"It's my home." Clearly, Jez could do this all day.

"Jez," Burn turned to him, clasping her hands in front of herself as if she were praying, "why are you taking us to Videre? What is it you plan to do with us there?" She spoke slowly and evenly, enunciating through her mask, which she'd pulled back over her mouth to keep out the sand.

Sensing that Burn was in no mood for his games, Jez turned to look at her, heaving a sigh.

"Look, I don't know what they're gonna do with you. If you're useful, they'll probably let you stay. If you're worthless – or worse, a Peace Officer – they'll kick you out and let you fend for yourself out here."

"Who's 'they'?" Burn asked, her voice wary.

"Oh, the others that make up Videre. There are a couple hundred of us now. We're one of the largest exile camps outside of Kasis. Got some of the best mutants, too. That's what makes us so powerful. The others wouldn't dare attack us."

Jez smiled at this, like he had singlehandedly made Videre what it was today. Despite her lack of knowledge on the subject, Burn had a feeling that was not the case.

Yet her mind reeled at all he had said. Hundreds. There were hundreds of exiles in their camp alone. How many Kasians were out here? And how did they survive in this bleak and barren landscape? And, a voice chimed in at the back of her mind, was she useful or would she be deemed worthless and chucked back into these unforgiving wilds?

She looked around at the lifeless mounds of sand, which all but sizzled in the heat of the sultry suns. This was an infinite wasteland, a sinister scene, and it whispered a forbidding song of predators and prey. This was not a place she wanted to find herself stranded, alone and defenseless. But if what Jez had said was true, then the decision wouldn't be up to her.

"Thank you," she managed to whisper, grateful for the information despite its gravity. Jez just nodded, giving her a small smile before returning his gaze to the desert before them.

They traveled in silence for a time, with Burn lost in a blur of foggy thoughts and Jez seemingly content with the lack of conversation. Burn guessed he was the kind of man who would be content in any situation, equally comfortable talking or not, alone or in the company of others. As if to emphasize this point, he began to whistle. It was a tuneless song, something made up on the spot rather than a familiar melody, but it was pleasant enough that Burn didn't protest.

She wasn't sure how long they traveled for. Burn had lost sight of the dome within minutes of their departure, with the sand rising up in dunes to cloak them in the shroud of the desert. Now when she looked back, she could no longer say with certainty from which direction they had come. Any hope of getting back, of somehow returning to Kasis and sneaking into the city, faded with a painful sinking feeling that bordered on despair.

As Burn gradually pushed through the haze and confusion, her chest ached for everything she was leaving. Her home. Her mission. The Lunaria. The thought of never seeing them again, of not being able to talk to them or help them or fight beside them, was almost too much to bear. They would presume she had died. They would mourn her. Then they'd go on with their lives, relegating her to the past and pressing on with their futures – futures without her in them.

A stab of pain shot through her at the thought of Scar. Her heart constricted as the image of her sister's face, lost and broken, floated into her mind. It felt like an invisible line had been strung between them, and as the distance mounted it was slowly pulling her apart.

A sudden, irrational urge came over her to jump from the cart and run, to tear through the desert like the pain tore through her. She had to stop herself from vaulting over the side, holding onto the wood of her seat until splinters dug into her palm.

She closed her eyes, fighting back the tears that threatened to break free. She couldn't show weakness, not here. She had to be strong, had to show these people of Videre that she was clever and useful. There would be time later to mourn. Right now she had to focus on survival.

The path ahead of them gradually changed, morphing from desolate dunes of sand to packed earth and rocks. Outcroppings of stone rose from the horizon, resolving into hills and plateaus as they grew nearer. Sand still blew around the cart and climbed the rock faces in an attempt to consume them, but its power was diminished, beaten back by the sheer cliffs and immovable boulders. Everything coalesced to paint a picture of a world that was ragged and rigid and utterly foreign.

As the cart departed its sandy path in favor of more level ground, its speed increased, the creature leading it spurred into a jog. Although Burn had no idea where they were headed, it felt like they were getting close, and the tension in her veins increased to a hum. Despite her wild imagination, she had no idea what she was walking into, and the precarious nature of the unknown frightened her.

Feeling more alone than she had since she'd jumped into the Pit, she risked a glance back at Hale. His breathing was regular, yet his eyes remained shut, blocking out the world. Burn couldn't tell if he was still unconscious or merely feigning it in order to gain some element of surprise, but he stayed immobile save for the light rise and fall of his chest. The sight did nothing to cure her loneliness, and she returned her attention to the road ahead.

Jez had stopped whistling by that point, instead concentrating on something unseen in the distance. Burn followed his gaze but couldn't make out anything other than rocks and mounds of sand. So she closed her eyes, centering herself and focusing her thoughts on the path. At first she could hear nothing besides the lonesome cries of the wind and the restless movement of sand across the surface of the planet. As she listened closer, however, she began to hear voices.

They were distant and quiet, mere murmurs among the

landscape, but they were there – and there were a lot of them. They were nearing Videre. Burn opened her eyes and sat up in her seat, craning her neck in an attempt to discern the village and its people. The voices grew louder, but Burn still couldn't see anything that resembled a town, at least not the type she was familiar with.

Then it struck her: The rocks and piles of sand in the distance were Videre. Her suspicions were confirmed when what she had thought were natural formations resolved into buildings and homes. Since they were made out of the same substances as their surroundings, they were nearly indistinguishable from the undulating tan landscape, blending seamlessly with the surrounding dunes and hills.

As they approached, Burn began to make out more details of the camp. The whole thing was nestled into a vast V-shaped cliff face. Two other man-made walls comprised of stone and clay were attached to the cliffs and closed off the area, with only one gate allowing entrance or exit. The gate currently lay open, and Burn could just perceive people as they went about their daily lives, their small forms looking like ants from her perch on a hill above them.

There were many buildings within the enclave, but they weren't like anything she had ever seen. In Kasis, houses were built from steel and glass and concrete, one on top of another with more to the sides. But these were different. For one thing, they were spaced out, with gardens and clothes lines and sheds between one house and the next. For another, they were composed of warm desert earth and clay. The result was buildings that seemed to rise from the sand, as if the desert itself had produced them and could just as easily swallow them up.

There must have been nearly a hundred buildings of varying shapes and sizes, not just houses, but shops and workspaces, all interspersed with roads and alleys. This was more than a camp, Burn realized with a start; it was an entire city.

Chapter 4

Burn wondered how long all of this had been here. It was clearly not a new development, but rather one that had sprouted over time, adding buildings and people over years and decades.

Did the Peace Force know about Videre? Burn couldn't imagine they did. If they had, they would never have allowed these people to exist outside of the bounds and laws of Kasis. They would never be able to resist exerting control, dominating these people just like they did to everyone under their dome.

Then again, if what Jez said was true, this was a city of freaks, of mutants, of outcasts who were no longer wanted in Kasis. If the Peace Force had learned about them, they would have attacked and killed every one of them just to eradicate the threat.

As their cart drew closer to the sprawling city, Burn noticed a raucous band of children playing in the streets, laughing and chatting and running around. The sight was almost foreign to her, and it brought a shadow of a smile to her worry-stricken face. Kids in Kasis learned quickly to be quiet, to do what they were told, to not make a nuisance of themselves lest they anger someone in charge. Yet these children were free; they were happy.

They also weren't Kasians. While the Peace Force was corrupt beyond her knowledge, they rarely took children. When they did, they "re-educated" them or used them to further their own endeavors – they didn't chuck them down the Pit. No, these were children of the wildlands, a new breed born and raised outside of the dome.

Despite her fear of the unknown – and of what might become of her once they reached the city – a tantalizing thrill of curiosity rang through her. What else was Videre hiding? How had it survived all these years? And what was life like inside its walls?

If Burn's fate weren't currently being held in the balance, resting on some faceless jury, she might even consider this an adventure, a new place to explore with new people to meet. Except she didn't yet have that luxury. Not until they decided she could stay. *If* they decided she could stay.

The thought was sobering, and she sat up straighter, alert and on her guard. She even rehearsed what she would say, crafting her case on how she could be an asset to such a city. She could act as a guard – or a spy. She could scan the city for plots to seize power. She could assist in trade negotiations – if there were any – by listening for the other side's true desires. She was useful, she told herself, repeating the phrase like a mantra in her head.

As they reached the gate, Jez looked up, and Burn followed suit. Guards armed with deadly sharp spears manned the walls on either side of the entrance. Recognizing Jez, they nodded him through, keeping a wary eye on Burn and Hale as the cart rolled into the city.

"We should find Imber at the town hall," Jez stated as they made their way down the main thoroughfare. "He'll decide what happens to you."

"Is he your leader?" Burn asked, trying to get a lay of the land.

"Yes and no," Jez said cryptically, then went on to explain. "We all have a say in what goes on here. As you can see, Videre is not like Kasis. We all do our part to keep it running. In return, we share in the city's food and resources, helping others when they need it and knowing they'll help us in return. It's a good system."

"So...how does Imber factor into it all?" Burn queried.

"Well, Imber is sort of our unofficial representative," Jez explained, trying to find the right words to describe the man's position. "His gift is water. Because of him, we're not dependent on external water sources and complex irrigation systems. We have a well, of course, but it's sort of a backup in case anything happens."

He pointed over to a corner of the city, although Burn's view of the well was obscured by houses and shops. She made a note of its location anyway, figuring any knowledge about Videre's layout might come in handy.

"Since Imber was so crucial to the city's success, he sort of became our decision-maker. He's pretty good at determining who's gonna be useful – and who might end up being a problem."

Jez smiled at that, seemingly proud that he'd summed up the city and its politics so simply for her. But Burn still had so many questions smoldering within her. This time, however, she kept them to herself.

Instead, she took in her surroundings. By then, evening had settled softly over the city, and people flowed busily through the streets. She spotted men and women removing laundry from clothes lines, shaking the items vigorously to dislodge the sand. Around them, kids chased each other with glee, shrieking and laughing as they ran.

Farther afield, men knelt in gardens, pulling weeds and putting produce into baskets. Somewhere toward the back of the city, more strange animals loitered in pens and cages, tended to by gangs of teenagers. And all around them, old ladies sat on stoops, sewing and chatting and criticizing the world.

As their cart rolled by, heads popped up and people peeked between buildings to stare at Burn and Hale, their gazes eager and curious. As newcomers, they were fresh meat, a novel source of intrigue and amusement. They were entertainment, at least for the time being, and their fates were a drama that would unfold before the masses.

Burn felt like an animal being led to the slaughter. People watched her with looks ranging from pity to hunger, lining the roads in a menacing sort of welcome. She tried not to look at them, tried to keep her eyes and her thoughts on the task at hand, but their murmurs and jeers were difficult to ignore.

They soon arrived at the end of the road. Looking up,

Burn saw a long, low building stretching out in front of her, its surface carved with intricate designs that almost resembled a story, although Burn couldn't quite follow its plot.

Stopping the cart, Jez disembarked from his seat and offered a hand to Burn. She accepted it without protest and jumped lightly onto the packed dirt road, sending up a small plume of dust. He then moved toward the back of the cart, but before he could reach it, Hale sat up and leveraged himself over the side, standing menacingly over the skinny man.

So he'd only been feigning unconsciousness, after all, Burn thought, wondering what his plan was – and hoping it wouldn't get them into even more trouble.

For the moment, though, he didn't move or speak. Instead, he stood there, taking up space and staring at Jez as if inviting him to fight. Jez, knowing what was good for him, backed away, moving closer to Burn and the building.

"Glad to see you're awake," he said with forced cheerfulness. "Sometimes it takes newbies a couple of days to come back around. But I can see you're a strong one. That's good." His nervousness seemed to be causing him to ramble, temporarily sidetracking him from his agenda.

Once he'd recovered, he went on, "I would appreciate it if y'all would follow me inside. I know Imber will be delighted to meet you."

Hale stared at him for a heartbeat longer, obviously weighing his options. Apparently deciding that playing nice was the best policy, he nodded at Jez, who visibly relaxed. Turning, Jez headed toward the building's entrance. Burn moved to follow him, but Hale put a hand out to stop her. She looked up for an explanation, but Hale merely put himself between her and Jez in their informal lineup, no doubt thinking he could act as her unofficial bodyguard.

While Burn bristled at the idea that she needed protection, in this instance the gesture was reassuring. They still didn't know what they were walking into, and as much as she hated to admit it, Hale was better equipped to take on opponents if the situation arose.

As they entered the cavelike building, the temperature around them plummeted. Gone was the glaring heat of the desert suns, which beat down mercilessly onto the sand. Now, it was as if the walls themselves had leeched the warmth from the air, creating a dry coolness that made her shiver.

Jez led them to the left and down a hallway, and Burn caught glimpses of various rooms as they walked. Desks constructed of large slabs of stone occupied most of the spaces, accentuated by elaborately carved chairs, while parchments were strewn haphazardly across the surfaces and floors. They were offices, she realized, craning her neck to see more.

They seemed simultaneously archaic and brand new, with fresh, intricately painted designs contrasting the antiquated furnishings. It felt as if an ancient civilization had been reborn and transposed into the wildlands of Kasis. It was astounding.

Since it was nearing the end of the day, most of the rooms were empty. Most, but not all. Burn, whose senses were on high alert, picked out the sound of movement from the room at the end of the hall. That's where they must be headed, she deduced, training her eyes on the monolithic door. Behind it, someone was waiting for them, waiting to dole out their fates.

Just as she had expected, Jez stopped at the end of the long building, rapping his knuckles quickly on the large wooden door. A muffled "come in" issued from within, and Jez ushered them inside.

This room was bigger than the others Burn had seen, taking up roughly double the space. It was cluttered with round tables surrounded by chairs, in addition to a long desk set against the far wall. Just like the others, this room was adorned in intricate patterns, with brilliant blues and yellows and oranges painted onto the walls in minute detail.

There was also a man. Burn sized him up, studying his appearance in hopes of discerning something useful. He was tall, although nowhere near Hale's size. His thick dark hair was graying at the temples, and his tanned skin was just beginning to wrinkle. Judging from the calluses on his hands and the muscular set of his shoulders, he looked like the kind of man who liked to labor alongside the people rather than above them. Burn could work with that.

Jez spoke first. "I'm glad I caught you, sir. I was afraid I'd have to go on another scavenger hunt through the city to track you down." He spoke in a respectful yet familiar tone, one that suggested they were, in fact, on fairly equal footing.

"I'm happy I could make things easy for you today, Jez," the man responded lightly. "Now, who do we have here?" He indicated Burn and Hale, looking inquisitively between them.

"Ah, yes. These are the latest victims of the Pit. Found 'em as they were leaving the tunnel. They got a bit loopy from the air out here, but they seem to be coming around now."

"Wonderful," said the man, whom Burn took to be

Imber. He made his way around the desk and stood before them, looking them up and down as if appraising their value. "Now, tell me what you can do. Or, better yet, show me."

Right to the point, then. Burn briefly considered how she could demonstrate her ability in a way that would impress this man, but before she could land on anything, Hale lurched forward and strode past the group toward Imber's desk. Without a word, he grabbed the heavy stone that made up the desk's top and lifted it above his head. He held it there for a minute, no obvious strain evident on his face, before placing it gently back down on its legs.

Imber appeared suitably impressed. "A strong man. Nice. Well, that should come in handy. Our construction crews are always looking for better ways to transport materials. And I bet our citizen militia could use someone like you. I think we'll keep you."

With that declaration, he pivoted in place, turning to face Burn. "What about you?"

This was her moment, her chance to shine. But suddenly, she couldn't think of a single thing to say. Her mind went blank, devoid of everything she had prepared in her defense. Imber began to look annoyed, obviously growing impatient with her silence. So she did the only thing she could think of: She closed her eyes.

Clearing her mind, she opened her ears up to the world. She sifted through the conversations of the city, trying to find anything that could be useful in proving her case.

"Dinner is ready in the mess hall," she began, roving through the city with her mind. "One of Mendas' pigs has escaped, and he's recruited some of the children to help get it back. And there's a storm on the horizon. It should be here a little after nightfall."

Burn opened her eyes again, hoping she'd heard enough to convince him, but Imber didn't seem impressed.

"So...you're a psychic?" he asked dubiously.

"No," Burn shot back, trying to remain calm. She didn't like people judging her, and so far that was all this man seemed to do. It put her in a foul mood. She took a breath to steady herself before continuing. "I hear things. Secrets and plots and approaching enemies. Things that are coming – and things people want to keep hidden."

To Burn's consternation, Imber did not look enthused about her gift – or what it could bring to Videre. He scrunched up his face in consideration, gently shaking his head.

Burn tried again. "I can act as a guard up on the walls. I saw them as we were coming in. I can hear beyond what the human eye can see. I can tell you when danger is coming before any of them can."

To her dismay, Imber's headshaking became more pronounced. "We already have someone with enhanced sight. I don't know what you could provide that she can't. Besides, if you're that good of a guard, how did you get caught back in Kasis? Shouldn't you have heard them coming?"

Her eye twitched in fury, but she bit her tongue, straining to remain calm despite his condescension.

He considered her for a few more seconds before going on. "Everyone here has a role. For their service, they get food and shelter. They get to live in safety. But we're not a charity. We have limited resources and can't go around giving them to everybody. That's why..."

Yet Burn never learned what it was he was going to say. At that moment Hale stepped in – literally. He placed himself between Burn and Imber, crossing his arms in his best "imposing" pose.

"She's also my wife," he said matter-of-factly.

Chapter 5

Burn couldn't move. Or speak. Or think. She merely stood there, so surprised by Hale's declaration that her body seemed to have gone numb.

His wife? Why had he just said that she was his wife?

Hale looked down at Burn, clearly trying to communicate something, but she was at a loss. Then he opened his mouth a fraction and shut it hard. Burn realized that her mouth was hanging open and closed it, trying to adopt an expression of nonchalance.

"Well then, that's a different matter entirely," Imber stated, his voice abruptly losing its stiffness. "I would love to have you and your wife join us in Videre as our newest citizens. Welcome to our little slice of paradise, Mr....?"

"Just call me Hale," he said firmly. He glanced at Burn and, upon observing that she was still too stunned to talk, he introduced her, as well. "And my wife here is Auburn. Although most people call her Burn. And thank you for your hospitality. We're delighted to have found such a welcoming place in our time of need."

"No, thank you, Hale. I'm sure we're the lucky ones," Imber said smoothly. "Now, Jez will show you to your accommodations. Once you have a chance to clean up, it would be a pleasure to have you join us for dinner. As your wife so accurately deduced, the food is ready and waiting. I'm sure the rest of the townsfolk will be delighted to meet you. Then tomorrow, you'll start work! Now, if you'll excuse me, I have a few more matters to attend to before supper."

With a nod, Imber shepherded them out into the hallway and shut the door behind them. Next to them, Jez looked inordinately pleased.

"I was hoping you two would get to stay," he whispered conspiratorially as they walked toward the entrance. Neither Hale nor Burn replied, so he kept going, "I could tell from the moment I met you that you two are incredibly powerful. Imber likes the powerful ones. And the great thing about living in the wildlands is that our gifts become even stronger."

Hale latched onto that the second it was out of Jez's mouth. "What do you mean we become stronger?"

"Oh, of course. I should explain. You should probably know what you're in for. Yeah, it's something about the atmosphere out here. Maybe the radiation is higher. Maybe there's something in the air. We're not entirely sure what causes it, but everyone with gifts seems to get stronger. I imagine you'll be able to move heavier and heavier objects. And Burn...well, I don't know. Maybe you'll be able to hear even better?"

Jez led them out onto the street, still talking merrily.

"For me, it's animals. I could kind of communicate with bugs and the like in Kasis. Out here, though, I can connect with almost anything. It's not talking." He gave a short, dry laugh. "Animals can't talk, obviously. It's more general ideas and such. But now I look after the animals here – and there are so many more types of animals to look after! I'll have to show you sometime. It'll blow your minds."

He walked them down the main thoroughfare for a minute before making a sharp right turn between two buildings, leading them down a semi-shaded lane. As the suns dropped below the horizon, the air was rapidly cooling, and Burn found herself shivering in her thin garments.

Of course, Jez noticed. "The temperature change is always a bit of a shock to our new residents. They're so used to the temperature-controlled Kasis, where it never drops below freezing. Out here, the nights can be brutal. Just be glad you got to stay! Otherwise you'd have had to find your own shelter for tonight. And don't worry, we'll get you some warmer clothes. There should be a few spare items at the boarding house you can use for the time being. That's where we're headed – the boarding house."

He took a few more turns, and Burn, coming back to herself slightly, tried to commit them to memory.

"You'll stay in the boarding house until you can build a house of your own. Or until one of the others becomes free. But the boarding house is nice enough – indoor facilities and a comfy bed to sleep on. Plus, you'll get to meet some of the other newbies. It's a great bonding opportunity."

While Burn appreciated the intel he was providing, Jez's incessant chatter and unending optimism were beginning to get on her nerves. She was obviously glad they hadn't kicked her out, but she resented being deemed unessential and considered "less than" Hale.

While Jez had been talking, an overwhelming exhaustion had overcome her, seeping into her bones and leaching into the crevices of her brain. All she felt like doing was locking herself in a room, collapsing on the bed, and not moving until tomorrow. Yet it didn't look like she was going to get that luxury.

Jez stopped in front of a sturdy two-story building capped with a small patio. Two stone columns rested in front, holding up a cantilevered room that provided shade to the entrance.

Jez knocked briskly on the front door. "I hope the landlady's in," he said to no one in particular. "There's a chance she's already gone down to dinner. In that case, we might be out of luck."

But his fears were for nothing because a few seconds later, a round woman with long gray hair and sharp eyes opened the door and stared up at them.

Jez stepped back, addressing her. "Evening, Luce. I'd like to introduce Hale and his wife, Auburn. They're our newest residents – and they'll be your new tenants. You do have a spare room, right?" She nodded once, almost reluctantly, and Jez went on, "Marvelous. Well then, I'll let you take it from here. See you two at dinner!" With that, he strode off, leaving them at Luce's mercy.

Luce didn't move aside to let them in. Instead, she looked them up and down, her expression turning into a sneer. Burn didn't know how, but they already seemed to have made a poor impression. She sighed, the full force of the day's events catching up to her and worming its way through her body.

Once again, Hale did the talking for both of them. "It's a pleasure to meet you, Luce. We're so grateful that you're letting us stay at your wonderful property. But it has been a long day, and my wife and I would truly appreciate it if you could show us where we'll be staying."

Burn guessed he was trying to sound charming. She didn't think it was working. Yet after a moment, Luce gave them another small nod and gestured for them to come inside – although she still didn't appear happy about their presence.

"You'll be sleeping in one of the upstairs rooms," she said, her voice high-pitched and crackling. She led them up a creaking staircase and down a short hallway, stopping outside a closed door with the number four painted on it in a garish green paint.

"I expect you to clean up after yourselves. I don't tolerate messes, and I don't tolerate loud tenants. If you disrespect me or my house, you will find yourselves on the streets. Do you understand?" She looked back at them, and they nodded mutely, both too startled to talk back.

"Good. Now, here is your room and here are your keys." She handed each of them an old-fashioned iron key before abruptly turning and heading back down the stairs.

She was almost as bad as Scar, Burn thought – then immediately regretted it. Thinking of Scar and what she must be going through was too painful, and Burn pushed it to the back of her mind. Now was not the time to dwell. She would save that for later when she was alone.

But, as it turned out, she wouldn't be getting that much-needed solace. Because as Hale turned the knob and opened the door, they were met with the sight of a tiny room equipped with a single lumpy bed, a shabby desk, a wardrobe, and one solitary window. This was going to be a problem, Burn thought tiredly.

Hale, however, didn't seem to see the issue. He strode forward and collapsed onto the bed, the furniture groaning and sagging under his weight. Gathering herself, Burn followed him, shutting the door behind her.

"So, we're married, huh?" Burn asked, her annoyance on full display.

Hale sighed, turning onto his back and putting his hands under his head. "Imber wasn't going to let you stay. He was going to kick you out into the desert. It was the only way to ensure that you'd be safe."

Burn chafed at the idea that she needed a man to keep her safe. Hale was, after all, the reason she was out in the wildlands in the first place. If he had been able to protect her, wouldn't they still be in Kasis? She opened her mouth to say just that, but closed it again, her common sense getting the better of her.

She was angry, yes, but it wasn't anger toward him. Well, it wasn't *all* toward him. She was angry at the Peace Force, at Imber, at these people of Videre who would judge her without even knowing her. And she was angry at herself.

Letting out a deep breath, she rubbed at her tired eyes, resigning herself to the situation at hand.

"So," she began, seating herself on the bed next to Hale, "how should we do this?"

A short while later, Burn and Hale made their way to the mess hall. They still didn't know the layout of the city, but Burn was able to navigate them in the right direction, following the sounds of raised voices and cheerful conversation.

The hall turned out to be a large square building near the center of town, its entrance marked by two towering stone statues. Just like the city itself, the statues seemed to rise from the ground, as if they were carved directly into the sand, and both depicted fearsome fantastical creatures. Well, Burn hoped they were born from fantasy and not reality, although after her experience with the donkey-ram, she couldn't be quite sure.

The creature on the left appeared to be a bear, although its neck and head were that of a vulture. In its left paw, the creature held a trident – a strange choice, given the arid landscape around them. Guarding the other side was a beast with the body of a man and the head of a deer, with striking antlers branching out above it.

Hale and Burn stood at the doorway for a time, taking in the peculiar specimens. They were intricate, even beautiful in a way, but also altogether alien, and Burn felt achingly out of place. Everywhere they turned, there was another reminder that they weren't in Kasis anymore. Burn wondered when the shock of their surroundings would fade – and the homesickness along with it.

The pair roused themselves from their momentary stupor and entered the mess hall, with Hale once again leading the way. The room inside was cavernous, consisting of one space with dozens of wooden tables. Each table was equipped with long wooden benches that spanned its length, providing seating for hundreds.

As they entered, a fragile hush fell over the room, all eyes turning in their direction. Burn felt exposed, like she was on display, and she instinctively tried to shrink behind Hale's large form. She was used to being the one doing the observing, not the one being observed, and the reversal of roles made her uneasy.

Just as she was considering turning around and leaving, a cheerful voice broke the silence.

"Hale and Auburn, welcome! I'm delighted you could join us. It was getting so late that we were beginning to think you wouldn't make it."

Burn peeked around Hale to see Imber coming toward them from a table at the far end of the room. Burn couldn't help but notice that his demeanor toward them had changed entirely. He was no longer the same man who had judged them and calculated their worth. Now he addressed them with kindness and mirth, a wide smile lighting up his face. She couldn't tell if they were real emotions or merely an act he was putting on for his audience.

"Everyone," he said, turning around to address the gathered crowd, "I'd like to introduce you to your new neighbors: Hale and his wife, Auburn. Oh, sorry, Burn," he said, correcting himself. "Hale will be joining our construction team and helping out in the militia when needed, and Burn here will be an excellent addition to our town guard."

A smattering of applause rippled through the crowd,

and Burn decided to play along with the charade. She held up her arm and waved at the room, giving them her best glowing smile. Taking her cue, Hale did the same, grinning warmly and waving while wrapping his other arm around Burn. She tried not to flinch at his unexpected touch.

Clearly pleased with their play-acting, Imber concluded his public address. "I know you'll all be the best neighbors you can be, helping out this delightful couple in any way you can and showing them all the wonderful things Videre has to offer."

With that, he turned around and lowered his voice, speaking directly to Hale and Burn. "It would be my honor if you'd join me at my table tonight. Although most of us are done eating, I'm sure we can scavenge up a few more plates from the kitchen. I'd love to get to know you both. And I'm sure you have plenty of questions about us, as well." Without waiting for a response, he turned on his heel and walked back to his table, evidently expecting them to follow in his wake.

After a moment's delay, they trekked after him. Arriving at the table, the pair took their seats across from Imber, who was situated next to a genial middle-aged blond woman. She looked up as they sat down, smiling at them and exposing her slightly crooked teeth.

"Hi! I'm Mags!" she said excitedly as two plates of food suddenly appeared before them.

Burn didn't know what to focus on first – Mags or the food. Her stomach growled as the savory scent of meat and grilled vegetables wafted up to her, but Mags' look was so insistent that Burn turned her attention to the woman first.

"It's lovely to meet you, Mags. Thank you for letting

us join your table." Burn wasn't entirely sure what the right pleasantries for this situation were, and she hoped she'd provided a suitable enough response to placate the woman. Apparently she had, because the smile never left Mags' face.

"Oh, don't you worry about it. We don't have any seating plans around here. Just sit where you want. You're guaranteed to make friends wherever you find yourself. That's how I got to know my husband. I just sat down and started talking. Isn't that right, hun?" She turned to face Imber.

Burn was caught off guard. She hadn't taken Imber as the marrying type – especially with someone as light and cheerful as Mags. But Imber smiled softly at his wife and nodded.

"I was a goner the second she opened her mouth," he said sweetly, bestowing a light peck on her cheek.

"Oh, you are the charmer, aren't you?" she said to Imber before turning her attention back on them. "Come on, eat! I'm sure you're starving after what you've been through, but you can relax now. You're home. Eat, eat!"

She was so insistent that Burn scooped up a bit of food and put it into her mouth before she even had time to assess what it was. Thankfully, it was delicious. Although after the excitement of the day, Burn was certain that even a bowl of plain porridge would have tasted delicious.

She glanced down and saw that she was eating some sort of thick stew, with large chunks of multi-colored vegetables and a meat Burn couldn't quite place. Given Videre's strange animal collection, though, she wasn't entirely sure she wanted to place it.

Despite the mystery meat, the soup went down easily

– and quickly – warming Burn's insides and clearing some of the remaining fog from her brain. Next to the stew was a chunk of warm, crusty bread, and Burn tore off a piece and dipped it into her soup.

As they ate, Mags talked. And talked and talked. She seemed to be the unofficial one-woman welcoming committee, explaining the general layout of Videre, the division of labor, their agricultural pursuits, and their enviable spot in the wildlands.

"But you have to be careful after dark, of course," she went on. "We're lucky here because we're walled in and we close the gates at night. Some other camps aren't as fortunate."

"Why? What's out there?" Hale asked in between large spoonfuls of stew. His bowl was disappearing twice as fast as Burn's, and she kept a possessive hold on hers in case he got any ideas.

"Oh, of course you haven't heard. It's not safe out there at night," she said, pointing in the direction of the city's gates. "For one thing, it gets mighty cold. As Jez probably told you, as the suns set the heat goes with them. Plus, we get some of the worst dust storms at night. More than once I've woken up to find half the house covered in sand. Had to dig myself out!"

She laughed lightly at the memory, although Burn couldn't quite see what was so humorous about the incident.

"Then there are the creatures," Mags said, shaking her head at the thought.

It was Burn's turn to ask. Swallowing a bite of food, she inquired warily, "What creatures?" Once again, she wasn't entirely sure she wanted to know.

"Oh, there are all sorts. We don't even know everything that roams around out there. It's too dangerous to go and investigate, but there seem to be a lot of wolves. You'll hear them howling at night. Although 'wolves' isn't quite the right term. They're much bigger than we'd thought, and faster, too. Then there are the sand bears."

Burn didn't ask about that one. Neither did Hale. But Mags explained anyway.

"We call them sand bears because they live in the dunes and come out at night. Well, mostly at night. They're angry creatures, with sharp claws and big tufts of white fur. If you're ever out there and you see a glimmer of white, you run. Run fast."

Burn and Hale stared at her, neither sure what to say in response. A response didn't prove necessary, however, since she simply went on without them.

"I look forward to seeing what you both can do. It's always exciting when we get new recruits. My husband's told me about your skills, of course, but I do enjoy seeing them in action – especially after you've been here a couple days and you start to get stronger. People love that part. They never want to go back."

Mags' seemingly offhand remark sparked something in Burn's mind, a question she'd wanted to ask since the moment she'd found herself alive at the bottom of the Pit.

"Has anyone ever gone back?" she asked, trying to hide the eagerness in her voice. Because that was her goal. That was her plan even if she couldn't verbalize it. She needed to go home, and she would do whatever it took to get there.

"People don't go back," Imber said firmly. His face had

lost the jovial quality he'd had when talking to his wife. Now he was all business.

Burn turned to Mags, hoping for a different answer, but Mags just looked at her sadly. She was oddly quiet for a minute, and with each second that ticked by, Burn's hope decreased little by little. Then Mags shook her head almost imperceptibly, and Burn's heart sank.

"No one has ever gotten back in, at least not that we know of. Plenty have tried. Some failed. Some died. Some never returned. But don't go looking for that. I know you don't know me well, but I pray that you'll take my advice. There's nothing for you back there. You could have a real future here, you and your husband. You could have a good life."

Burn nodded in response, as if taking her words to heart. Yet her mission remained firm in her mind.

No matter what they said, she was going back to Kasis. She was going back to Scar.

Chapter 6

Scar knew something was wrong. Burn hadn't returned the night before, and for some reason the messages Scar sent kept bouncing back. And now the Peace Force-sponsored news was reporting terrorist activity. She turned up the volume on her tab and listened to the bulletin that had been playing on repeat since early that morning.

"Yesterday afternoon, two terrorist operatives, who are believed to be working with the extremist Lunaria organization, attacked the ventilation system that feeds the upper levels. Their motives for doing so remain unclear. The pair was apprehended by local Peace Force patrols and immediately sentenced to the Pit. We congratulate our brave officers who put their lives in danger to tackle this radical threat."

Scar's heart pounded as she listened to the broadcast, certain they were talking about Burn and Hale.

The news reader went on, "Minor damage was done to the air supply points that service the upper levels. The ventilation department has informed us that the area's air quality may degrade slightly in the coming days. Citizens from those tiers are encouraged to stay inside and keep their doors and windows securely shut. Please be assured that crews are working night and day to restore order. As always, if you have any information regarding this or any other plot against our great government, you're advised to contact the Peace Force immediately. Your safety is our top priority."

Minor damage. Yeah right, Scar thought. She'd bet anything that most – if not all – of the system was currently offline. It would take more than a few days to get that functioning again. At least she had that fact to hold onto. At least their mission hadn't been a complete failure.

Scar didn't believe that Burn was dead. Surely she would have felt something – like a sudden emptiness or a desperate yearning. Yet she hadn't felt a thing.

She knew she had to move, though. Disappear. If the Peace Force had discovered that Burn was behind the attack, it was only a matter of time before they came for her. It didn't matter that she hadn't done anything wrong. Well, at least not anything they knew of. What mattered was that she might have information – and they would do anything they could to get it.

Scar packed quickly. She didn't need a lot of things. Clothes and jewelry and trinkets didn't matter to her. She did, however, grab as many of her tools and gadgets as possible, the things that couldn't be easily replaced. What she couldn't pack she stowed in secret cubbies under the floorboards, hoping the Peace Force wouldn't be thorough enough to find them.

Before leaving, she activated a few "special" security measures. They wouldn't stop the Peace Force entirely, but they would definitely frustrate their attempts for a while. She also placed a few red herrings around the house, technological clues that, once deciphered, would lead them in all manner of wrong directions. Needless to say, Scar was pleased with herself.

She left the house without looking back. There was nothing there for her anymore.

Tucking her wild curls into the hood of her cloak, she made her way softly through the streets. Scar didn't like being outside, didn't like the way people looked at her – like she was a freak, like she was dangerous. Like she wasn't even human.

She tugged involuntarily at the fabric around her neck, making sure it covered the sleek metal of her skin. If she wore enough clothing, she could hide it – and hide herself in the process. If she didn't...well, people didn't take kindly to metal women, especially when they were afraid. And nowadays, people were terrified.

The Peace Force had once again increased their patrols, interrogating anyone who looked out of place. Or anyone who looked like an easy target. It was best to stick to the shadows if you could. Thankfully, she'd had plenty of practice. She'd been slinking about in the shadows for as long as she could remember.

It wasn't difficult to find her destination. In reality, she'd only been there a handful of times, but she'd traced the route so often in her head that it felt like going home.

The flowers and vines decorating the red door greeted

her cheerfully, as if nothing bad had happened. Once upon a time, behind that very door, she had believed that nothing bad could happen, that she was invincible. She had been proven wrong in so many ways.

The sight of it twisted something inside of her, and her throat constricted, making it difficult to draw breath. She had to force herself to breathe, in through the nose and out through the mouth. There was nothing hiding behind that door, nothing that could hurt her. Well, nothing besides memories. But sometimes those could hurt more than anything.

Scar pushed the feelings down, relegating them to a deep, dark place within herself. She didn't need to examine them now. Now was the time for a plan.

Using the biometric bypass device she'd created, Scar let herself into the small house. She was sure Symphandra wouldn't have minded. In fact, she probably would have been thrilled to see her home used as a safe haven. That's just the kind of person she'd been.

Inside, the home felt musty, as if no one had been there in months. Although, to be fair, no one had. Yet somehow, despite the stale air, it still smelled like Symphandra: citrusy and spicy, like an exotic tea. Despite the memories that attempted to break free, the smell was comforting and familiar, providing a little bit of consistency in a world of unknowns.

Scar turned on the lights, blinking as the soft yellow bulbs sprang to life and illuminated the rainbow of colors that decorated the small space. Scar had always liked it here. It felt like Symphandra – warm and welcoming and colorful. Symphandra hadn't worried about standing out, even in a world as cruel as this one.

Scar dumped her luggage onto one of the brightly colored couches. Unzipping one of the bags and digging through its contents, she emerged with a compact silver box, which she immediately took to the door. After pressing a few hidden buttons along its side, a small steel bar shot out. She affixed the contraption tightly to the door and its frame, creating a virtually unbreakable seal, like a mechanical deadbolt. It was one of Scar's own inventions and would keep out even those who managed to bypass the biometric scanner. One could never be too careful, especially in such dangerous times.

With the house secured, Scar began to unpack. Her tools and contraptions and gadgets posed a stark contrast to the soft furnishings in the space. The well-worn steel and mess of wiring seemed so strange lying amongst the pillows and rugs and tapestries.

That was what she and Symphandra must have looked like – a mismatched combination of pretty colors and hard metal. But despite their differences, they had fit. And now, so did her things.

After she'd finished emptying her luggage, Scar got down to business. Her only goal now was to find her sister – find her and bring her home – but she couldn't do it alone.

Scar whipped out her tab and began typing. She read the message once, then again, making sure it was perfect. Encrypting the text to hide it from prying eyes, she hit send.

Throughout the city, in houses and factories, on street corners and thoroughfares, the Lunaria were called to action. "Tonight at 7. They've taken Burn. It's time for a plan."

Burn couldn't breathe. She lurched up in bed, coughing and sputtering, trying to draw air into her lungs. Its strange chemical makeup made the process difficult, and she had to force herself to take long, steady breaths rather than frantic gulps. She hated this place.

Next to her, Hale slept soundly, oblivious to her struggles. She wanted to kick him, to literally roll him off the bed and onto the floor, but she knew she couldn't. It wasn't because they had to maintain the charade of being married. She was certain that plenty of couples kicked each other out of bed. It was more that Hale had the body mass of a small to medium boulder, and she couldn't budge him if she tried. And, yes, she had tried.

Burn couldn't tell what time it was. The light streaming in the window was bright and consistent, but she didn't know what that meant out here. Back home, it was always a little bit dim, with the light from the suns broken by the tiers above them and the smog around them. But here, with nothing to block the rays, the suns seemed too bright, too direct, as if their light wasn't meant to be experienced without a shield.

She thought back to what Jez had said about the radiation enhancing their gifts. The suns were, in fact, mutating them more, taking them even further from the norm and placing them forever in the category of "other." She didn't need that. She was fine with the way she was. Besides, hearing more wouldn't help her get home. Unless she could hear all the way into Kasis, enhanced hearing wouldn't do her much good. Not in this barren wasteland.

Burn gave up on sleep and rolled out of bed, her feet hitting the floor with a loud thud. She glanced over at Hale, hoping the sound might have jarred him awake, but he remained where he was, his eyes shut and his breathing even. This marriage was already getting on her nerves, and they hadn't even been married a day. Burn briefly envisioned spending a lifetime with him and flinched. She definitely needed to find a way out of there.

She padded to the bathroom, listening to the world around her as she walked. Everyone else in Videre already seemed to be awake. The city was abuzz with life and conversation, plus all manner of sounds Burn wasn't accustomed to. The oinking of piglets in a pen. Sand being swept off porches. Rocky soil being tilled for crops. The foreign sounds made Burn feel all the more out of place, as if these noises belonged to someone else's life and not hers.

Entering the bathroom, Burn shut the door behind her and sighed, enjoying the brief solitude. With Hale always by her side, she'd hardly found a moment for herself. Finally alone, she let down her guard, giving in to the feelings that lurked like an ever-present shadow in her mind.

She missed Scar bitterly. Burn felt hollow in her absence, and her heart pounded an aching melody of loss and regret. She allowed a single tear to escape and roll down her cheek before composing herself.

Burn turned on the taps connected to the small tub, and a meager stream of water spilled out into the basin. It wasn't much, but it was enough to wash away the sand and dirt and sweat that had accumulated on her skin. With the help of a sweet-smelling soap, she rubbed off the traces of the previous day, leaving herself feeling almost normal. Almost, but not quite.

She changed into some of the clothes that Luce had left for her, which included a thin white blouse and tan linen pants. They weren't new by any means, but they were clean and soft and relatively free of holes. Imber had informed them that the city's seamstresses would deliver some new clothes to them in the coming days, but for now they had to content themselves with castoffs.

Looking at herself in the mirror, Burn saw the same short brown hair, narrow chin, and dark eyes that always stared back at her. Today they were set in a somber expression, some combination of mourning for her old life and a steely resolve to get it back. To most people, she probably just looked angry. That wasn't a bad thing, she decided. She didn't need to make friends here.

Her morning routine complete, she crossed back to the bedroom. She was glad to see that Hale was finally up, yawning and rubbing the sleep from his eyes.

"Morning," she said briefly by way of a greeting.

He grunted in response, giving credence to Burn's theory that he wasn't a morning person. Turning away from him, she put her head in her hands, rubbing her face and trying to quiet the headache that had emerged behind her temples. She tried to clear her thoughts, pushing the noise of Videre to the back of her mind.

"I could really go for some breakfast," Hale mumbled, almost too low for Burn to hear.

"What?" she asked, spinning around to face him.

Hale looked at her, confused. "I didn't say anything," he said, his face a mask of innocence.

Burn shook her head, certain that she would never understand men.

Sighing, she said, "Well, I think breakfast is over anyway. It seems we've slept in a little late. Everyone's already up and about. I hope Imber doesn't kick us out if we're late on our first day of work."

Hale, still looking perplexed, opened his mouth to speak but shut it again without saying anything. Burn made a mental note not to engage with him after he'd just woken up. It seemed he required more time than most to get himself together.

"Fine," she conceded, taking pity on him. "Go clean yourself up, and I'll see if Luce has any spare food lying around. But in the future, when you're hungry you get your own food." She left the bedroom without waiting for a reply and climbed down to the first floor.

Luce was out front, sweeping the sand from last night's storm off the stoop and muttering to herself. "Damn sandstorms. Can't even go one day without sand getting into every corner of this godforsaken place. Might as well live inside a sand dune and be done with it."

Burn had to clear her throat to get Luce's attention. The woman spun around at the sound, brandishing the broom like a weapon, and Burn put her hands up in surrender.

"Hi, Luce," she started warily. "We know we missed breakfast, but we were hoping you might have a bit of something to tide us over? We'd appreciate any food you could spare." She tried to sound sweet and sincere, but it was difficult given Luce's obvious dislike of her.

Luce considered her for a moment, sizing her up as if to determine whether Burn was trying to fleece her out of her daily rations. Apparently she decided that Burn was trustworthy because after a few seconds she lowered the broom and steered her inside.

"I have a few things tucked away for emergencies," she said, opening a squeaky wooden cabinet in the corner of the kitchen. "But don't get used to this. If you miss breakfast again, you'll have to fend for yourself."

Luce pulled out a few bruised apples and a muslin bag and thrust them into Burn's hands before closing the cabinet and stalking back outside. Burn stood there for several heartbeats, trying to regain her bearings after the abrupt conversation.

Peeking inside the cloth bag, she saw it held a mixture of toasted oats, seeds, and miscellaneous dried fruits. It wasn't much, but it would be enough to tide them over until lunch. Assuming Hale didn't eat it all. Having seen the large man eat, she knew he had quite the appetite.

Burn shoveled a few handfuls of the oat mixture into her mouth as she climbed the stairs, determined not to let her faux husband bogart the meal. Only after she'd sufficiently satisfied her own hunger did she enter the bedroom and toss the remaining foodstuffs to Hale.

He had changed in her absence, donning a simple tan shirt and an animal hide vest over loose pants of a deep brown hue. Burn found it amazing how much a change of outfit could change a person. Hale now looked like all the rest of the men in Videre, like he had always been there.

She imagined she must look the same, like she was one of them. Like she belonged. That thought was an unwelcome one, and Burn chastised herself for even considering belonging in a place like this. She belonged in Kasis, not here.

As she watched, Hale dumped the contents of the muslin bag straight into his mouth, emptying the sack in a matter of seconds. Then he got to work on his apple, with that, too, disappearing faster than Burn could have imagined. She was glad she had taken her share when she did, and she made another mental note to never leave him alone with a plate of food – at least not if she wanted it to be there when she returned.

Done with his meal, Hale turned to her and asked, "So what now?"

Burn shrugged, glancing out the window to the city beyond. "Now I think we have to go to work."

Chapter 7

Burn had never done an honest day's work in her life. She preferred to pay the bills in a somewhat less conventional way: blackmail. Targeting the rich and powerful, it turned out, was a great way to curry favors, gain intel, and sustain a comfortable lifestyle with a little cash to spare.

In Videre, however, blackmail wasn't a viable career path. Which was a shame because with her gift, Burn had become a master of discovering people's darkest secrets. Now she needed to learn a different trade entirely. She was going to be a guard. The thought did not appeal to her.

She enjoyed the freedom of blackmail – the varied hours, the different settings, the myriad people she could meet and extort. Yet up on the wall, guarding the city from intruders, she'd have none of those things. It would be the same place and the same people day in and day out.

Naturally, she wasn't in a hurry to get to the wall. But sooner than she had expected, she found herself standing before it, squinting up in an attempt to find someone – any-one – who could show her the ropes. Or at least show her how to get up.

"Hello?" she yelled, hoping her voice would carry along the wall's wide expanse. She waited a minute, but no one responded. "Is anyone up there?" she tried again.

This time, a head surrounded by a tangle of black hair poked out over the side. "You Burn?" the woman shouted. Burn nodded. "You're late," she stated before promptly ducking out of sight.

Burn remained where she was, flummoxed by the strange interaction. Should she stay and try to find a way up? Should she yell again? Should she leave and call it a day?

A few seconds later, however, her questions were answered for her when a small door opened in the wall nearby and the black-haired woman stuck her head out once more.

"Follow me," she said before disappearing into the gate's interior.

Burn did as she was told, entering through the almost-hidden door and finding herself in a dimly lit passageway with a single staircase. Seeing no other options, she climbed the stairs and soon emerged on top of the city's wall.

The woman was waiting for her there, leaning against the parapet with her arms folded in front of her. Burn approached warily, considering the woman. The woman considered her right back.

This guard was tall and muscular, with wavy black hair that cascaded down her back. She had a wide nose and strong jaw, paired with dark eyes that saw far more than Burn was comfortable with.

"I'm Nara," she said after reaching the end of her inspection. "I don't need another guard. I can see beyond the horizon in every direction. If anyone approaches Videre, I'll be the first to know. But Imber says I need to let you play along. So here we are."

There was no malice in her voice, merely conviction. The bluntness and self-satisfaction almost rivaled Scar, and Burn couldn't help but smirk. Despite her best efforts, she liked Nara and found her clear-cut demeanor refreshing.

"OK," Burn said, shaking her head. "You seem like you have this whole guard thing under control. But I do have to earn my keep. So I'll be here. Every day. And while I'm here, I might listen for anything out of the ordinary, just to keep myself occupied. And who knows? I might hear them before you see them."

Burn strolled past her, looking out into the wildlands. Yes, she was baiting Nara, but if the woman was anything like Scar, then she thrived on a little friendly competition.

Nara was at her side in an instant. "You're on," she whispered into Burn's ear. Burn smiled, relieved. Maybe this whole "work" thing wouldn't be as bad as she'd thought.

Scar wove through the dim streets, her head covered and her hands thrust into her pockets. Being outside for a second time that day made her uncomfortable, as if she were tempting fate and enticing it to bite her, but she had no other choice. She had to get to the Lunaria's meeting. She had to convince them to save Burn.

This meeting was located a few tiers beneath Symphandra's house, although not quite at the bottom of the city. This particular safe house had been used as the command center for the ManniK Battles, and they'd converted it to a hospital in the battles' wake. It still held painful memories for Scar – memories of Burn, small and broken, lying unconscious in bed.

Scar had feared that Burn might never wake up, that she would be left alone to deal with the aftermath. Thankfully, that hadn't been the case then. But it was now.

She made it to the safe house in good time, scanning her finger on the pad outside to gain entry. Per usual, she was one of the first to arrive. Not wanting to draw attention, she tucked herself into a chair in the corner of the room and waited, observing each member as they entered.

As more people trickled in, whispered conversations emerged and spread, creating a buzz that rippled through the space. It seemed that Burn and Hale were the topic of the night, with their names sprouting from most people's lips.

Theories on their capture mingled with gossip on what had happened to them to form a curtain of rumors, which blanketed the room. Scar bristled at how brazen they were, how crude and unfeeling they acted about two of their own. Yet she remained silent, waiting for her moment.

That moment came a quarter of an hour later. Half of the Lunaria were late, which grated on Scar's nerves, but she knew she couldn't start without all of them present. When the last member finally closed the door behind her, Scar stood up abruptly, drawing the room's attention.

"Yesterday, during their mission to sabotage the

ventilation system, Burn and Hale were captured by the Peace Force and thrown down the Pit." Scar didn't see the purpose of pleasantries or beating around the bush, so she got straight to the point. "I believe they're still alive. I don't know what's out there, but it's likely bleak. We need to find a way to get them back."

Titters of laughter rolled through the room. Scar swiftly turned her head to face each culprit, intent on staring them down. This was not a joke. Her sister's life hung in the balance, and she was deadly serious.

"We don't know what happens when someone gets thrown down the Pit," she continued, her tone grave. "We've only assumed that it leads to certain death, but no one knows for sure. It was built long before our time, and no information regarding its creation exists in the public record. That, in itself, is suspicious."

No one spoke up to disagree with her, but she could tell they were dubious. Convincing them to help her – and to help Burn – was not going to be easy.

"Burn and Hale led many of you through the ManniK Battles. They saved the lives of thousands of people down on the lowest tiers. If there's a chance they're alive, we need to do everything it takes to bring them back."

"But what proof do we have that they're still alive?" Raqa piped up from his seat on the floor. "I mean, wouldn't our time be better spent ensuring that they didn't die for nothing? We should capitalize on their progress, strike again while the top tiers are still reeling from the last hit."

For a man who always acted shaky and timid, he certainly wasn't afraid to speak up, Scar thought. Other heads around the room nodded at his words, and Scar had to stop herself from visibly sneering. This was what she'd been afraid of.

"If they're alive out there," she began, but she was cut off before she could continue.

"That's a big 'if.' I'm with Raqa," said Ansel, one of the men who had fought alongside her in the ManniK Battles, utilizing his potent gift of fire to torch his opponents. "Our mission should be to keep going, keep fighting back. It's what Hale would have wanted."

Scar tried to speak again, but Ansel held up his hand. "If you can bring us proof that they're alive, that there's something out there beyond the Pit, then we'll act. We'll mobilize a team and do everything we can to get them home. Until then, we can't waste our resources on a hunch."

The rest of the room murmured their assent, and Scar's vision went red with rage. They couldn't do this to her. No, they couldn't do this to Burn, to someone who had sacrificed so much for them. They had no loyalty, no allegiance.

The wires that threaded through Scar's curls began to spark, and she could hear them sizzle as they telegraphed her anger. She wanted to scream, to demand they help her, to pin every one of them to the wall until they agreed to her plan, but she couldn't. She was helpless, and that was the worst part of it all.

She took her seat in silence, the crackle of her hair the only sign of her fury. Patience was not her strong suit. Neither was taking orders. So if they wouldn't help her, she would rescue Burn on her own – no matter the stakes.

The rest of the meeting passed in a blur. Scar didn't listen to their discussion, nor did she take part in their plans. She didn't volunteer to help or lend her expertise. This was not her fight, not anymore.

She knew it was selfish, forgoing their battle in favor of her own, but she didn't care. As far as she was concerned, they'd betrayed her and Burn and, in doing so, had shown their true colors. Leaving an ally behind wasn't the mark of a courageous team. It was the action of a frightened band of rebels who were too concerned with losing to ever truly win.

The instant the meeting ended, Scar was out the door. She needed to get away, to clear her head and figure out where to go next. Pulling up her hood, she stalked through the darkening lanes, conscious of the fact that curfew was drawing near but too incensed to care.

Pausing at the mouth of a narrow alley, she felt a sudden presence at her elbow. She spun to find Kaz standing beside her. Without hesitation, she pulled out her pen and held it to his neck, pressing the trigger.

An electrical pulse shot through Kaz's body for the barest fraction of a second, and he crumpled to the ground. Satisfied with herself, Scar dragged him deeper into the alley, out of sight of the connected street. Looking down, she considered her handiwork.

Kaz was a Peace Officer, albeit a familiar one. Burn had found herself in his company several times before the ManniK Battles, having used him to gain inside intel on the Peace Force's plot.

That didn't mean Scar trusted him. When he'd learned about Burn's true allegiances, he'd turned on her. Despite that, Burn had let him go, freeing him and allowing him to return to his corrupt little Peace Force – even though he possessed a particularly useful gift.

His gift of stealth must have been what allowed him to sneak up on Scar. Yet she had been prepared. She was always prepared. And now he was unconscious – and would be for several more minutes.

Seizing the opportunity, she patted him down. Finding a gun strapped to his belt, she carefully removed it, holding it up as a warning. She didn't like guns, but she respected the authority they bestowed – and she wasn't against using that authority to further her own ends.

Towering above Kaz, gun in hand, she waited for him to regain consciousness. As she waited, the light around her dimmed and the sirens sounded throughout the city, indicating that curfew had begun. Scar didn't care. She had a feeling this was going to be worth the risk.

Eventually, Kaz stirred. He groaned and put his hand to his neck before slowly opening his eyes. He followed the line of Scar's body up to the gun in her hand, and his eyes went wide. Scar was pleased at his reaction.

Kaz looked tired. There were bags under his eyes, and his thick dark hair was unkempt. He even had hints of a scraggly beard poking through his normally clean-shaven skin. He looked like a mess.

"What do you want?" Scar asked, her voice all business.

Kaz took his time before responding, no doubt still disoriented. After blinking at her a few more times, he straightened, holding his hands up to show he wasn't planning to attack.

"I was waiting outside the safe house," he began in a

husky voice. "That was where I was kept during the battles. It's the only meeting place I know about."

"Have you told anyone else? Does the Peace Force know about it?"

Kaz shook his head emphatically. "No. I didn't tell them. I didn't tell them anything. After the battles, the force was in such disarray that they didn't even realize I'd been gone. Cross only told a few officers that he thought I was a traitor, and Hale dealt with them when he freed me during the prisoner transfer. I was able to go back to work without anyone being the wiser."

"You ran right back to them," Scar said in disdain. "Burn never should have let you go."

Kaz stared up at her, his look pleading. "That's not it. I was...confused. I didn't know what to think or believe. I wanted things to go back to normal. I wanted everything to feel like it had before, like I was the good guy and I could make a difference."

"And you thought you could do that with *them*?" Scar spat back. "You're even more naïve than I thought."

"Listen, I want to help you! That's why I followed you tonight. I want to help you find Auburn!" He was frantic now, desperate for Scar to believe him.

"What?" That hadn't been what Scar was expecting. Her heart was hammering in her chest, with rage and adrenaline and a small tinge of hope mingling in her mind. She didn't fully trust this man, but if he was serious, he could be the key to bringing Burn back.

"I heard what happened to Auburn," he said, his voice cracking. "I know you don't trust me, but I did care for her. I *do* care for her."

"So you think she could still be alive?" No one else had believed her. No one else was on her side. No one but him.

"Yes. If anyone can survive whatever's in the Pit, it's Auburn. She's strong and resourceful. She's not like anyone else I've ever met. But if she is still alive, she needs our help."

Scar considered him for a long moment. She didn't know if she believed him. This could easily be a trap, a way to trick her into revealing more about the Lunaria and their plans. Still, she wanted to believe him, if only to have someone else on her side.

"Prove it," Scar demanded. "Prove you're willing to do what it takes to bring Burn back."

"How?" Kaz asked, his voice still shaky.

Scar smiled beneath her mask, a plan forming in her mind. "Find out what's on the other side of the Pit," she commanded.

Chapter 8

Burn awoke suddenly. At first, she couldn't tell what had startled her. The room was calm and cool, and Hale was breathing gently beside her.

Then she listened, truly listened to the world around her. Something was tapping on the roof. The sounds were gentle and inconsistent, but the longer she listened, the faster they got. Curiosity got the better of her. Slipping on a pair of loose shoes over her woolen socks, she crept out of bed and down the stairs, quietly unlatching the door and sneaking outside.

A cold breeze brushed across her face, bringing with it scents of damp sand and minerals. All around her, small divots were appearing in the dirt as water began to fall from the sky. It was raining.

She stepped out from the protection of the cantilevered roof, placing herself in the storm. With her hands held out to the sides, she lifted her face to the clouded sky. She had never felt rain before. She had only ever heard it from a distance, pummeling the glass of the dome. Now, in this place, she let it flow over her, savoring the feel of the cool droplets splashing on her skin and running down her body.

Burn heard his footsteps before he emerged. She didn't turn around. Within a minute, Hale was beside her. Without saying a word, he mirrored her stance, putting his arms out and his head back as if trying to drink in the rain.

For the first time in a long time, Burn laughed – a real laugh, not one tricked out of her by the chemical imbalance of the wildlands. For the first time in a long time, Burn felt free.

They stood like that for some time, until the rain began to splash down in earnest, soaking through their clothes and into the skin beneath. Wet and happy, they took shelter under the roof, settling themselves on a step to watch the rain fall around them.

After a time, Hale spoke. "It's not half bad here," he said gently, as if trying to convince her to stay.

Burn glanced over at Hale, considering him and everything they'd been through. Sure, he was impulsive. He could be pig-headed. And he liked to be in control – a trait they both shared, which was definitely an obstacle.

But he was here. Over the past few days, there had been many times he could have left her to fend for herself. It would have been easier for him if he had. Yet he had stayed by her side. He had fought for her when no one else would.

He caught her looking at him. She didn't shy away. They stared at each other for a moment, each trying to read the other's thoughts.

Finally, Burn said quietly, "We can't stay."

"Why not?" He sounded sad but like he already knew the answer.

"They need us. The Lunaria need us. And no matter how much we try to deny it, we need to be part of that fight. It's rooted in us now. It's part of who we are."

"It doesn't have to be."

Burn smiled at that, a sad smile full of things left unsaid. "I wish that were true."

With that, she rested her head on his strong shoulder and watched the rain fall.

Time on the wall passed slowly. It turned out that guard duty wasn't half as much fun as it sounded. Very few people traveled in and out of the gates, and those that did were definitely no threat to the community. More shepherds and tradesfolk than wild barbarian raiders.

Thankfully, Nara had a solution for the boredom: She was teaching Burn how to fight.

Long ago, Burn's father had shown her the basics of hand-to-hand combat, drawing on his Peace Force training to demonstrate blocks and blows. But Burn was out of practice. It had been many years since she'd sparred, and her brawls during the ManniK Battles had shown her just how rusty she was. When she'd come up against Cross, she'd barely made it out with her life. If it ever came to that again, she wanted to be ready.

Burn still knew surprisingly little of Nara's past, of who

she had been before coming to Videre. However, it did seem that her role had included a substantial amount of fighting. She was good. Her movements were fluid and precise, with fists and knees and elbows finding their way past Burn's defenses more often than she cared to admit.

The training was grueling, especially in the heat of the mid-afternoon suns, yet Burn found it exhilarating. For so long, she'd lain in the shadows, listening to the action from the safety of her perch. Now, she was learning how to be a part of it.

Nara didn't limit herself to hand-to-hand styles. When she'd tired of traditional sparring, she would transition them to sticks, teaching Burn how to wield a wooden baton to inflict maximum damage. Then she'd move on to knives. Or bows and arrows. Or spears.

Videre didn't often deal with guns, much to Burn's relief. It wasn't because the city was morally opposed to the deadly weapons; it was more that they were difficult to come across outside of Kasis. The few that the city possessed were locked up in the armory and only used for special occasions – like trips to the Pit to scavenge for new residents.

So Burn learned to fight with the classics, honing her skills and strengthening her muscles atop the city's parapets. Sometimes, people came to watch them, lured by the sounds of a struggle and mesmerized by the speed of their movements. They'd gasp when one of the women came close to injuring the other, and they'd cheer when Nara would inevitably disarm her. Thus, through no effort of her own, Burn became a part of the city, a familiar feature and a welcome inhabitant.

Still, she preferred the times when they were alone, when she could concentrate on the sound of Nara's knife slicing through the air or the thwack of stick hitting stick as they deflected and parried. Little by little, she got faster and stronger, her strikes gaining precision and her movements fluidity.

In between their training, they would talk. Or, at least, Burn would talk. It wasn't easy getting anything from Nara, but once again, Burn was up for the challenge.

"Have you ever thought about going back to Kasis?" Burn asked one morning as they took a break from their training.

Nara sat opposite her on the wall, staring out into the desert. She was quiet for a while, her sights focused on the horizon. Burn wasn't sure she had heard and was about to repeat the question when Nara spoke.

"No," she said simply, not bothering to elaborate.

"Why not?" Burn pressed, looking for more.

"Because it's not possible."

Burn considered that for a moment. "When I was in Kasis," she said pensively, "I didn't think it would be possible to exist out here. But here we are. Some things aren't as far-fetched as you think. There has to be a way to get back."

"No one has ever done it," Nara said plainly.

"Really? Because Imber's wife said that some of the people who went searching for a way in never came back. How do you know they didn't find what they were looking for? How do you know they're not in Kasis now?"

"I don't," Nara said softly. "But what's the likelihood of that?"

"Then let's go! You and me. Let's go to the dome. We could hop on Jez's cart and see for ourselves. You can see farther than anyone, and I can listen for weak spots. Together, we could find a way back in."

Despite Burn's eagerness, Nara seemed unmoved. "It's not going to work. A trip around Kasis on foot would take days, and there are things out there that even I don't want to face."

Nara pushed herself up, hopping to her feet and walking forward to Burn's side of the wall. She looked out at the landscape, seeing more than Burn could possibly imagine.

"I do want to go back," she said so quietly that Burn nearly missed it.

Burn rose and stood next to Nara, gazing out at the lonesome expanse of sand and rocks and sky before her. "I'm going to find a way," she said confidently, turning to her friend. "And when I do, I'll let you know."

Just like Jez had promised, the radiation in the wildlands began to change them – Hale especially. While Burn found that she could hear somewhat farther than before, Hale discovered that he could now lift nearly anything he found, whether it be rocks, planks of wood, or, on one occasion, a cart full of sheep.

He enjoyed his newfound strength, and he found any opportunity to show it off around the city. He gleefully helped erect buildings, move tables, and excavate dig sites for new materials. One afternoon, he even began splitting boulders of mountain stone apart with his bare hands.

And with each passing day, his desire to return to Kasis seemed to wane a little more. As he found his place in this new society, his role in the old one faded, gradually disappearing into the past. Yet Burn remained resolute. She was going to find a way back, and if she had to do it without him then she would.

Unfortunately, she had no idea where to start. Everyone she talked to gave her the same answer: "It's not possible. Forget about your old life. You'll grow to like it here."

But that's precisely what she was afraid of: that she would forget about her life in Kasis and grow to like Videre. She fought against it, every day reminding herself of what she'd lost and who was waiting for her back home. She even went as far as repeating their names in her head, picturing their faces as she went. Scar. Meera. Ansel. Crete. The list went on and on.

"They're probably fine without us," Hale said one morning as they lingered in the mess hall after breakfast. "The Lunaria can take care of themselves. I bet they've already capitalized on our success with the airflow systems and moved on to bigger things."

"And you're OK with that?" Burn shot back, a fire beginning to smolder in her chest. "You're OK with them going on as if we never existed, finishing the work we started?"

"It's just how things are. We're here. They're there. We all have to do what we can to survive."

"Argh!" Burn yelled, threading her hands through her hair in agitation. "That's not good enough. We can get back. I know we can. We still have so much more work to do there.

We just need to think! Stop sitting around and help me. Please," she begged.

"I bet your precious Peace Officer would know what to do," Hale said acidly.

Burn stared at him, confused. She could have sworn that his lips hadn't moved…but she'd heard him loud and clear.

"I doubt it," she responded warily, still uncertain. "Kaz was never one for plans."

The look Hale gave her then confirmed her fear. He hadn't spoken out loud. The two stared at each other for a long moment, their mouths open in shock.

Had…had she just heard his thoughts? No, that was ridiculous. And impossible. Her gift was being able to hear things others couldn't – not hearing inside their minds. She must be going crazy.

"Burn…" Hale started to say, his eyes wide.

Without waiting for him to finish, she turned on her heel and stalked out of the mess hall, her mood suddenly soured. She didn't even greet Imber and Mags as she passed them in the entrance, breezing around them as if they didn't exist.

Burn stormed to the wall, her thoughts in a jumble. As she reached the top of the stairs, she went straight for the sparring sticks. Grabbing both, she tossed one to Nara and attacked.

Despite her shock, Nara was ready. Burn wasn't thinking clearly. Her mind wasn't focused on moves or footwork or hand positions. All she wanted to do was attack. She hit hard and fast, her confusion and frustration morphing into fury as she struck.

She wanted to go home. She wanted to see Scar. She wanted things to go back to the way they had been.

Then, all of a sudden, she was on the ground and Nara was yanking the stick from her grasp. She pointed both weapons at Burn, but all Burn could do was stare at them mutely. Her anger faded into numbness as her friend towered over her.

Seeing the look in Burn's eyes, Nara sighed and tossed the sticks aside. Taking a seat next to Burn, she waited. And waited. Burn had the feeling she could wait an eternity, staying silent until the other person spoke. Only, Burn didn't know what to say.

"How did you end up here?" she finally whispered, her eyes fixed on the ground. Her mind was tired. She didn't want to think about her own life anymore. Maybe hearing about someone else's would be enough to distract her, if only for a while.

Nara was silent for time. Burn didn't know if she was thinking about how to answer or if the silence was her answer. After a few long moments, however, she spoke, her voice low and dreamlike.

"I was young. And I was angry," she began, gazing in the direction of Kasis. "My dad was sick, and my mom couldn't find a way to support us. I was old enough to help out, but I didn't know how. No one wanted to hire a kid from the bottom tiers. In the end, I had to start stealing just so we'd have enough food to get through the day."

Nara closed her eyes for a minute, as if watching the story play out on the inside of her eyelids.

"I fell in with a violent crowd. They told me they

appreciated my gift, that I was special. What they really meant was that they could use me. I became their lookout, their spy. They'd have me scout out the places they wanted to rob, then make sure the coast was clear so they could go in and do the job.

"That's where I learned how to fight. They taught me how to protect myself...and how to hurt people. We didn't care who we stole from – rich, poor, good, bad. If we wanted something, we took it."

Nara shook her head, her eyes unreadable. "We started making a name for ourselves. People were afraid of us, and it felt good. It felt like we had power. But being feared isn't the same thing as being powerful. And one night it all went wrong. Horribly wrong." She took a deep, shuddering breath before continuing, as if building up her strength.

"We were targeting this house. They didn't have a lot, but they had more than we did so they were fair game. We went in at night when they were all asleep. Thought it would be an easy job, just in and out and no one would get hurt. But I didn't see the Peace Officers. They must have been waiting for us. They knew we'd be there.

"When we went in, they followed after us. And that's when they started shooting. I ran and I hid as they shot my crew." A single tear rolled down Nara's face, and she hastily wiped it away with the back of her hand.

"The noise woke the family. The mother came down to see what was happening, and the Peace Force shot her. They didn't even hesitate. Their little girl must have been at the top of the stairs because she ran down, screaming 'Mommy!' over and over again. They raised their guns at her, too. I knew

I couldn't stand by. So I jumped out and put myself in front of her.

"They tackled me almost immediately. Took me straight to the Pit and tossed me in. The whole time I was thinking I deserved it; I deserved to die. But I didn't die. I ended up here. Imber didn't care about my past, about what I'd done, and neither did anyone else. I got to start again, become someone new, someone better."

They lapsed into silence as Burn considered what she'd learned and Nara tried to bring herself back to the present. Her experiences were heart-wrenching, yet they explained so much about her and the person she'd become. However, something still nagged at Burn, forcing her to speak.

"But I heard you the other day," she said tentatively. "You said you wanted to go back." A sudden realization dawned on her as she spoke. "You didn't say that out loud, did you?"

Nara shook her head, her eyes meeting Burn's for the first time since she'd begun her tale. Burn took a deep breath, realizing what that meant. She was, indeed, beginning to hear people's thoughts. Her mind started to race, but she clamped down on it, relegating this new information to the background.

"After all that," Burn said gently, "why would you want to go back?"

"When I first got here, it felt like I was given a second chance at life, a chance to do things better. The longer I stayed, though, the more it felt like I was running away," she explained slowly. "My problems didn't go away because I'm not there. The things I did didn't just disappear. They're with me, but I can't do anything about them here. If I could get back...maybe I could make amends. Maybe I could do something that would make a real difference."

Burn smiled sadly. "I think I know exactly what you mean."

Without invitation, Burn embarked on her own tale. It felt like she owed it to the woman – a story for a story. Their pasts were somehow so similar despite their differences. They had both wanted to create a better life for their families and had both found a group that would help them do it. They'd both hurt people along the way – and gotten hurt in return. But unlike Nara, Burn had been fighting to change the system. Now she had a way to help her friend do the same.

When she'd finished her story, she paused, letting Nara soak in everything she'd said about the Lunaria, Scar, the ManniK Battles, her capture. It was a lot to take in. Burn rubbed at her eyes, her mind swimming with memories, painful and bittersweet.

"If only my father were here," she said absentmindedly. "I bet he'd know what to do. He always had a plan."

All at once, the idea came to her. It had been lingering there, in the back of her mind, since she'd found herself in the wildlands, yet for some reason she hadn't been able to grasp it. Now it was as if the fog had cleared and she could finally see through the haze.

Her father. Before his death, Cross had admitted that he'd had her father thrown down the Pit. And if she'd survived the fall, then Arvense must have, too. He could still be alive. He could be out in the wildlands right now. He could help her get home.

Chapter 9

Scar prowled through the lowest tiers of the city, mentally mapping the streets and buildings around the base of the dome. She'd never been one for exploration, much preferring the confines of home to the perils of the unknown. Now, however, with Burn gone and the Lunaria unwilling to help, the job fell to her.

It was slow going. She'd already been at it for days without success. The edges of the dome were inaccessible at best and dangerous at worst. It was as if the long-ago architects had foreseen her search for a weak spot and done everything they could to prevent it.

On top of that, the areas were heavily guarded, with roaming PeaceBots patrolling the borders. But a handful of electrified gates and a few robotic soldiers couldn't stop Scar. They could slow her down, though. And they could frustrate her to no end.

On this particular evening, she'd made her way down

below the Corax End. The seedy back alleys and dirty lanes weren't directly against the walls, but they were close enough to make a passable starting point. Within no time, she'd found herself alone, lost amongst the maze of small passageways and cramped tunnels that led to the outer limits of the city.

She checked her compass often, changing direction to correct her course. If she wasn't careful, she could easily end up back where she'd started. There were no maps of these sinister paths, no electronic records she could follow. It was up to her to find her way through the chaos.

Coming to a tall wired fence, Scar stopped to listen. She heard no hum indicating it was electrified, but she wasn't willing to take any chances. She'd already learned her lesson once.

Rifling through her bag, she pulled out the makeshift voltage reader she'd cobbled together from spare parts and held it to the fence, waiting impatiently for a reading. After a long pause, the device beeped, indicating it was safe. Sighing in relief, she took out another gadget – a small black tube equipped with a powerful laser cutter – and got to work carving a small, Scar-sized hole along the fence's side. After she'd squeezed through, she replaced the portion of fence, making it whole once again.

As she was now in a restricted zone, Scar kept her movements quick and light, checking around every corner before darting out from behind it. Now more than ever, she missed Burn and her gift, how she always knew what was lurking in the darkness even before turning on the light. Without her, Scar's own senses felt dulled, as if she had lost one of them without even realizing it.

She pushed the thought from her mind, throwing herself into the task at hand. She was close now. She could feel it.

While she'd been working, dusk had arrived. Down in the polluted bowels of the city, that didn't mean much. The streets here were always drowned in the same murky shadows, the voracious grime clinging to everything and everyone. But it did mean that she was now breaking curfew as well as trespassing. Two crimes for the price of one. If she were caught now, the Peace Force would have no qualms about chucking her in a cell – or into the Pit. She wouldn't be much use to Burn then.

It was quiet here, bordering on calm, but Scar knew better than to trust it. Silence didn't mean safety; it just meant your enemies knew how to hide. And down here, there were plenty of places to hide.

Disused generators rose around her like monoliths, while hunks of old iron bridges and walkways leaned against them, creating a vertical maze to nowhere. Rats and rodents squeaked within piles of rubbish and refuse, claiming the area as their own. Even the streets petered out, disintegrating into small footpaths through the rubble. It was an eerie place, this graveyard of the past, and despite the clammy warmth she couldn't help but shiver.

Scar picked her way through the debris, her progress slow. As she worked, the air around her subtly changed, morphing into something heavy and oppressive. It felt like the world was closing in on her, squeezing its dirty fingers around her unwelcome form. Curious, she looked up.

It wasn't the world closing in on her after all. Peeking through the mounds of metal and brick was the gently sloping curve of the dome. The discovery spurred her on, and she increased her pace through the wreckage. Skirting a wall of rotten lumber and ducking beneath a makeshift passageway of gears, she wound her way closer and closer to the glass that encapsulated the city.

Then, almost without warning, she was standing before it. Scar had only ever glimpsed the dome from afar, its surface intangible and nearly invisible against the sky. Yet now it was right in front of her, smooth and solid and all too real. And, apparently, impenetrable.

Two layers of thick glass curved up from the ground, cemented in place and protected by a buzzing forcefield. Scar could feel its power from several feet away, her skin tingling and the hairs on her arms standing on end.

The world beyond the dome was quiet and still. Since Kasis was built on a small platform, she wasn't level with the ground. Instead, she stood several stories above it, looking down on the sandy desert below. There was nothing out there, she realized with a shock. As far as she could see – which wasn't far amidst the darkness and the haze – there was nothing.

Scar adjusted her goggles, tailoring their settings to the scene. Increasing the contrast and brightness, she zoomed in on the bleak landscape, scanning the area for signs of life. But there were none. The only thing to move was the sand, blown across the boundless vista by mighty gusts of wind.

There were no traces of people, no buildings, no tents, no footprints in the sand. And there were no doors or portals either, no means of entry or escape. It was a wasteland, inexpressibly desolate, a place which she could never enter – and from which Burn might never escape.

Shaking slightly, Scar walked along the edge of the dome, following the curve. There had to be a way out. There just had to be. The longer she walked, however, the more certain she was that Kasis was a fortress, an impenetrable city forever separated from the outside world. She could see no weak spots, no cracks in the façade, no way out.

Outside the dome, night had fallen in earnest. Some part of her knew that it was late, that she should be getting back. Yet she couldn't seem to pull herself away from the wall, believing that the key to saving Burn could lie just beyond her line of sight.

She didn't know how long she'd been walking – maybe minutes, maybe hours. The view outside never seemed to change, with the swirling sand and dunes forever beyond her reach. If she had stopped to look around, she would have realized she was lost, but she couldn't stop. A trance had taken hold, cupping her in its thrall and coaxing her ever onward.

It was only when a thundering crash rang out behind her that she finally came to, whipping around to search for the source of the commotion.

"Halt! Trespasser!" a mechanical voice shouted, its words echoing off the piles of junk and debris. "You have broken into a restricted area. You will be detained for questioning. Stay where you are!"

Naturally, Scar ignored the PeaceBot's warning and fled. Jumping over a low pile of bricks and rubble, she moved away from the edge of the dome and into the junkyard beyond. She couldn't see the PeaceBot, but she knew it was close and that it could hear every sound she made. Escaping it wouldn't be easy.

She wove around walls and under railings, up stacks of concrete and over rickety bridges, but its warnings were getting closer, stalking her through the night.

"I am authorized to use force, if necessary," it warned in a monotone voice, enacting its brutal programming. "I am armed. If you do not cooperate, I will begin shooting."

Scar wasn't going to win this one – at least not if she played fair. She wasn't fast enough to outrun this machine, nor stealthy enough to hide from it. But, thankfully, those weren't her only two options.

She cast her eyes around for a weapon, something she could use to stun the PeaceBot and give her time to work. It wasn't a foolproof plan, but it was all she could think of in the moment. Her eyes landed on a severed mechanical arm sticking up from a nearby heap. Taking a breath, she lunged for the pile, narrowly missing a hail of gunfire as her hands closed around the appendage's cool surface.

Rolling over and getting to her feet, she ran, snaking between rows of rusted beams and dangling chains with her weapon clutched tightly in her arms. Sounds of bullets ricocheting off steel clanged around her as she sprinted through the perilous lanes and passages, looking for a spot to hide. She narrowly avoided tangling herself in a spider's web of cables, sliding under it at the last second and coming to rest under a low canopy of sheet metal.

Out of breath and out of time, she lay there, waiting. It wasn't long before the PeaceBot came, tracking her movements like a dog with her scent. Scar pulled herself up to a crouch, her heart beating wildly. The PeaceBot neared, sensing her presence, and it sped up to catch her. That was its first mistake. And its last.

The bot ran straight into the crisscrossed cables, tangling itself in their web. Without hesitation, Scar leapt toward the robot's back, striking it repeatedly with the mechanical arm and feeling the clangs reverberate through her body.

With a few more blows, she loosened its head and reached into the cavity, feeling for the wires that gave it life. Yanking them out, the PeaceBot slowed, then stopped, its movements frozen. Letting go of its mechanical innards, Scar slumped to the ground, her breathing ragged.

She knew she didn't have much time. If there were other PeaceBots around, they had almost certainly heard the exchange and would be coming to scour the scene. Scar had to act fast.

Carefully, Scar removed the bot's head unit and plugged it into her tab. Getting to work, she bypassed its firewalls and tapped into its mainframe. Her fingers moved rapidly, rewriting the bot's core code and reprogramming its commands. She didn't have time for a full overhaul of its systems, but she could alter just enough of the data to put the machine under her command. It was a rough job, but it would have to do.

With only seconds to spare, Scar reaffixed the head and lurched into the shadows, barely managing to stow herself before three more PeaceBots appeared on the scene. Sensing no immediate danger, they waited, poised for an update.

Scar's nimble fingers flew over the keys as she gave her

bot its first command.

"Everything is under control," its inflectionless voice began. "There have been no trespassers here tonight. Go back to your posts."

For a small eternity, the three bots remained immobile, digesting the new information. Then, just as quickly as they had come, they left, quietly departing in different directions to retake their posts. Scar sighed as a wave of relief washed over her. She was safe.

Now all she had to do was find her way back.

Except, as it turned out, that was easier than she'd thought. While *she* might not have a map of this outer wasteland, her new bot did. These machines had patrolled the area for years – maybe even decades – and were equipped with an internal diagram of its mazelike passages. All she had to do was input her destination and it would oblige, acting as her very own guide and escort. She wondered why she hadn't thought to do this before.

The journey back took longer than she expected, and she realized just how far she'd traveled in her search for a weak point. She must have canvassed miles of the dome, finding no way through and nothing to suggest that life could survive beyond it.

For the first time since Burn had disappeared, Scar felt truly alone. What if there was nothing out there? What if Burn was, in fact, dead? It was a heartbreaking thought, and Scar wished that her father were there to tell her what she needed to do next. He'd always had a plan.

She could practically hear his voice in her mind, even after all these years. "Be strong. Stay together. Keep fighting."

And she would. She would keep fighting until she couldn't fight any longer. The echo of his words spurred her on, and she lifted her head to take in the world in front of her.

Almost without her notice, they'd left the city's outer limits, with the PeaceBot granting them access into the inner streets – no electric fences required. Scar could have taken it from there, ditched the bot and found her own way home, but with the PeaceBot by her side, she had protection. The robot was her ticket home, and she stayed close behind it as it led her through the city.

Up and up they rose, steadily making their way back through dim streets and polluted alleys. Most of the world was quiet now, scared into the safety of their homes by the curfew and its enforcers. One or two stragglers still skulked about the city, drunk or high or on the hunt for an easy mark. Yet when they caught sight of the PeaceBot, they fled, scurrying back to their burrows.

Scar was growing to like her new toy.

A few tiers below Symphandra's house, however, they ran into a different sort of problem, one that wasn't so easily solved: Peace Officers. A pair of them emerged from around a corner, instantly spotting Scar and sauntering toward her.

"Halt! Who goes there?" one of the men shouted, gripping his holstered gun in warning. Scar kept her mouth shut and her eyes glued to the ground, letting the PeaceBot do the talking.

"I have apprehended a curfew breaker," the PeaceBot said, following Scar's script to the letter. "I am taking her to the station to be processed."

The Peace Officers considered her for an inordinately long time, circling her like hungry dogs.

"I don't know, friend," the second officer said to the bot. "This one looks like she might be too much for you. Why not hand her over to us? We'll make sure she gets to the station. She'll be in extremely good hands." He wiggled his fingers in Scar's direction, driving home his crude meaning.

Underneath her cloak, Scar typed, feeding the bot its lines. It was a dangerous game, but unless she wanted to find herself escorted to a seedy alleyway by these two degenerates, it was a game she had to play.

"I have had no problems with this woman. She has come willingly. I thank you for your offer of assistance but will kindly decline. I have already contacted the station, and they are expecting her imminently."

They wanted to fight back. Scar could see it in their eyes. Still, they knew better than to argue. If the Peace Station really was expecting her, then they'd never have enough time for their fun. So they gave in.

"Fine, have it your way," the first man said, turning to leave. The second followed, but he couldn't resist giving Scar a little slap on the backside as he passed.

A surge of anger rocketed through her, and she wanted nothing more than to knock that salacious smile off his face. Yet she kept her head down, silently signaling for the Peace-Bot to move. It did as it was bid, taking her away from the officers and their dangerous ideas.

Scar's skin crawled as she considered how close she had come to being their plaything. All she wanted now was to go home, to lose herself in her work, to forget that a world existed outside her door.

Coming up to Symphandra's house, Scar unlocked the door and dashed inside to safety. A moment later, the Peace-Bot followed.

Chapter 10

"No," Hale said firmly, his tone resolute. "I don't want you poking around in my head."

"Please?" Burn all but begged. They had been having this conversation for a quarter of an hour, and his answer hadn't changed. "I just need practice. I won't hear anything you don't want me to."

She didn't know that for certain. In fact, she still had no clue how her radiation-enhanced gift worked. It wasn't like there was a manual for mind reading, a beginner's guide to telepathy. But if she didn't try to explore its limits, she would never learn what she was capable of. And it was best to start with a willing volunteer.

"I know you better than I know anyone else here," she tried, hoping this line of reasoning would work where the others had failed. "There's a reason I heard you first. We're connected. We have a history."

"It doesn't matter. My thoughts are my own. They're

private." Hale glared at her coolly, a warning in his eyes. Most people would have backed down at a look like that – especially when coming from someone like Hale – but Burn wasn't like most people. She wasn't afraid of him.

"Well I'm going to hear them anyway. If I don't practice, I'll keep hearing random thoughts that run through your head, which could be anything," she warned. "But if you help me, I'll be able to control it. I can put up a barrier so I don't hear anything I shouldn't."

He grumbled under his breath, less a word than a growl. Burn could tell she was wearing him down.

"Hale, please. I need to learn about my father, and Imber isn't going to tell me the truth, not willingly," she explained, trying to drive him that last little bit to acceptance. "He wants to keep us here. We're useful. He won't like it if we go looking for a way back. If I can hear what he's thinking, though, I can learn anything he doesn't want us to know – about my father, about getting back to Kasis. All of it. It could be our key to getting home. But I won't be able to look into his mind if I don't know how!"

Hale put his head in his hands. With him seated on the bed and Burn pleading before him, the scene was so domestic that they almost seemed like a real couple. Almost.

"And what if I don't want to go back?" Hale asked, refusing to look at her.

Burn had been afraid of this. She'd also come prepared. "This isn't about what we want," she said, settling herself beside him. "It's about doing what's right. We may be free of the Peace Force's tyranny, but what about the tens of thousands who aren't? Sure, staying here would be easy. We wouldn't have to fight to get through the day. Yet we would have to live with the fact that we abandoned those people just so we could live a comfortable life."

Hale didn't move, and she couldn't tell if she was getting through to him, so she continued, "I'm going. Whether you help me or not, I'm going. You can come if you'd like, but I won't force you. I won't wait for you to make up your mind, either. If I have to leave you behind, I will. But my fight is there – my life is there – and I won't stop until I find a way back."

The pair lapsed into silence as Hale considered her words. Burn wanted him by her side. He had become a friend, an ally, and he had proven himself loyal. Still, she meant what she'd said: She wouldn't wait for him. They had wasted too much time already. It was time for action.

Hale shifted his position beside her, and she looked up, hopeful.

"Fine, I'll help you," he said grudgingly. "But that doesn't mean I'm coming with you."

Happiness and disappointment warred in Burn's mind. She was one step closer to finding a way back, but from here on out she would need to walk alone. She nodded slowly, accepting his answer.

"We start now," she said, letting go of her sadness and allowing the excitement to take over. This was going to be fun.

Except it wasn't. As it turned out, reading someone's thoughts was hard. It was nothing like listening to the world around her, which happened so effortlessly that she sometimes forgot she was doing it. No, mind reading was more like learning how to fight: long, arduous, and requiring lots of practice.

"What color am I thinking of?" Hale asked tiredly. It had been several hours since they'd started this game, and Hale's patience was growing thin.

Burn stared into his eyes, willing the thoughts to come to her. She visualized a beam of light connecting his mind to hers, transporting the knowledge across the ether. A minute ticked by, then two, and still nothing happened.

"I don't know!" she finally shouted, throwing her hands in the air. "Blue?"

"No," Hale said brusquely. That had been his go-to answer throughout their session. No, that's not the person. Or the number. Or the animal. Or the godforsaken month of the year.

If it was at all possible, Burn was getting worse. Maybe the thoughts she'd heard had been a fluke. Maybe she had imagined it. Maybe they really had spoken out loud and they were just playing with her, tricking her into believing she could do something that was obviously impossible.

"I don't care what color you're thinking about. How is a color going to help me get out of here?" she groaned, rubbing her temples. Her head hurt, and she wanted nothing more than to lie down and go to sleep. This was obviously a bust, and she needed to come up with a new plan, but she was too tired to think.

"Maybe we're going about this the wrong way," Hale tried, shaking his head. "Think back to the times you heard me and Nara. What was different? What were the circumstances?"

Burn sighed, closing her eyes and picturing each instance in her mind. "You were hungry and wanted breakfast. Nara was homesick. You were jealous of Kaz."

"I wasn't…that's not the point," Hale said haltingly. "What did all of those situations have in common? Why could you hear me then and not now?"

"I don't know. You were feeling something, I guess. You weren't thinking of a random number or color. There was an emotion attached to it, a desire." She turned away from Hale to stare at the wall, trying to organize her thoughts. "It was like you wanted something, and that need was enough to amplify your thoughts so I could hear them."

Silence descended on the room as they both thought about what that meant. Then, without warning, Hale's quiet voice broke through.

"I want *you*. Is that enough desire for you?"

Burn spun around, shock plastered on her face. "What?! How...why…what?!"

Hale smiled, a look of triumph in his eyes. "Well, I think we've figured out how your gift works."

Burn couldn't think. Her mouth remained open as she stared at him, and her body felt frozen in place. Hale laughed lightly at her, his expression playful.

"Now that we've figured that out, I'm going to bed. Are you coming?"

Burn had to make Imber angry. That was the emotion she'd decided would work best for her purposes. If she could make him angry, maybe he would drop his guard enough for her to see what he truly wanted – and what he was hiding in order to get it. And with any luck she could use that information to find a way home.

She didn't relish the thought of making him angry. With a flick of his wrist he could knock her to the ground with a jet of water. Or he could just as easily have her chucked out of the city. The stakes were high.

Imber wasn't a cruel man. He wasn't anything like General Cross, who had led with fear and violence, leaving a trail of people cowering in his wake. Imber was a quiet leader, a man who preferred to stay in the shadows rather than take the spotlight.

In the weeks since she'd arrived, Burn had studied him, making note of his interactions and decisions. He loved the city, that much was clear, and he wanted it to thrive, along with its citizens.

That wasn't to say that he didn't strive for power. Yet it was power as a collective he was after, power that would boost the fortunes of the city as a whole rather than him as an individual. Anything that threatened that power – like the possibility of his citizens leaving to return to Kasis – he took as a direct threat against himself. That was her way in.

"So, what's the story with Imber?" Burn asked Nara one day while they sat atop the wall, their legs dangling over the edge. "How did he get here? And how long has he been here?" She figured it was worth the effort to learn more about his background before accosting the man. A little insight into your target was never a bad thing.

"He's been here a while. Decades," Nara replied. "I think

he got chucked out of Kasis when he was a teenager. Don't know why. He doesn't like to talk about it. Even Mags doesn't know the whole story, and they've been together for years."

He was secretive about his past, then. That sounded like someone Burn knew. And she'd managed to get through his defenses, so that boded well for her dealings with Imber.

"How did he become the 'unofficial representative,' then? Is that a recent thing, or has he always been in charge?"

Nara mulled over the question, thinking back. "From what I've heard, Videre used to be a very different place. Well, it wasn't actually a place at all. It was more like a group of nomads who traveled around in search of water. Once the stream or the well dried up, they'd move on. In fact, most of the other exile groups we know of still live like that.

"But when Imber came, his gift with water changed things. They didn't have to rely solely on their wells or streams anymore. They didn't deplete the area's natural resources, which meant they could stay in one place. Back then there weren't as many of us, but people began coming, and Imber was put in charge of deciding who could stay. People trusted him, and eventually he became the man you would go to if you had a problem. He's been in the role so long now that people don't even question it."

Burn considered Nara's story, slotting it in with her own experiences with Imber. It fit with her perceptions of him – a man who wanted to protect the city he helped build. It made sense. Although she didn't quite know how she could use it to her advantage.

"Has he ever…acted rashly? Hurt someone? Or made a controversial decision?" If he had a temper, she might be able to exploit it.

"Not really," said Nara, shaking her head. "He's thrown a few people out of the city over the years, but that was always warranted. Like if they stole something or endangered someone's life. If it's something small, he'll usually let us decide for ourselves."

For all intents and purposes, he sounded like a fair and levelheaded ruler. Maybe that meant he would tell Burn the truth, and she wouldn't need to go poking around in his head. But, based on her experiences, when people wanted to maintain the status quo, they'd tell all the lies they needed to.

"What happens when someone wants to leave?" Burn queried, trying another line of thought.

"Not many people want to. Or at least not many people admit it." Nara gave Burn a wry smile. "But he'll try to talk them out of it. Tells them horror stories of the people who go back and are never seen again, likely eaten by bears or wolves. If they're determined to go, though, he'll give them a pack and tell them to leave. It's like he doesn't want the disease to spread. If you cut off the arm, send out the people that want to go, then the desire to return to Kasis won't linger."

It was just as Burn thought, then. Keeping Videre strong was Imber's priority, and he took any threat against the city seriously. She could work with that.

Looking down at the desert below her, Burn braced herself. She had one last question.

"Did you ever come across my father? His name was Arvense. He was a Peace Officer and was sentenced to the Pit about five years ago. I need to find him."

Burn looked up into Nara's eyes, but they only held

sadness and pity.

"It would have been before my time," she said apologetically. "But I haven't heard of him. It's possible he's in another camp. Or that he didn't survive. People don't take kindly to Peace Officers out here. He may have even changed his name so no old enemies would come looking for him."

Great. Now she didn't even know the name he was going under. That could make finding him nearly impossible.

Groaning, Burn leveraged herself up onto the walkway, heading in the direction of the sparring equipment. Grabbing the wooden sticks, she tossed one to Nara, who caught it with ease. If she couldn't get anywhere in her search, she figured, the least she could do was work on her fighting skills.

With her newfound talent for getting into people's heads, Burn found that her ability to predict Nara's attacks and parries was vastly improving. Now when Nara feigned left or tried to sweep her legs, Burn could sense it, as if she were seeing each move a second before Nara made it. So every time Nara struck, Burn blocked, and every time she ducked or rolled in evasion, Burn caught her.

For the first time, as people gathered to watch them, Burn disarmed Nara, striking the baton out of her hand and sending it flying. It was a small victory, but it emboldened her. For the first time since she arrived, she felt like she could do anything.

That evening, still high on her success, she walked across the city toward the offices, where she and Hale had been taken on their first day. Weaving between buildings and greeting familiar faces, she considered how much had changed in only a few weeks.

She was no longer a stranger in this place; she was a part of it. And, despite her short residence here, it was already a part of her.

She felt a pang of sadness at the thought of leaving. It was, after all, a comfortable enough life. They had a roof over their heads, food on the table, friends and neighbors who liked them. And, unlike in Kasis, they had the freedom to be who they truly were without hiding. Burn could see why Hale wanted to stay. In fact, if the Lunaria had meant less to her – and if Scar weren't in the equation – she could even see herself staying, building a life within Videre's walls.

Maybe in the future, when they'd tried and failed to bring about a revolution, she and Scar could come back here together. Or maybe they could break down the dome and spread out into the desert, merging Videre and Kasis into an unbreakable whole. It was a nice thought, although Burn doubted very much that either would truly come to pass.

All she knew was that she couldn't stay, no matter how much she might want to. So she savored the moment, drinking in the dry air and the friendly greetings, trying to memorize this place and these feelings so she could hold onto them in the darkness.

As she approached the long, low building, she spotted Jez coming out. Like always, he had a smile on his face and was whistling a pleasant tune into the evening air.

"Hiya, Burn!" he greeted her, waving cheerfully in her direction. "Whatcha doing in this neck of the woods? It's almost time for supper. I heard a rumor that Dagon plans on serving up some of his homemade beer," he said excitedly, referring to the town's blacksmith, who had a side business of brewing experimental creations in the back of his shop.

"I'll be over in a bit," Burn replied. "I need to have a quick word with Imber. But why are you here? Bringing another load of newcomers from the Pit?"

"Nah, nothing like that," Jez said, waving a hand to dismiss the idea. "No, I'm going out on a trade mission tomorrow. Gonna swing by one or two of the nearby camps and do some bartering. I like to bring 'em some fresh water as a goodwill gesture. Keeps things flowing smoothly, if you know what I mean." Jez chuckled lightly at his own joke before continuing. "I was just organizing things with Imber to make sure everything's set before I leave."

"Hmm," Burn mused, taking in this new information. She'd assumed that the city traded with the other camps, but she'd never known the specifics. She wondered briefly what kind of goods were on the trade lists – and how friendly the negotiations were – before coming back to the present and reminding herself of her task.

"What kind of mood is he in?" she asked, trying to sound nonchalant despite her nerves.

Jez shrugged noncommittally. "You'll be fine," was all he said before walking past her with a wink. "See you at dinner! If you don't show, I'm drinking your portion of beer." Burn had no doubt that he would.

She took a deep breath to calm herself before stepping into the building's cool halls. Looking around at the offices, images of her first day in Videre came flooding back, and she shuddered. There had been so much fear and uncertainty and doubt. She could almost sense it now, like a ghost of her former self.

But today she held her head high as she walked to the end of the hall, finally certain of her purpose – although slightly doubtful of her ability to achieve it. Raising her hand, she knocked lightly on Imber's door and waited as he got up and opened it for her, ever the gentleman.

"Auburn. How nice to see you. Have a seat, won't you? What can I do for you today?" He was jovial and kind, and Burn felt a pang of guilt about what she was about to do.

For a moment, she wavered in her resolve, hating herself for rewarding his kindness with her lies. Yet if she wanted to get out of there, if she ever wanted to find her father, then she had to act.

"I want to return to Kasis, and I'm not alone. There are a number of people in Videre who feel the same, who have family and friends and unfinished business there. And we think you know a way back in."

The smile remained on Imber's face, but Burn could have sworn that something cold flickered across his eyes. He stared at her for a few long seconds, as if testing her veracity. She stared back, unblinking, opening herself up to his thoughts.

Yet she heard nothing. No matter how hard she concentrated, she couldn't break through his guards, couldn't tell what was running through his mind. She silently cursed herself, regretting the whole plan. If she played this wrong, she could end up in the desert, powerless and alone with nowhere to go and no one to help her. She swallowed, trying to suppress the sudden anxiety that thrummed through her.

"If you want to leave, I will not stop you," Imber said flatly, as if lifelessly following a script. "But I ask that you not take the others down your futile path. Because it is futile. You won't find what you're looking for. This is the best place for you now, but if you can't see that then maybe you don't belong here after all."

"I don't believe you," Burn shot back, trying to get a rise out of him. "You know something that could help us get back, but you can't stand the thought of giving in and relinquishing your power. Because if we leave, there'll be nothing left for you to rule over. You'll be alone and weak, overseeing a city of ghosts."

A muscle in his jaw twitched, and Burn prayed that it would be enough, that she would be able to get past his defenses and discover what she needed.

Yet when he spoke, his voice was calm and level. "There is no way to get back into Kasis. I am not keeping anything from you or the people of Videre. Anyone who wants to leave is free to do so. Yet they don't because they know that if they walk out of here, they'll never again have the peace and freedom that they've had here. Kasis isn't a dream; it's a nightmare, one that we were lucky to be stripped of. If you wish to play make-believe then go right ahead, but I cannot help you make it into a reality."

Nothing. There was nothing under the surface of his words that Burn could grab onto. He was either telling the truth or he was so poised that she'd never be able to break through the walls of his mind. Either way, she was losing this battle. She only had one more trick up her sleeve, the wild card that could be the difference between sinking and swimming.

"I believe you. You can't help me. But there is someone

who can." Burn paused, watching as Imber's eyebrows rose in curiosity. "His name was Arvense Alendra. I believe he came through here five years ago. He was also looking for a way back – a way back to his daughters. I think you knew him."

It was a longshot. It was entirely possible that Imber had never met Arvense, that her father had never even set foot in Videre, but she needed to know for sure. She needed to find out what had happened to him, if he was still alive, if he'd found a way home…and, if so, why he'd never come back.

At her question, something shifted in Imber's expression. He pressed his lips together, smothering all traces of his earlier smile. His light blue eyes squinted slightly, as if he were truly seeing her for the first time.

"You're mistaken. I have never heard of an Arvense Alendra," he said tightly.

Something tingled in Burn's mind, a hint of something beyond his words, something he wasn't saying. She concentrated harder, willing the information into her mind.

"It's possible he was going by a different name," she pressed on, ignoring his dismissal. "He was a Peace Officer, after all. Still, he would have been hard to miss. Tall, red hair, a penchant for discovering people's secrets."

That got a reaction from him. It wasn't a physical reaction. Outwardly, nothing changed, but mentally, something was ticking.

"Like I said, I am not aware of any such man having been to Videre," Imber said out loud. But it was what he wasn't saying that Burn was truly interested in.

"Arvense," came the quiet murmur of his thoughts, which Burn could just make out beneath the surface. "I thought I'd heard the last of him."

Burn beamed, elated. "You see, I think you're lying," she goaded him, trying to elicit more. "I think he came here and you two didn't see eye to eye. I think you know what happened to him."

"How does she know?" he thought, the words getting louder as his tension and anger mounted. "He left. I thought I was rid of him."

"He left?" Burn queried. "Where did he go? Why did he leave Videre?"

Imber stared at her, his mouth open. She realized she'd shown her hand and revealed her gift, but she didn't care. She just wanted answers, and it didn't matter how she got them.

"You're like him," Imber said, his eyebrows knitting together in bewilderment. "You can hear secrets."

"What?" Burn shot back, the confusion knocking her off course. Her father had been a master at *discovering* secrets, not hearing them. "What do you mean I'm like him? What could he do? And what happened to him?"

Imber's mind was a jumble now, a mess of memories and biting comebacks and denial. He was arguing with himself, trying to decide whether or not to lie – and whether or not she could detect it if he did.

"It's no use pretending, Imber," she warned. "If you try to keep something from me, I'll hear it. I'll know the second you even consider it. So you might as well tell me everything." It was possible she was overselling her abilities, but he didn't need to know that.

Imber rose and turned, breaking eye contact with her to peer out the window.

"He wasn't here long – a week, maybe two," Imber started, his voice distant. "We didn't find him at the Pit. He found us. One day, he simply walked through the gates and into the city. I don't know how long he'd been out there, but the desert had taken its toll."

Burn could see it in her mind as he spoke. She didn't know if it was her vision or Imber's, but it played in such detail, telling the story she'd sought for so long.

"He asked to see the person in charge, and someone brought him to me," Imber continued, still not looking at Burn. "He told me his sad tale – about his daughters back in Kasis and how he needed to get back. I told him what I tell everyone: There's no way back. But, much like you, he didn't believe me.

"He didn't seem like a particularly useful addition to the city. Most of the people here have a rather negative view of Peace Officers. And he didn't seem to be gifted, at least not in any way I could see. I was about to have him escorted out of the city when he asked me point blank who Mags was. Yet I hadn't mentioned her. I hadn't told him a thing about myself, but he knew her name. I thought it was a fluke, that maybe he'd heard about her around the city, but he kept going, revealing more and more about me."

"He could read your thoughts?" Burn asked, enthralled by the story.

"More like he could read my secrets," Imber said, shaking his head. "At that point I hadn't even admitted my feelings for Mags to myself, but he read them like I was an open book. It was as if he could see anything you wanted to hide simply by looking into your eyes."

The resemblance to Burn's gift was uncanny. Back in Kasis, he'd been normal, for lack of a better word. He'd been skilled at sleuthing, adept at uncovering the truth, but it wasn't a gift – at least not one like Burn's. The atmosphere in the wildlands must have changed that, just like it had changed her.

"I thought he could be useful," Imber continued, turning back around and settling himself in the wide windowsill. "Having someone who could uncover secrets would give us an advantage with the other camps, make sure they weren't trying to pull anything over on us. So I let him stay."

"I should have tossed him right back out," he thought coldly, but Burn decided not to comment. She wanted to hear the rest of the story, to discover what had become of her father and why he'd never made it back to them.

"It turns out he wasn't looking for a new home. He was looking for people to join him. And his newfound gift allowed him to find just what he was searching for. He located every single person that had ever wanted to return to Kasis, and he convinced them that he could make it happen. He told them they could finally see their families again, everyone they'd left behind when they were exiled. And they believed him."

Imber massaged his temples with his fingertips, as if the memories hurt to recall. Burn could see why that might be the case. Videre was his family, and her father had wanted to break it into pieces.

"So what happened?" Burn asked, eager to hear the story's conclusion. "Did they go? Did they find a way back in?"

Imber shrugged, sighing loudly. "From what I gathered,

he thought that if they had more people, it would be easier to find a way back into the city. So he set off for one of the nearby camps to get more recruits. He told everyone he would be back within a few weeks, but he never returned. He either died or got captured or went back without them. Or the whole thing was a joke to begin with and he never intended to return."

Burn got defensive at that, her temper flaring. "If he said he was coming back for them, then he planned to come back. He wouldn't have intentionally left them. He was a man of his word."

"He was a Peace Officer," Imber countered angrily, spitting out the words like they were poison in his mouth. Checking himself, he took a deep breath, then another before finishing his story. "I don't know what happened. I was just glad to be rid of him. He was a danger to this city and our people."

Burn scanned his mind for lies or omissions, but she found none. He was telling her the truth – or at least his version of it.

"Thank you," she said stoically as she rose from her seat and made her way to the door.

As she was about to leave, his voice stopped her. "What are you going to do?" His tone held a note of warning. While he may have given her the information she was searching for, he wasn't about to give in and let her take over her father's plan. His thoughts were clear on that point.

"I'm going to find out what happened to him. And I'm going to figure out what he had planned," she said simply.

Burn heard Imber move behind her, and she felt his

presence at her back. Yet she didn't turn around.

"I will fight to keep my people," he whispered down to her. "If you try to break up this city, I will break you."

Burn turned around at that, shocked by the nearness of Imber's face to hers. Yet she didn't flinch. Instead, she inched even closer before responding.

"Is that your definition of 'peace and freedom'?" she asked, using his own words against him. "Why not let your people decide their own fate? If you can't even do that, how is Videre any better than Kasis?" With that question hanging in the air, she turned around and walked out the door.

She could really use that beer now.

Chapter 11

PeaceBots were the solution. Scar couldn't believe she hadn't thought of it before. The answer had been staring her in the face. Literally. The PeaceBot she'd abducted had been looking to her for instructions since the moment she'd put its reconfigured head back onto its body. Even back at Symphandra's house it just sat there, staring at her. It was unnerving.

She'd already written the code that would bend the bots to her command. It was essentially the same thing Raqa had done to the two PeaceBots they'd reprogrammed together, albeit with a few improvements. There were certain things that she hadn't shared with Raqa. It was always useful to have a few secrets up your sleeve.

All she needed to do now was get her hands on more PeaceBot units. Then she could alter their core imperatives, changing them from spies to scouts. Equipped with her own army of explorer bots, she could canvass the entire perimeter of the dome, searching for weak spots without even leaving home. It was genius – and she wasn't ashamed to say so.

The only issue was how to acquire more. She didn't relish the thought of reenacting the plan she'd used last time – the one that had nearly resulted in her arrest. So she needed to come up with something new, something that would lead an army of willing PeaceBots right into her hands. And she had just the thing: She was going to create a trap.

Trapping PeaceBots followed many of the same principles as trapping mice. All you needed was something to lure them in and something to immobilize them. Although in this case, cheese wasn't going to do the trick. No, she needed something that the PeaceBots wanted, something they were programmed to go after.

That's where their communication system came in handy. Separate from the Peace Force comms, the bots had their own way of signaling to each other through the ether, communicating distress, requesting backup, and acting as a beacon that would lead others to their exact location. So, naturally, once one bot arrived at the scene of a crime, the rest would follow. Good thing Scar already had that one bot. Now she simply needed the crime.

If it was anything too serious, she ran the risk of them alerting their human counterparts. So kidnapping and murder were out. That left the small-scale offenses, like trespassing, breaking curfew, and petty larceny. Since she'd already done the first two, she was leaning toward the last one.

Of course, she wasn't actually going to commit the specified crime. She just had to make the bots *think* that she had. That was the fun part.

She'd decided that the upper tiers would be the perfect place to enact her plan. Since Burn's attack on the airflow points, the area had been crawling with the latest model of PeaceBots. And, since the Peace Force still hadn't gotten the ventilation system back online, the smog in those sectors would provide the perfect cover.

With her plan sorted, her main problem now was finding a way to blend in on the upper tiers, amongst the rich and the powerful. That was harder than it sounded. Up there, they had no fear of standing out. Their costumes were colorful, the uniforms unique, and they bathed in the envy of their peers. If Scar wanted to assimilate, she'd need to take their lead.

Thankfully, she had Symphandra's closet to assist her. Left to her own devices, Scar wouldn't know the difference between cotton and couture. But Symphandra had been a true visionary, crafting intricately colorful creations that entranced the eye and flattered the body. Her wardrobe was a thing to behold, stuffed to the brim with shades and fabrics Scar had never even seen, let alone considered wearing.

Now was her chance – a chance to become someone else, to step into another's shoes, and, in the process, perhaps feel closer to the extraordinary woman who had once worn them. Lightly fingering the rainbow of dresses, skirts, and blouses that hung in Symphandra's bedroom, Scar marveled at their beauty. The garments held a part of Symphandra, capturing her vivacity and playfulness, and, just like the house itself, they still held her scent, giving off a sweetly spicy aroma that was achingly familiar.

As Scar perused thc clothing, her sights landed on a

pair of deep purple pants and a silky cream-colored blouse, both of which played coquettishly with the light, making it bounce off their surfaces and absorb into their folds. She carefully removed the garments from their hangers, draping them softly over the nearby bed. Checking the closet again, she added a midnight blue cloak that bordered on black and a hand-etched leather mask that was alive with flowers and vines – Symphandra's signature style.

Donning the clothing, Scar felt as if she were donning a disguise, putting on a new visage to camouflage her own. She buttoned the blouse over her shiny metallic collarbone and twisted her hair back, covering it with a scarf to hide the silvery wires. Stepping back, she considered herself in the mirror.

She almost looked normal, like one of them. She didn't like it. Yet it would have to do.

Shrugging into the cloak, she woke her new pet Peace-Bot from its mid-day charge and gave it its instructions. She'd been careful to spell out its role in detail, programming every response and eventuality in case something went wrong.

"Now you behave yourself," she added out loud, as if the bot were capable of doing otherwise. "This is an important day for both of us. I'll need you to be at your best." She nodded to enforce her words, entirely cognizant that she was talking to a machine.

As expected, the bot said nothing in return.

Satisfied, Scar led the creature out the front door, fastening it securely behind them. Slowly, the pair rose through the tiers, with Scar staying a respectable distance behind so as not to raise suspicions. Once again, her unofficial escort was a handy one, clearing the streets with just a glance from its robotic eyes. No one wanted to be the subject of its gaze – or its guns.

Within no time, they reached the upper echelons of the city, where the rich and powerful spent their days – and their money. Or, at least, they once had.

The transformation it had undergone stopped Scar in her tracks. No longer was the area pristine and bright, dominated by shiny buildings and gleaming surfaces. The smog had taken care of that.

Now the tiers were drenched in gray, covered in a curtain of dust and grime. It coated every window, concealing the high-class shops and their overpriced wares, and it floated in the air, limiting visibility to a street or two at most. If it hadn't been for the lighting overhead – all working and all turned on to max intensity – Scar might have believed she'd stumbled into the Corax End.

Even the people here had changed, their appearances and behaviors altering to match their environment. No longer did they seem bright and shiny, a paragon of health and well-being. The few that ventured onto the streets now looked beaten and worn, their dry coughs echoing through the dull and lifeless roads.

Scar smiled to herself under her mask, secretly pleased. Burn and Hale had done quite the job here, that much was certain. It would take the Peace Force weeks to undo this level of destruction. Even if they were able to clean the air, its lingering effects might be seen throughout the city – and the people – for years to come.

Slowly, without urgency, Scar ambled through the barren streets, drinking in the eerie stillness. Eventually she came to a stop beside her PeaceBot in a narrow dead-end lane behind the shops and shuttered stalls of the tier's main thoroughfare.

Breaking out her tab, she set the events in motion. With the tap of her finger, her PeaceBot enacted its role, sending out a localized distress call that alerted nearby units to the presence of a thief. As soon as she'd finished, Scar got into position, tucking herself just around the corner, out of sight of the street.

In her right hand, she gripped her trusty stun gun pen. She'd made a few modifications to it since her run-in with Kaz. Most notably, she'd upped the voltage, increasing the level until it could take down a horse. She'd have to be quick – and very precise – but if she managed to press the pen directly to the base of a PeaceBot's neck, its systems would overload, forcing a shutdown. She'd tested the device on her own PeaceBot (several times), and it had been an unqualified success. Plus, it was incredibly satisfying.

Several seconds ticked by, with Scar's anxious heart beating out the time. Gradually, an all-too-familiar hum filtered into the alley, telegraphing a PeaceBot's approach. Scar readied herself for battle, moving her finger to the trigger.

The moment the robot rounded the corner, Scar stuck out her hand, jamming her weapon roughly into the hard steel of its neck. A loud buzzing noise reverberated through its shell as the electricity coursed through its system. A few seconds of contact was all it took for the machine to go silent, the electronic lights disappearing from its eyes.

With a grunt of effort, she shoved the now-lifeless bot

farther into the lane and reset herself behind the corner. It was time for round two.

Except this time, the match wouldn't be so easily won. One PeaceBot she could handle. Two at once was doable. But three was a bit much, especially when they all turned the corner at the exact same time.

Scar signaled to her trusty PeaceBot, which sped toward her with alacrity. As she dealt an electric blow to the first foe, her bot put itself between her and the others, forming a shield with its body.

Upon seeing the distress of their comrade, the two remaining bots naturally began shooting. But instead of hitting her, the bullets ricocheted off her personal bodyguard, filling the alley with resounding clangs.

With one bot taken care of, Scar moved her attentions to the second. The spray of bullets, however, somewhat hindered her approach. Thinking fast, she reached into her bag and pulled out a small, round ball. She threw it to the pavement at the robots' feet, sending a thick cloud of smoke swirling around them and obscuring their vision of the alley.

With no time to spare, Scar darted behind the second bot and jammed her pen in the direction of its neck. Yet with the smoke clouding her vision, as well, her aim was less than accurate, and the weapon discharged uselessly into the robot's back. Going on the defensive, the bot swung around, knocking the pen out of Scar's hand.

Scar dropped to the pavement, evading the bot's next attack and scrambling to find her weapon. Her eyes locked on the pen a few feet away, and she dove for it, her fingers closing around its smooth surface just as one of the bots rammed her in the back, sending her sprawling.

The bot reversed, intending to hit her again, but she managed to roll out of the way, narrowly avoiding the second strike. Jumping to her feet, she lunged behind one of the immobilized creatures as another volley of bullets echoed around her.

Whipping out her tab, she executed a series of commands to her own bot, which complied obligingly. Within moments, it began firing on its former cohorts, gradually drawing them away from Scar's position. Momentarily free of foes, she jumped out and grabbed the nearest bot, forcing her weapon into its neck. Two down, one to go.

She knew she had to work quickly. The commotion had no doubt caused some curiosity among nearby residents. Soon there'd be more PeaceBots than she could handle – or, worse, Peace Officers. And the latter were a good deal more difficult to get rid of.

So Scar pounced, grabbing the last bot and plunging the pen into its neck. The weapon, however, did not seem to have the same urgency as she did. The pen sparked then went out, fizzling into nothing. Caught off guard, Scar just stood there. The bot, on the other hand, swung its top half around, colliding with her body and knocking her against the wall. The air escaped her lungs in one painful breath.

It was a good thing that her backup plan was still intact. As she struggled to regain her composure, her own PeaceBot slammed into the side of her foe, sending it careening down the alley where it collided with two of its now-defunct brethren. Seizing the opportunity, Scar ran up behind it and positioned her pen for the kill.

This time, the stun gun sprang to life, sending waves of electricity into the PeaceBot's core. She breathed a sigh of relief as the bot slowed and stopped, its body giving out under the force of the current.

Scar wanted to revel in her victory, to delight in their defeat, but time wasn't on her side. Grabbing her tab, she canceled the distress call and promptly got to work updating the bots' core commands, giving herself complete remote access to their systems and their cams. Now whatever they saw, she saw, and whatever she wanted, they did. It was the perfect robotic army, with four new soldiers at her beck and call.

Within a few minutes, she'd managed to reprogram all four bots, putting each under her control before sending it into the world. Then she, too, took her leave, her original PeaceBot traveling in her wake. Several pairs of curious eyes poked out as she passed, but Scar kept her head bent, letting the smog conceal her identity – and her indiscretions.

The next morning dawned cool and bright. Before the suns had even cleared the horizon, Burn was out of bed, dressed and ready for the day. Slinging a light pack across her back and fastening her knife belt around her waist, she took one last look at Hale, who was still sound asleep.

Burn had the sudden urge to wake him and beg him to come with her. Yet he'd made his feelings clear: He wanted to stay. So she would do this on her own. Turning her back on the sleeping giant, she shut the door quietly and snuck down the stairs, carefully sidestepping the creaky floorboards. She opened the front door without a sound and stepped into the shy morning light.

Videre had yet to awaken. She'd never seen the city so still, so tranquil. Burn drank in the silence, enjoying the calm feeling that blanketed her mind.

Instead of heading toward the gate like she usually did, Burn weaved her way through the city toward the stables. As she approached, she heard the familiar sound of Jez's whistling wafting through the cool air. Turning the corner, she spotted the man, who was carefully inspecting each animal with the eye of a jeweler.

"Not today, my lovely lady," he murmured gently to one of the donkey-rams. "You just rest and regain your strength, and soon you'll be as strong as an ox again."

It was a strangely endearing sight, and Burn suddenly felt as if she didn't belong. She wavered for a moment, uncertain whether to intrude, but she was soon spared the choice.

"Hello, Burn," Jez said without looking up.

Coaxed from the shadows, Burn stepped forward and joined Jez amongst the animals, giving him a nod in lieu of a greeting.

"How did you know I was there?" Burn asked, genuinely curious.

"The animals," he replied simply. "They get spooked by strangers."

Of course. The animals acted as his sentinels, alerting him when anything – or anyone – was out of place. What a useful gift, Burn thought, eyeing the creatures around her.

"What are you doing here, Burn?" Jez asked, efficiently getting to the point.

"I'm here to join you on your trade mission. I have business in the other camps. I figured since we're both headed in the same direction, we could share a ride." Well, she could share his ride – and his knowledge of the desert, since hers was practically nonexistent.

Jez considered her for a moment, taking in her pack and weapons belt. "Did you tell Imber about your business?" he queried, a hint of suspicion creeping into his voice.

"He knows," she replied simply. It was technically true. Imber did know what she was planning, although he hadn't officially signed off on it. Still, he hadn't physically stopped her, so that was good enough for her.

Jez seemed to accept her answer, shrugging his shoulders. "Why not? It'd be nice to have some company out there. It can get a touch lonely in the wildlands."

He let go of the creature he'd been petting and sidled up to Burn. "But if anything happens, anything that puts us in danger or hampers our trade talks, you're on your own. My priority is and will remain the safe transport and sale of our goods. You got that?"

Burn was taken aback by his sudden seriousness, but she nodded in assent. As if to emphasize his point, Jez leaned over and picked up his rifle from the ground, shouldering the weapon.

"Great," he said, his voice reverting to its normally jovial tone. "Give me a hand loading up the cart and we'll be off."

Burn did as she was bid, hoisting bags of grain and barrels of water onto the nearby cart while Jez carefully selected the creature that would be leading them through the desert. Within no time, her muscles burned from the effort of transporting the hefty cargo. She briefly considered fetching Hale to assist her but quickly banished the idea from her mind. After all, she needed to get used to a life without him in it.

Fifteen minutes later, the cart was packed and ready to go, with Jez sitting happily in the driver's seat. Burn climbed up next to him and gave him a short nod, a nervous excitement growing in her chest. With a small flick of Jez's wrist, the cart began to roll, and they took off in the direction of the gate.

As they moved toward the wall, Burn spotted Nara seated atop it, her still form keeping watch over the equally still desert. At their approach, she turned to inspect them. Burn smiled at her friend and nodded, knowing that Nara could see the gesture even from her perch.

In return, Nara whispered, "Good luck," knowing that Burn – and only Burn – would be able to hear her. With that, Jez and Burn and their cartload of goods rolled through the gate and into the desert beyond.

Chapter 12

Burn marveled at how much had changed since her first cart ride through the desert. The landscape itself was exactly the same, with its flowing dunes, stoic plateaus, and unrelenting heat. However, she was no longer the same woman who had once traveled through it.

For one thing, she was stronger. Her training with Nara had begun to chisel her body, with lean muscles now apparent on her arms and a new sharpness in her face. Yet it was more than that. Cloaked in the familiarity of Kasis, she'd been afraid – afraid to lead, to choose a path, to act when action was needed. Now, surrounded by nothing but uncertainty, she knew her purpose, and she finally felt strong enough to see it through.

"So where is this camp anyway?" she asked, curious how far they'd have to travel before they happened upon another living soul. It had already been over an hour since they'd departed, and the suns were creeping up in the sky, their bright heat unbroken by clouds.

"Callidus. They call it Callidus. And it's a few hours thataway," he stated, pointing ahead of them.

Burn wasn't a navigational expert, but she knew that when they'd exited Videre, they'd headed off to the right. From what she knew, it wasn't in the opposite direction of Kasis, but their route wouldn't take them any closer to the city. Which meant that, despite their progress, she was still nowhere near home.

She glanced toward the space in the distance where she knew Kasis lay, the blank landscape tugging at her heart. She imagined the domed city sitting on the horizon, glinting in the suns, and it filled her with an immeasurable longing. Tearing herself from the daydream, Burn refocused her attention on the path ahead.

"What's it like, this Callidus?" she asked, trying to prepare herself.

"It's...different than Videre," Jez responded slowly. Burn waited for him to elaborate, but he remained silent, his eyes fixed on the skyline.

"How so?" Burn prodded, hoping for more.

"Well," Jez began, pausing to collect his thoughts, "they've had a tougher time of it. They don't have the luxury of staying in one place, which means they can't build up defenses like we have. They're at the mercy of the desert."

"So? What does that mean?" Jez's patented version of storytelling made it difficult to get a clear answer from him, so Burn pushed on, attempting to ferret it out of him.

"They're not as friendly, shall we say," he replied lazily. "They've had to fight for what they have, and they'll fight to keep it. They're not too keen on outsiders. Heck, they only tolerate us because we're good trade partners. They know if they did anything to Videre or one of its people, they'd never see another bag of grain again." Jez chuckled lightly, seemingly unconcerned with the city's violent tendencies.

Burn mulled it over, forming a picture of the city in her head. Tents, crude weapons, a hunter-gatherer society. It sounded like a tedious existence – one that could be wiped out by one bad sandstorm or a mild depletion in wild game.

"Do they have a leader, then? Someone like Imber?" Burn went on, trying to solidify the image.

"Yes and no," Jez said, sighing. "They have a leader, but he's nothing like Imber. Thestle is…strict with his people. He doesn't let them decide their own fates. They do what he tells them."

Burn was about to ask about his gift and how he had come to dominate Callidus, but something at the edge of her vision caught her attention. She whipped her head around, not quite sure what she was looking for. At first, she thought it had been a trick of her imagination, just the suns and the sand playing games with her eyes, but then she spotted it again: a small patch of white peeking through the sand.

Curious, she leaned toward it, sticking the top half of her body out of the cart to get a better view. It looked like an anomaly in the sand, a place the gods forgot to color in when they'd shaped the desert floor. It was probably just a rock or a plant or the skull of a poor creature who had perished in the sun. Then again, none of those things tended to move – and this thing was moving.

"Jez…" Burn said loudly, her eyes trained on the rising

figure. He followed her gaze, his eyes going wide as sand streamed off the growing shape like water down a mountain. Whatever this thing was, it was huge.

"Run!" Jez screamed to the animal tethered to their cart.

In an instant, they had doubled their speed. The cart bumped unsteadily over mounds of sand, sending grain bags and fruit crates rocketing into each other and over the side. Jez didn't even notice the lost cargo. Instead, he frantically switched his gaze back and forth from the desert ahead of them to the creature behind.

Burn, on the other hand, couldn't take her eyes off the enormous shape. It had stopped rising from the ground now, and it paused to shake the remaining sand off its colossal body. Burn's mouth went dry at the sight.

It was a bear – or at least it had the general shape of a bear, except it was at least three times the normal size. It also appeared to be balding, with patches of rough, hairless hide interspersed with tufts of thick white hair. Then the pieces came together in Burn's mind, and she realized what it was: a sand bear.

Terror pulsed through Burn's veins as she watched the creature sniff the air and languidly turn its head in their direction. It's piercing blue eyes locked on the cart, and it actually seemed to smile at the sight. With a feral leap, it began its pursuit.

Fueled by its powerful legs, the creature bounded toward them, letting loose a guttural growl. Jez glanced back, his eyes wild. He flicked the reins, urging the animal at the cart's helm to accelerate, but Burn knew with a savage certainty that it wouldn't be enough. No matter their speed, they'd never be able to match the beast at their back.

"Use the gun!" Jez yelled to Burn as he drove, swerving to avoid a large dune that could have upended them.

Burn ripped her eyes away from the sand bear to search for the weapon within the wreckage of their goods. After a few seconds, she spotted the rifle lodged under a crate of pears near the rear of the cart. She strained desperately to reach it, but her arms weren't long enough to make contact. Giving in, she vaulted over the seat and into the storage area, grabbing the gun and aiming it at the bear.

The heavy rifle felt foreign in her hands. She'd only ever used a handgun – and even then she'd been out of her mind on ManniK. Still, she knew she had to do something. The bear was nearly upon them now, only a few strides away from the back of the cart. Burn took aim, struggling to steady herself amidst the jostling, and fired.

The force from the shot sent her sprawling, and she landed in a pile of grain on the cart's bed. Picking herself up, she got to her knees and peered through the detritus. Her heart sank as she saw that the sand bear was still in pursuit, with only a few feet between them.

She grabbed the gun from beside her and steadied it on a crate, aiming the muzzle toward the beast's enormous body. Taking a shuddering breath, she fired again. This time the bullet flew straight, striking the bear in the chest.

Burn felt a brief moment of elation before she realized that the bear wasn't slowing. It was close enough now that she could see the spot on its thick, calloused hide where the bullet had struck. It had barely left a mark.

"It didn't work!" Burn began, but before she could finish

the bear reached out one of its massive paws and sent the cart flying – along with its inhabitants.

Burn's world spun as she flew through the air. Her back hit the sand with a muted thump, stunning her, and she looked up just in time to see the cart sail overhead and land behind her with a furious crash.

As her world fell back into place, she realized with heart-stopping clarity that the bear was still coming. Knowing she could never escape in time, she rolled into a ball, making herself as small as she felt. Peering through her hair in hopeless terror, she watched as the creature thundered toward her. Yet right before it reached her, it lurched into the air, landing heavily on the cart behind her.

Relief surged through her, but it was painfully temporary. She knew it was only a matter of time before the bear finished with the cart and made a move for her. So she pushed herself up and ran. The sand clung to her feet, making every step torturously slow, but she kept going, kept moving, putting more and more distance between them.

She didn't know where she was going. All that mattered was that she got away – as far away as possible. In the moments between utter panic, her thoughts turned to Jez. Where had he landed? Was he safe? Had he gotten away? Or was he there, in the cart, facing the sand bear alone?

A bubble of guilt swelled in her chest, but she tamped it down, telling herself that there was nothing she could do. One person couldn't take on that bear alone. Nor could two.

A deafening growl split the air behind Burn, and she turned to see the bear standing on its hind legs amidst the remains of their cart. Her mouth dropped at the sheer scale of the creature, its muscular body nearing the height of five men. She raised her eyes to its head and realized with a jolt that the animal was staring straight at her.

Stumbling, she turned and fled, picking up speed. The bear followed, its paws striking the sand with loud thumps as it gained on her. She didn't know what to do. She had no plan, no place to hide, no clear means of escape. Her mind reeled, searching for a way out.

In the distance, Burn spotted a crack in the sand. Putting on a burst of speed, she drew nearer, watching as the crack widened into a canyon. A very large canyon.

Burn had an idea. It was a stupid idea, but it was all she had. The bear was practically on her heels, and she had no other options. Fumbling, she drew one of the long knives from the belt around her waist. But instead of throwing it at the creature, she ran forward, carrying it to the mouth of the canyon.

Right before the sand dropped away beneath her feet, she plunged the knife into the desert floor. Then she hurled herself off the edge and into the chasm. Holding fast to the knife, she dangled over the cliff's side, her feet flailing in mid-air as her arms absorbed the shock.

Unable to stop its momentum in time, the sand bear careened over the edge, narrowly missing Burn as it fell. Out of the corner of her eye, she saw it thrashing, pawing in vain for purchase in the empty air. A moment later, Burn heard a resounding thud as the bear collided with the canyon's hard rock floor.

She felt like she couldn't breathe, couldn't get enough air into her lungs to stop her world from spinning. Her arms ached, and she tried and failed to pull herself up the cliff face. Finding a foothold, she finally managed to drag herself over the ledge and onto the safety of the sand.

For a small eternity, Burn lay there, panting. Despite the heat, she suddenly felt numb, her body and brain sapped of all their energy. She couldn't find the strength to move or shout or cry. All she could do was stare up at the sky, her mind blank.

Some time later, knowing she had to move, Burn got to her feet. She couldn't bring herself to look down at the creature she'd killed. Instead, she simply turned away. Only, she didn't know what direction they'd come from. The wind had long since erased their tracks from the sand. So she picked one that felt right and walked. And walked. And walked.

After a time, she stopped. Glancing around her, nothing looked familiar. There were no signs of Jez or their cart. She was lost. She tried calling for help, shouting Jez's name as loud as she was able, but the wind stole her words just as it had stolen her tracks.

She cried then. Falling to all fours, she let the tears come. They flowed freely onto the sand, creating dimples in its golden surface much like the rain had all those weeks ago.

The thought of the rain – and of Hale – sobered her, and she climbed to her feet, wiping the sand off her hands and her pants. She might not know where she was, but she knew where she was going. Jez had pointed out the direction of Callidus, indicating a space to the right of the twin suns. Although the suns were somewhat higher in their arc now, Burn could still follow the path, using the sky as her compass.

Steadying herself, she set off toward the horizon, her head held high.

Burn huddled in her cave, shivering. The suns had long since disappeared and the heat had gone with them, leaving a howling wind that bit through her clothing.

She was lucky to have found the cave at all. Before she'd stumbled across it, she had been seriously considering burrowing into the sand, much like the bear that had left her stranded. But as dusk had set in across the desert, she'd detected an outcropping of stone in the distance. Desperate, she'd made her way toward it, unwilling to look away in case it evaporated in a blink or faded with the ever-dwindling light.

Yet as the light died, the stone mound had remained. Burn had eventually reached the rock face, running her hands along it to convince herself that it was real. Under her calloused fingers, its cool surface had felt surprisingly reassuring.

She'd discovered the cavern after following the rocks for some time. The darkness had obscured most of the cave's features, but light echoes of sound bounced off its walls, helping her form a picture of the space. It was small and low and – thankfully – unoccupied. Carefully examining it, she'd found no bones or droppings to suggest it had a current tenant, so she'd made her move, claiming the area as her own.

Despite the chaos of the day, she had somehow managed to keep hold of her pack, which was a small kind of miracle.

Of course, her pack didn't hold much, as she'd assumed her journey would be a short one. Still, she'd possessed enough foresight to bring a meager supply of food and water, along with a few items of warm clothing to shield herself from the evening chill.

She'd nearly finished the water. The food was easier to ration, although the temptation to eat it all in a few quick handfuls was strong. The gnawing in her belly was difficult to ignore, its volume and ferocity rivaled only by the howls of predators lurking somewhere outside the cave.

Sleep would be impossible. Even without the terrible cries of the creatures prowling in the night, Burn was certain that her chattering teeth would hamper her ability to drift into a dreamless sleep. So she sat there, her back against the hard stone, listening to the night.

She couldn't light a fire. For one thing, she didn't know how. Wildlands survival skills hadn't been required learning in the urban jungle of Kasis. For another, the light could attract predators, luring them out of their comfort zones with the promise of easy prey. The last thing she needed was another sand bear barreling toward her, intent on ripping off her extremities.

Alone in the darkness, with nothing to distract her, she couldn't help but worry about Jez. Was he alright? Had he made it back to Videre? Or had he met a grisly fate, crushed under their cart or mauled by their attacker while she ran? Burn imagined every possibility in gory detail. No matter how many times she told herself that it wasn't her fault, the guilt still lingered, aching in her chest.

The cold worked its way into her muscles, melding with

her exhaustion to make her body feel stiff and sore on the hard ground. In a way, she felt like she deserved it, like the pain was her reward for cowardice. Then again, her reward might well be that she would wander forever in the desert, never finding Callidus or the safety of Videre. She wouldn't last long in a place like this, that was certain. Not alone, at least.

Suddenly, Burn heard something move in the darkness. There were no howls or snarls to accompany its approach, only a quiet crunch of sand and a low rush of breath. Its footsteps were slow and even, but they grew louder with every second that ticked by, telegraphing the creature's approach – along with its considerable size.

Burn stood, clutching her knife with a fervor that made her knuckles go white. Her breathing sounded too loud in the stillness, but no matter what she did she couldn't seem to quiet it. She faced the mouth of the cave, her shaking arm held out in warning. If she was going to die, she'd die fighting. This time, there would be no running.

"Burn!?" a voice called from the darkness, and she nearly crumpled in relief.

Burn stumbled to the mouth of the cave, sticking her head into the night. She couldn't see the figure, but she knew he was close.

"Hale?" she yelled back, trying to locate the man by the sound of his movements.

Upon hearing her voice, Hale's pace quickened, and within moments he appeared by her side. Burn couldn't stop herself; stepping out of the cave, she wrapped her arms around him in a hug. After a second of surprise, he returned it, snaking his broad arms around her in a tight embrace.

They stood there for several heartbeats, each absorbing comfort from the body of the other. Despite having lived together for weeks and sleeping side by side each night, the pair had never really touched, preferring to lead separate lives in their separate spheres. But now, here, away from everything and everyone, their closeness eased something in Burn, a tightness she hadn't known she'd been carrying.

It was Burn who eventually pulled away, stepping back out of Hale's strong arms. As they parted, the world fell back into place around her, dark and cold and all too real.

"How did you find me? And how did you even know to come?" she asked, just able to make out the outlines of his face in the darkness. His strong jaw and furrowed brow were tilted toward her, as if he were silently checking to make sure she was whole.

"Nara," he replied, inching closer as he spoke. "She saw the sand bear attack your cart. Then she lost sight of you. We didn't know…she didn't know if you'd made it." He paused, gathering himself. "I came as soon as I heard. I didn't think. I just grabbed a horse and rode off."

"Why?" It seemed like such a simple question, but Burn had to know.

"I needed to do something. I couldn't just sit there. I needed to help."

"I don't need saving," Burn said quietly.

"I can see that," Hale replied, his body closer to hers than she'd realized.

Burn's mind was spinning. She'd written Hale off, left him behind and relegated him to her past. Yet here he was, standing in front of her after riding across a barren wasteland to rescue her. She didn't know how to respond to his gesture, whether to thank him or send him on his way. So she said the only thing that came to mind.

"Where's your horse?"

A low rumble echoed in the darkness. Burn recognized the sound as a laugh, Hale's signature chuckle.

"I left her around the corner. I wanted to explore the rocks on foot. She should be fine until morning."

Morning. Hale was planning to stay until morning. Here. With her. She suddenly felt flushed, her cheeks warm in the cool night. A shiver went through her despite the fact that she no longer felt the cold.

"Aren't you going to invite me in?" Hale asked, his voice playful.

Burn let out a quick laugh of her own before showing him into her den, warning him to watch his head as he entered. With both of them fully inside, it felt even smaller, as if the cave had constricted and were pushing them together. Hale stood hunched over beside her, his tall frame too large for the low space.

"It's nice," he commented, turning in a slow circle before seating himself along one wall. "A little dark. Could be bigger. But all in all, not a bad cave."

"It does get quite drafty, though," Burn added, sitting beside him.

Without a word, Hale put his arm around her and drew her in, the heat from his body seeping into hers. Once again, his nearness felt strange and almost foreign, although not entirely unwelcome. Masked by the darkness and emboldened by her recent escape from death, she nestled closer, leaning her head against his broad torso. The rhythmic movement of his chest soothed her, and more of her tension faded into the night.

Burn didn't want to break the spell lingering over them. For the moment, everything was calm. The wind raged and howled outside, but it couldn't touch them, couldn't penetrate the barrier of their intertwined forms. Still, something nagged at the back of her mind, something she couldn't shake.

"What happened to Jez?" she asked, her voice barely above a whisper. "Did he…Is he alive?" She shut her eyes against his response, as if that would somehow shield her from the truth.

There was a moment's silence, and Burn wondered if Hale had heard her. Yet, after a pause, his deep voice rumbled to life.

"I don't know," he said honestly. "We lost track of him, too. I found the cart – or what was left of it – but he wasn't there. It's possible he got out and has since made it back to Videre."

He didn't mention the other possibility, but both of them were thinking it. It was just as likely that Jez hadn't made it, that the sand bear had swallowed him whole and left nothing to find. Burn didn't want to imagine it, didn't want the pictures filling her mind, but they appeared nonetheless, drowning her in guilt.

She swallowed, trying to rid her throat of its sudden tightness. Burn needed something to fill the silence, to wash away the sorrow that was clawing at her lungs and making it difficult to breathe. So, once again, she said the first thing she could think of.

"I'm still going to Callidus," she said into his chest, not daring to look at him. "I'm sorry you came all this way for nothing. But I'm not going back, not before I learn what they know about Kasis. And about my father."

Burn expected him to protest, to rant, to demand she return to Videre, but he didn't. Instead, he stroked her back lightly with his fingers, leaving a trail of warmth where they touched her.

"Then I'm coming, too," he declared evenly, his breath tickling her face.

She couldn't help but pull away, and her body was suddenly cold without the touch of his. She looked up at him, searching.

"Why?" she asked, not comprehending his abrupt change of heart. "You want to stay in Videre. You've made that clear. You could be happy there. If you come with me… well, Imber might not welcome you back with open arms."

Hale considered her question for a moment, trying to put his feelings into words. As he pondered, Burn listened, but she only picked up pieces and snippets of thought, as if his motives were a mystery even to him.

"You've always been so sure about things," he began slowly. "I envy that. You had such certainty that returning to Kasis – and to your sister – was the right path. It was just what you needed to do. But I never had that level of conviction. I guess…" he paused, searching for the right words. "I guess I didn't have anyone to return for."

Burn was stunned, both by his statement and his honesty.

She'd never known much about Hale's life or his past. When she'd joined the Lunaria, he'd just been there. Somehow, it seemed like he'd always been there – and always would be. Burn had never thought to ask about his life before, about who he'd been and how he'd gotten there.

"There's no one back there? No one waiting for you?" Burn queried, a sudden sadness sweeping through her.

"No," he stated calmly. After a beat, he went on, "My mom died when I was born. My dad was killed in a factory accident a few years later. I grew up alone. They tried to place me in St. Astiphan's Orphanage, but…" he stopped, shuddering at the memory. "That's no place for a kid, especially one with a gift. So I left. I learned to take care of myself."

"But there must be someone," Burn replied, searching. "A friend or a partner. Someone who misses you."

He shook his head softly, looking down at the cave's dirt floor. "There was someone once, but she's been gone so long that I don't think I can even remember her face."

Burn flashed back to a few months ago, when Scar had hacked into Hale's tab. She said she'd discovered something – someone – that shed light on Hale's aloof disposition. Apparently, this someone had died at the hands of the Peace Force, and Hale had never forgiven them – or himself. Burn's cheeks went red at the memory, and she regretted bringing it up.

"Listen," he said, drawing her attention back to him. "No matter what you say, I'm coming with you – to Callidus and to any other camp you need to scout. Then we're going back to Kasis. Together."

Burn opened her mouth to ask why, but Hale beat her

to it.

"Because now I have someone to return for."

He said it so simply, so matter-of-factly that it took Burn's brain a moment to process it.

"When I heard you'd been attacked," he continued, "I realized what an idiot I'd been. I couldn't stand the thought of something happening to you. I promised myself that if I found you, I'd never let you go."

Burn couldn't speak. She couldn't seem to think, either. This was Hale – big, lumbering, domineering Hale. The man who considered violence a suitable solution to any problem. And the man who had landed her out here in the first place.

But, her brain added, it was also the man who had stood up for her in Videre, putting his own life on the line to make sure she was safe. And it was the man who had helped her hone her gift, spending hours as her guinea pig with no promise of a reward. And it was the man who had ridden across a lifeless desert to save her, forgoing his own dreams for the mere chance of helping her achieve hers.

These past few weeks had been some of the most difficult Burn had ever faced. Yet she hadn't been facing them alone. He had always been there, taking on the world alongside her, but she hadn't even noticed. He'd simply been a comforting friend and a little piece of home. Until now. Now he was something else entirely.

Suddenly nervous, Burn could feel her heart hammering in her chest. Swallowing, she raised her eyes to find that he was looking at her, observing her face for any hint of a reaction. As their eyes met, he brought a hand up, brushing away a hair that had fallen into her eyes. Without thinking, Burn reached up and held his hand to her face, savoring the heat and the feel of his rough fingers against her cheek.

Without a word, Hale drew her in, his head coming down to meet hers in a tentative kiss. His lips were surprisingly soft against hers, forming a contrast to the rough stubble of his unshaven face. Burn closed her eyes, relishing the taste of him.

Sensing no resistance, he deepened the kiss. As if by instinct, her arms wound around his large form, pulling him closer until no space remained between them. He copied the move, twining his arms around her until she didn't know where her body ended and his began.

For a time, the world around them ceased to exist. There was no Kasis, no Videre, no desert. It was just them, together. And, for a time, that was all they needed.

Chapter 13

Scar's night was not going well. The PeaceBots she'd sent out to do her bidding had thus far been unsuccessful, finding nothing more than barricades and solid walls along the city's edges. Despite their widened search area, they'd discovered no weak spots, no secret doors, and no hints that life could exist outside the dome.

Naturally, she was more than a little frustrated. She'd done all that work, put herself in harm's way, and enacted an incredibly ingenious plan, yet she had nothing to show for it. She was no closer to finding Burn or uncovering a way back into the city. She couldn't even prove to the Lunaria that Burn and Hale were still alive.

Normally Scar wasn't given to flights of fancy, but for some reason, she couldn't stop herself from imagining the worst. She kept seeing Burn, all alone, pursued by some nameless evil that was inching ever closer.

To distract herself from the images, Scar threw herself

into her work. In normal times, she'd have had a backlog of projects for other people, from upgrading their tabs and hacker-proofing their goggles to creating some less-than-legal code to hide their activities from prying Peace Force eyes. She'd gained quite the reputation, too, and had been the go-to girl in all the least-reputable circles. Anyone on a Peace Force watchlist found their way to her door eventually.

Since Burn's disappearance, however, she'd shut herself away, eschewing the typical projects in favor of her own creations. In the span of a few days, she'd concocted a nearly imperceptible tracker, a jammer for Peace Force comms units, and an early prototype of a sonic blaster that would temporarily incapacitate attackers.

Yet none of those things would help her find Burn. So she turned to something that could – or at least something that could help her establish contact. Scattered around Symphandra's small table were the parts of Scar's tab, each chip and connector and bracket separated and categorized. She'd taken apart her first tab when she was only 3, so by now it was second nature to her.

Her previous tinkering had always been for fun, though, a curiosity-fueled exploration of the boundaries of technology. This was something else entirely. This was a lifeline to her sister, a link she could use to reel her back in and save her from the wildlands. This was Burn's salvation.

It also wasn't working.

The plan was simple: to extend the tab's transmission range beyond the dome, allowing Burn to receive her messages. The execution was a tad more difficult. She'd never before had to send data beyond the dome, through the thick glass that encased them and into the uncivilized world outside. The task was steadily driving her mad.

Every time she thought she had cracked it, she'd send another message to Burn. And, like clockwork, every time it pinged back, undelivered. It made her feel…normal. Like one of them – the ungifted, the powerless. She almost understood why they were so angry all the time.

Of course, there was the chance that it wasn't Scar's fault. Maybe Burn's goggles would never be able to receive a message no matter what she did. They could easily have been confiscated by the Peace Force and destroyed. Or maybe Burn was so far out of range that no transmitter created would ever be able to reach her. Scar's insipid imagination threw in another possibility: Maybe the goggles had been crushed or skewered or completely eviscerated in some other horrible manner – along with the person wearing them.

Yet she couldn't dwell on that. She had to keep her hope alive. Otherwise…well, otherwise she would turn off, shut down, withdraw from the world completely. It had happened before when they'd lost their father. Scar hadn't known how to process it, so she hadn't. She'd stopped functioning, stopped computing the data, like a machine whose battery had long since run dry.

Burn had been the one to pull her out of it. Slowly, over time, her sister had brought her back to life, coaxing her out little by little. But now, if it happened again, there was no one left to save her. So she had to keep going, keep trying until there were no options left. Burn would do it for her. Burn *had* done it for her. Now it was her turn to do the saving.

Scar redoubled her efforts, burying her head in a pile

of secondhand tab components. She was so focused on the task at hand that the sudden arrival of a message on her own goggles came as quite the shock. She was so startled that she nearly managed to set the table on fire – again.

For a second, she feared it was the Lunaria inviting her to yet another futile meeting to plot against the Peace Force. After their refusal to help Burn and Hale, she'd given them the same treatment, refusing to lend her particular set of skills in return.

As she skimmed the text, though, she realized it wasn't a Lunaria communique. In fact, it was quite the opposite; it was from Kaz. Scar hadn't heard from Kaz since that night in the alley. She'd almost given up on him, written him off as useless, just like she'd done with the Lunaria. Yet it seemed he was more capable than she'd thought.

"I've discovered something," the message began, getting straight to the point. "Can we meet?"

Cryptic yet intriguing. Scar couldn't stop the excitement from thrumming through her. This could be it, the breakthrough she'd been waiting for.

Without hesitating, she typed out a reply. "Meet me in 15. Come alone. Make sure you're not followed."

Since it was past curfew – and she didn't fancy the idea of another late-night rendezvous with the Peace Force – she gave him the address to Symphandra's house. She knew it was risky, but she needed to find out what he'd learned, and she couldn't wait until morning.

The following quarter of an hour was agonizing. Scar kept glancing at the clock, willing it to move, but it remained lethargic, ticking off the seconds in slow motion. Finally, with only a few minutes to spare, a light knock sounded on the door. Scar was there in an instant, checking the peep hole to make sure it was Kaz before admitting him inside.

Kaz didn't look any better than the last time they'd met. The bags under his eyes remained, while his hair and scraggly beard had grown out, adding several years to his otherwise young face. But there was a new light in his eyes, something Scar had never seen. He seemed energized despite his exhaustion, fueled by something that was bursting to get out.

Without invitation, he strode into the living room and began pacing back and forth like a caged animal. He wrung his hands in front of him while his eyes scanned the room, looking at everything but taking in nothing.

Burn would have been concerned for him. He was obviously experiencing some inner turmoil, no doubt some combination of guilt and regret and sadness, but Scar couldn't bring herself to care. True, he had once been close to her sister, but that didn't make him anything to her. For Scar, he was merely a source of information, a means to an end. Once he'd served his purpose, it didn't really matter what became of him – as long as he didn't sell her out, of course.

"What did you learn?" Scar wasn't one for small talk, so she asked the question on her mind.

Kaz stopped his pacing to look at her, startled to find her standing in front of him. Then, just as abruptly, he resumed his path, traveling back and forth from the kitchen to the bedroom door.

"I followed everyone who might know about the Pit," he began. "I hid in the shadows and listened, but they said nothing about it. Or about weak spots in the wall. Or the possibility that people could exist outside of Kasis."

Scar sighed. This was going to be a long story. She hated long stories. She much preferred it when people got to the point quickly and didn't waste her time with the backstory. Yet she deemed it in her best interest not to interrupt him. If she did, it might take even longer, and she definitely did not have the patience for that. So she sat herself down on one of the living room couches and waited for him to get to the crux of his story.

"I realized I needed to do something, to move things along somehow. I wouldn't learn what I needed to know by just lurking around people's offices. I had to force them to reveal their hand." Kaz lapsed into silence as the memories flashed through his mind. Scar waited for a moment before nudging him along.

"And?" she queried, trying to conceal her impatience. "What did you learn?"

"Well, I sent anonymous letters to a few of the most senior officers," he said, continuing his story but getting no closer to the point. "I told them that I knew their secret: When people get sentenced to the Pit, they don't die. They just end up outside of Kasis. I told them that I knew that life outside of the dome is possible and that there are people living and thriving out there as we speak."

He said the last sentence without breathing and paused momentarily to catch his breath. After he'd sucked in enough air, he continued. "I ended the letters by threatening to go public with the information. I told them I had proof and, unless they paid me, I would leak it to the Lunaria, who would, in turn, release it throughout Kasis."

"You asked for money?" Scar asked incredulously.

"I knew they would never give in to a bribe," Kaz explained hurriedly, trying to allay Scar's fears. "I just needed them to take the letters seriously. Once I delivered them, I staked out the offices, listening for any mention of the Pit."

Scar had to hand it to him – it was a clever plan. By threatening them, he'd forced them to confront the issue. She was impressed, although she'd never tell that to him.

"Did it work?" she prodded, attempting to move the conversation closer to its conclusion.

"Well, I delivered them gradually, over the course of a few days, so I could track each subject and monitor their conversations," he continued, eschewing the simple "yes" or "no" in favor of a long-form answer. Scar checked out for a brief period as she realized that the point was still a long way off.

"The first few were disappointing. They either didn't know anything, or they thought the whole thing was a joke – or both. I spent over a week following dead ends. Then, on the fourth or fifth try, I discovered something. I'd sent another letter, this time to Sergeant Radix. Except instead of laughing at it or throwing it in the trash, he called for another one of the sergeants, one who I've never seen before.

"He showed the letter to the sergeant – I think his name was Sergeant Bellis – and Radix asked him what he thought of it. Like the others, Bellis said that it was probably a joke. Radix agreed, but then he said that they couldn't be too careful. They had to make sure that none of the records were missing. He said that if they were all still in place, then they wouldn't have anything to worry about."

Scar perked up at the mention of records. Records meant that there was, indeed, something to record. And something to hide.

"And?" Scar queried, leaning over the back of the couch to get closer to Kaz, as if that would somehow get her closer to the end of the story. "Did you find the records they were talking about?"

"I followed Bellis down to the records room, deep within the Peace Station," he said, still pacing – and still not answering her questions directly. "He didn't bother with any of the typical records, the ones that catalog arrests and warrants and that kind of thing. He went farther back than I've ever been, and he opened a secret door tucked away and disguised to look like part of the wall. I managed to slip in after him before the door shut.

"It was a tiny room and I thought for sure that he would spot me. I'm still getting used to this whole 'gift' thing. Yet I managed to duck into one of the dark corners. I watched as he opened one cabinet and then another, flipping through the documents to make sure they were all in place. He was slow and thorough, reading every file before tucking it back. I don't know how long we were there. It felt like hours. But finally, he seemed satisfied that nothing was missing, and he left."

Scar was sitting at attention now. Surely he had to be coming to the conclusion of his story. He was in the same room as the documents. What else could stop him from getting to the point?

"I waited for a few minutes to make sure he wasn't coming back. When I was sure he was gone for good, I yanked open the drawers he'd been looking in and combed through every file. Most of them were old – very old – and they looked on the verge of disintegrating. They were hard to make out, but the majority of them were useless, just old plans of the city and construction invoices for different buildings. Then I saw 'the Pit' written on one of them. It turned out to be the original sketches for the Pit's design."

Scar couldn't take it anymore. "Where does it lead?" she demanded impatiently. She was done with his story and wanted the facts.

"You were right. It leads outside of the city. The creators of the Pit never intended it to be a death sentence. They just wanted a way to banish people to the wildlands. They thought the atmosphere and animals would eventually kill them in the end, but they didn't want to have people's deaths on their conscience."

Scar's heart soared. Burn wasn't dead. In fact, she could be right outside the dome now, waiting for them to find a way to let her back in. Scar wanted to laugh and cry and run to the dome's edge to find her. Yet all of those things seemed rather excessive, so instead she remained where she was, seated on the couch. The only outward display she allowed herself was a small, tentative smile.

Kaz, not realizing that his story should have concluded with that piece of information, continued talking. "It's been centuries since they built it. Over time, the truth about the Pit must have been corrupted, just like the Peace Force itself. As their purpose changed, so did their ideas of the Pit. Only a few officers seem to know the truth. I'm guessing they don't want people to know that life outside the dome is possible.

They want to keep people contained – and scared."

Scar agreed with his assessment, but she didn't really care why they'd done it. All that mattered was that she and Kaz could prove that they had.

"Did you take the documents? The Lunaria won't believe us without evidence. We need to prove without a doubt that there are still people alive out there and that there's a way to get them back."

Kaz gave her a self-satisfied smile. Reaching into an inner pocket of his cloak, he pulled out a thick stack of yellow parchment and tossed it blithely onto the couch next to her. He was so smug, so proud of himself for his sleuthing, and, flipping through the papers, Scar could see why.

He'd not only grabbed the documents on the Pit itself, but seemingly the planning documents for all of Kasis – blueprints, electrical grids, contracts, project specifications. The list went on. This was a gold mine of information, a rare glimpse into the inner workings of Kasis.

Scar didn't know where to start. She wanted to consume everything Kaz had brought, to absorb it into herself like light, but most of it meant nothing to her. Despite her technological brain, building schematics and contractor specifications didn't compute the same way chips and circuits did. It was like trying to read another language, one that looked strangely similar to a child's sketchbook.

"We need to tell the Lunaria," Scar said, glancing up from the documents for the first time in several minutes. "Tomorrow. We'll call a meeting for tomorrow. That should give us enough time to formulate a plan."

"We?" Kaz asked suspiciously. "I don't think the Lunaria

would be that fond of me attending one of their meetings. The whole Peace Officer thing might be a sore spot."

Scar sighed loudly, exhausted by his tedious dramatics. "It'll be fine. Just let me do the talking." She didn't think she could stand another tiresome recitation of his story.

"But..." he started to say, but Scar cut him off.

"Do you want to get Burn back?" He nodded mutely. "Then do what I say. You've done fine on your own so far, but now it's time to bring in people who actually know what they're doing. Apart, we have no chance of finding her. But if we combine forces with the Lunaria, we might have a chance of bringing her back alive."

Kaz just stared at her, his eyes wide. She took that as acceptance.

"Good. Now it's time to get to work."

Burn awoke with the suns, their unrelenting rays piercing the darkness of the cave and startling her into consciousness. She felt groggy and sore, the rough floor of the cave being ill-equipped to serve as a mattress. One of Hale's large arms lay across her stomach, pinning her to the ground. Gradually she managed to wriggle free, squirming out of his grip and crawling out of the cave.

The sight that met her outside was breathtaking. While the first sun had cleared the horizon and was beginning its trek across the sky, the second was just cresting, drenching the desert with shades of orange, yellow, and pale pink. It peeked tentatively over the dunes, creating a captivating portrait of shadows and light as far as the eye could see.

The early morning stillness made the whole scene feel serene and peaceful, as if there was nothing out there that could touch her. Gone were the howling wind and the howling creatures. In their place was a timid breeze that made the sand dance merrily around her feet. Tendrils of hair tickled her face as she settled herself in the sand and raised her head to the sky, drinking in the warmth.

With her eyes shut, Burn opened her mind to the desert, listening as the wildlands came to life before her. Small animals skittered from their holes in search of food as the birds provided a musical score in the background. Somewhere, far away, a faint trickle of water splashed across rocks as a stubborn stream tried to compete with the merciless desert suns. The thin, dry air brought with it the scent of sweet sand and dusty earth, filling her senses and uniting her with the landscape.

Sitting there, her eyes closed and head raised, she fell into a sort of trance, lulled into a gentle peace by the harmony of her surroundings. That's how Hale found her, seated on the desert floor with her hands buried in the sand beside her. Instead of rousing her, he took a seat next to her, mirroring her movements. They sat like that for some time, without speaking or needing to speak.

Eventually, though, thirst and hunger and the gradually increasing heat made speech and movement necessary, and Burn broke the idyllic stillness of the scene.

"We need to find water," she said, hating to bring reality back into their lives but knowing that it must be said. "I finished my canteen last night. Callidus is probably still a few hours away, even on horseback."

Her voice cracked as she spoke, emphasizing her point. Instead of responding, Hale lifted himself up and walked away, following the rock face out of sight. Unconcerned, Burn merely waited, certain he would return and explain.

After a time, he did return – but he was no longer alone. Walking sedately behind him was a tall, muscular horse with a reddish-brown coat that gleamed in the suns. Its mane and tail were a silky black, while a once-colorful woven saddlebag rested comfortably across its broad back. Pausing in front of her, Hale reached inside one of the pockets and withdrew a large canteen, which he offered to her wordlessly.

Burn took it, its fullness reassuringly heavy in her hands. She gulped down a few mouthfuls of water, its magical coolness washing the sand from her mouth and the prickles of thirst from her throat. Satisfied, she handed the bottle back to Hale before venturing cautiously toward the regal animal.

"She's friendly," Hale stated, noticing her interest. "And she's one hell of a runner. Didn't seem to mind my weight in the least, so she should be able to carry both of us without difficulty."

As Burn tentatively reached out to stroke the creature's neck, Hale withdrew a small bowl from its pack and poured some of the water into it. He offered the bowl to the horse, who obligingly dipped its muzzle in and drank. Burn smiled to herself as she watched Hale interact with the animal, his gentleness tugging at something deep within her.

"There's a bit of food, as well," he said, indicating the saddle bag. "It's not much, but it should last us for a bit if we're careful."

Burn rummaged through the pockets and discovered a small store of dried meat and nuts. Taking a handful of each, she offered some to Hale before digging in herself. Despite the meal's meager size, she felt her energy level rise – and her optimism along with it. They had food, water, a horse, and each other. The desert seemed a small foe in comparison.

Once they'd finished their meal and packed their limited belongings, they mounted the horse and set off in the direction Jez had indicated. Just as Hale had said, the horse had no problem supporting their combined weight, and it trotted easily through the dunes as it headed toward Callidus.

At first, the ride was jarring, and Burn found herself bouncing painfully in the seat. Hale, however, intrinsically understood the creature, and he shifted his body in sync with its movements. Burn could feel him at her back, his large form rising and falling in time with the beating hooves. After a while, she began to do the same, matching the rhythm of his body until they all moved as one.

It was thrilling. The desert air whipped around them, focusing the majority of its strength at their backs as if spurring them on. Beneath them, the path changed from dunes to dry, cracked earth, and Burn watched as brittle foliage, prickly cacti, and long stretches of nothingness competed for her attention. The uneven surfaces and varied terrain made their journey slow yet achingly beautiful.

Around midday, they stopped for water and lunch, and to allow their horse to rest. With the suns at their peak, the heat beat down on the trio, sapping their energy. Luckily, they found a spot in the shade of a high cliff face and took sanctuary in its cool embrace.

Yet their respite couldn't last. As soon as the horse was able, they took to the road once more. Burn and Hale rode in silence now, their eyes scanning the skyline. They knew that Callidus was close. Jez had said the journey was a few hours, and they were rapidly approaching that mark. Unless they'd veered off course, they would encounter the city before the suns commenced their downward arc.

After a while, the horse began to climb, its hooves clacking against the stone hill underfoot. The incline was subtle at first, but as it increased, Burn and Hale disembarked to walk alongside the creature, each panting with the effort.

Burn was so focused on setting one foot in front of the other that she almost missed the change in the air. Gone were the caws of birds and the skittering of lizards across the sand. The animals had gone silent, hushed by the presence of a larger predator in their midst: humans.

Burn paused, gesturing for Hale to do the same. Callidus was close. She could feel it now. A multitude of voices murmured somewhere beyond the ridge, beckoning to her. She had to stop herself from scurrying up the rock face to get a better view.

Jez's words popped into her head as a warning. "They're not as friendly...not too keen on outsiders."

She'd been so intent on getting there that she hadn't considered what would happen when she arrived. Burn's eagerness turned into nervous energy as she contemplated the camp's reaction to her and Hale's sudden appearance. Would they welcome the pair as citizens of Videre, accepting them based on their tentative peace? Or would they view them as outsiders, fair game to do with as they pleased?

"Callidus is just over that hill," Burn whispered to Hale as she listened, taking note of the people and their movements. There had to be at least 200 of them, all busily going about their daily chores. She suddenly felt extremely small and inconsequential, like a bug they could crush without even trying.

"What's the plan?" Hale whispered back, looking to her for direction. She shrugged, her mind devoid of any clever strategy.

Sighing, Hale straightened and continued his ascent. Burn's whispered warnings went unnoticed as he reached the peak and surveyed the land before him.

A strange whooshing noise erupted from somewhere to their right, and she had just enough time to yell "look out!" before a man stood before them. In a flash, he sized up Hale and – apparently determining him to be a threat – stabbed him in the neck with a small needle. Hale promptly fell to his knees before collapsing into the dust.

Unable to help herself, Burn let out a sharp shriek. The man, clearly gifted with outstanding speed, turned his head toward her. In a blink he stood before her, towering over her and blocking out the suns. Not knowing what else to do, she raised her hands in surrender.

"We're from Videre," she explained hastily. "We were part of a trade mission, but our cart got attacked by a sand bear. We come in peace."

The man let out a small "humph" at her words, but he didn't pull out another needle, which was a good sign. Glancing up at Hale's immobile form, she prayed that he was merely sleeping, knocked out by a tranquilizer rather than a deadly poison.

Turning her attention back to the stranger, she saw him scan the rocky hill, as if searching for someone. Sure enough, within a few moments more men appeared around her, creeping up one by one until she was surrounded.

"Take the intruders to Thestle," the first man commanded, gesturing to her and Hale. "He'll know what to do with them."

At his words, two men flanked Burn, grabbing her by the shoulders and pinning her arms to her sides. She tried to protest, tried to explain that she wasn't an intruder, but they promptly tied a gag around her mouth and pushed her up the hill.

Burn struggled to see past them into the valley beyond, but they blocked her view, turning to lead her down a perilously narrow footpath that wound into the city. Twisting to look behind her, Burn glimpsed four men hoist Hale's limp body onto their shoulders before her own guards forced her back around.

Panic welled up inside of her as she realized just how defenseless she truly was. She had no credible excuse for her presence there, no allies, and no exit plan. And now she didn't even have Hale to watch her back. This was definitely not the welcome she had imagined.

Chapter 14

Treating their prisoners well did not seem to be part of Callidus' strategy. On the way down the rocky trail, Burn stumbled and fell on more than one occasion, helped along by a push from the back or a foot placed conveniently in her path.

By the time she arrived in the city center, she was covered in dirt and bleeding, with a stone still lodged in her shin from a particularly unpleasant tumble. The guards seemed proud of themselves for her disheveled state. Hale still hadn't regained consciousness, and they roughly plopped his body beside her in the dirt, face down.

Stealing glances around her, Burn took stock of the city. Surprisingly, it was quite similar to what she'd pictured in her head. Tan tents flapped in the breeze as bedraggled people walked between them, lugging buckets of water, piles of dirty clothes, and animal hides still dripping with blood. Their weapons, however, weren't as crude as she'd hoped. As the guards encircled her, she saw the glint of more than one knife pointed in her direction, in addition to several long spears with hideously sharp tips.

As the two guards let go of her, one of them stopped to bind her hands in front of her. Then, with a harsh push on the shoulder, he forced her to kneel. Sharp stones bit into her kneecaps, but she refused to show weakness, keeping her head high.

The man gifted with speed, who had disappeared from the cliff's edge once they'd started their descent, emerged from the tent in front of her. As if on cue, everyone turned their attention to the dwelling, which was by far the largest in the village. Before long, a second man appeared, and the guards around her bowed their heads in respect.

Burn didn't see what was so special about this man. His rotund frame clearly wouldn't make him much of a hunter, and his bald head and round cheeks made him more akin to a baby than a leader. Despite the heat, he wore a long, colorful robe that was belted in the middle and left only his hands and head exposed. He clasped his hands in front of him, circling his large belly, as he took in Burn and Hale.

"These must be our new visitors," the man said in mock cheerfulness. "Welcome to Callidus, friends. I'm Thestle. I would inquire as to your names, but they don't really matter. All of our slaves get new names, after all. Although if being a slave doesn't suit you, we'd be more than happy to introduce you to our local carrion birds. They also don't need to know your names. They'll pluck out your eyes no matter what you're called."

A sudden revulsion rose in Burn's throat at his sickly

sweet threats. She wanted more than anything to grab one of the guards' spears and challenge him to a duel, the way she and Nara had practiced so many times. But the thick cloth that bound her hands prevented her from moving, so she simply glared at him, wishing her eyes had the power to burn holes into people's chests.

Undaunted by her glare, Thestle approached, bending down to get a closer look. Reaching out one of his pudgy hands, he tucked a lock of hair behind her ear before brushing off some of the dirt that had accumulated on her face. Burn tried to squirm out of his grasp, but he held her head in place, his grip surprisingly strong.

"Now this one I like!" he exclaimed to his men, who chuckled in response. "So much fire. It's adorable." Straightening, he continued, "Put her in my chambers. Throw the other in a cell. I'll deal with him later."

At his orders, two sets of arms grabbed her and dragged her to her feet. She tried to dig her heels into the dirt to slow their progress, but they merely picked her up by the arms and carried her forward into Thestle's tent. Without a word, they threw her onto the enormous bed that dominated the space.

She had a sudden surge of hope as they undid the cloth ties around her arms, but it dissipated almost instantly as they secured her hands to the bed frame behind her. Their movements were quick and efficient, and she got the feeling that they'd done this before.

Chuckling to themselves, they left her there, helpless. But Burn was never one to give up easily. She wriggled her body around, straining against her bonds in an attempt to loosen them. Twisting in every conceivable direction, she pulled at the fabric, hoping either it or the bed frame would give out and release her. Yet nothing budged. The guards had done their job well.

It was during this futile attempt to escape that Thestle re-entered the tent. In her heated desire to free herself, she didn't notice his presence for several seconds. Instead, her focus was consumed by her attempts to deal a kick to the wooden frame behind her in hopes of weakening the planks. It was Thestle's light throat-clearing that ultimately got her attention. Twisting her body back around, she glared at him and readied a kick in case he came anywhere near her.

"Oh, how I love the plucky ones. It's so much fun to break them," he said, as much to himself as to Burn. "There's no use fighting, my dear. Even if you managed to get yourself free, there's nowhere to go. You might as well make yourself comfortable."

He approached the bed but stayed clear of her legs, as if he knew her intentions. Thestle took his time looking her over. Burn tried to block out the lecherous thoughts that were emanating from his mind, but they screamed at her, demanding she listen.

He wanted to take her, and he wanted her to struggle. He enjoyed it when they fought back.

Thankfully, Burn could also see that he wanted to take his time, to enjoy the atmosphere of tension and hatred before subduing her. That would give her a chance to think, to construct a plan. Because she would never let this bastard lay a hand on her.

"I don't think we're going to be needing this anymore," he said, reaching up to untie her gag.

Burn sucked in a deep breath. The heat mingled with the sweet smell of the tent to choke her, and she coughed and gasped in an attempt to breathe. Thestle looked on, a satisfied smile tugging at the corners of his lips.

"I'm a citizen of Videre," Burn managed to get out in between coughs. "If anything happens to me, Imber will never trade with you again. And without his help – and his water – you and your people will die. Now let me and my friend go, and maybe we can come to an arrangement." She tried to put all of her strength behind the words, willing them to work.

Yet the smile remained on Thestle's face, growing wider as she spoke. He waited for her to finish, leisurely walking to the other side of the bed to stare down at her.

"You're so cute," he said, his tone thick and greasy. "But we both know that's a lie. Imber would never send anyone like you, and you've clearly brought no goods to barter with. No, I bet that they tossed you out of Videre – you and your little friend. And now you're crawling around the wildlands in search of another camp to take you in. So pathetic."

"We were part of a trade expedition," Burn tried again, a hint of impatience creeping into her voice. "We were traveling with Jez when our cart was attacked by a sand bear. We managed to escape, but we lost Jez and the cart in the process. Callidus was nearby, so we came in search of help."

It was close enough to the truth that she could sell it convincingly. She decided to leave out the bit about her search for her father, at least for the moment.

Part of her brain – the part that wasn't frantically searching for a way out – wondered if her father was indeed in Callidus. Had he come here in search of information and found himself pressed into slavery? Had he been here for years, forced to do their bidding and unable to escape? The more she considered it, the more likely it seemed. Despite her panic, she felt a glimmer of hope spring to life in her chest.

What if Arvense was right around the corner? What if he could save her? If that was the case, she just needed to stall until he could get there, until he could find a way to free her. It was a longshot, but more impossible things had happened.

Meanwhile, Thestle was shaking his head at her tale.

"I applaud your creativity, girl," he said derisively. "A sand bear! What a story. Maybe I should keep you on as my personal court jester. You obviously possess a flair for the dramatics. Unfortunately, though, that won't save you now."

He licked his lips as he looked her over, a chill going up her spine. She had to keep him talking, even if no one was coming to her rescue. Maybe, if she was very, very clever – or incredibly lucky – she could even turn the situation in her favor.

"OK, OK! You caught me," she said, feigning resignation. "You can clearly see right through me. I thought I could fool you, but you're obviously too clever for that." Thestle paused in his approach, enjoying the boost to his ego.

"I'll tell you the truth, the real reason I came to Callidus," Burn continued, watching as he tilted his head in curiosity. "I'm looking for my father, Arvense Alendra. I believe he came here around five years ago looking for a way back into Kasis. And I believe you knew him."

Burn listened intently to his mind, scanning it for any hint of recognition. All she needed was a flicker of acknowledgment, a single sign that her father had once set foot in the city. But Thestle was already too far gone to care about anything she'd said. He had one thing on his mind, which overpowered every other thought or need.

"I never knew an Arvense," he said, brushing her words aside. "I'm afraid your trip was in vain. Although I must admit that I'm delighted you came. If you hadn't, we wouldn't have gotten the chance to get to know each other so...intimately." Putting a finger on her chest, he trailed it down to her stomach, tracing the curves of her body.

Disgust warred with red-hot anger in the pit of Burn's stomach. She wanted this man to suffer, to feel what it was like to be powerless. A harsh scowl contorted her face as he moved closer, placing himself on the bed beside her.

"You have so much anger for someone so young," he purred into her ear. "It's not very becoming, you know."

Burn felt like she was going to be sick. She tried to twist her legs up to kick him, but she couldn't quite reach. All she managed to do was elicit a small chuckle from the round little man.

"Now, now. That won't do you any good," he said in reprimand, as if talking to a child.

Placing his hand back on her stomach, he began to move it lower and lower, savoring her expression. When his hand reached her hips, however, it paused, lingering.

"But what do we have here?" he asked almost gleefully. Lifting up her shirt, he revealed her knife belt, taking his time to run his hand along the strip of leather.

His eyes lit up as he took one of the knives from its sheath and playfully tossed it above her, nimbly catching it mere inches from her skin. He laughed jovially, like it was all some sort of game.

"Well, now I have to make sure there's nothing else you're hiding," he continued. With a quick swipe of the knife, he cut through her shirt, exposing her chest.

Burn lunged for him. The ropes bit violently into her wrists, but she no longer felt the pain. Boiling rage consumed her, removing any hint of logic or common sense. It felt like her humanity was slipping through her fingers, replaced by pure animalistic hatred. She wanted to claw at his eyes until they bled, to tear him to pieces with her teeth. He didn't deserve the privilege of sight or sound or taste. She yearned to leave him crippled and bleeding, a feast for the carnivores of the wildlands.

"If you touch me again, I swear to the gods you'll pay," she growled through clenched teeth.

"You're not really in a position to make threats, now are you?" Thestle cooed. "Although it's endearing that you're still fighting. Most people give up by now. Don't you worry, though. I'll take care of that."

He swung his leg over her body and mounted her, subduing her with his considerable weight. She tried to lash out, to headbutt him or twist out from beneath him, but he held her down.

"Now, I'm sorry to have to do this, but I don't want you to scream," he said, lowering his head to hers. Right as she opened her mouth to do just that, he put his lips on hers and sucked.

Burn felt her throat go dry as he raised his head, a white, gauzy haze traveling from her mouth to his. Within an instant, it was over.

Burn tried to shout. She tried to ask what he'd done. She tried to whisper. But nothing came out, not a hint of sound. Thestle had stolen her voice.

"There, now," he said enthusiastically. "That's much better."

Burn screamed at him, using every profanity she'd ever learned. She called him a coward and a cad and cursed him to rot in hell for an eternity. Yet silence covered the room, blanketing her in its cruel embrace.

She felt violated. He'd taken something so precious, so tied to her identity that it felt like he'd stolen a part of her soul. Despite her rage, she felt her energy begin to fade. The fight gradually drained from her body, leaving her weak and broken. He had won – and he knew it.

As the last of her resistance left her, a figure burst into the tent, drawing Thestle's attention. Peering around her attacker, Burn saw that it was one of the guards who had escorted her into the city. The relief that had momentarily flashed before her eyes faded as she realized that he wasn't there to rescue her. No one was coming to save her.

"What do you want?!" Thestle cried in irritation. "You know that I'm not to be disturbed when I have company!"

The guard bobbed his head in apology but kept venturing deeper into the room. He glanced at Burn, and she could have sworn that a look of pure hatred flashed across his face before his features went blank. She wondered what she'd done to garner such emotion from a man she barely knew.

"I'm sorry, sir," came the man's low voice as he approached. "But there's a problem with one of the prisoners. We need your assistance in the cells."

By this time, the man was nearly upon them, and Burn could see that he was clutching something behind his back. He shot a quick look at her, clearly trying to communicate something, but she couldn't interpret it.

"Damn it, man! You should be able to take care of that..." Thestle's words drifted off as the guard raised a large baton.

With an effortless swing, he clubbed Thestle on the side of the head, eliciting a satisfying thud as the wood struck the man's thick skull. He swayed precariously for an instant before collapsing on top of Burn, knocking the wind out of her lungs.

The guard shoved Thestle off of her, moving the body as if it were nothing more than a pebble. Getting to work on her binds, he swiftly undid the fabric, freeing one arm then the other.

Burn's mind felt sluggish. It didn't make sense. Why was this guard helping her? She watched suspiciously as he checked her for injuries, not trusting him in the slightest. He seemed to understand her hesitation, though, and made no move to touch her.

"So," he began, his low voice rumbling to life, "tell me again how you don't need saving, Burn."

Burn's mind went blank, confusion clouding her thoughts. It couldn't be. It was impossible. But yet...

"Hale?" she asked tentatively, relieved to find that rendering Thestle unconscious had also returned the use of her voice.

The guard smiled sweetly at her and nodded.

Chapter 15

It didn't make sense. None of it made sense. It wasn't Hale's face staring down at her, and it wasn't his voice that emanated from the guard's thin mouth. Nothing about this man was familiar. Yet it was Hale.

Burn didn't know how to react. Fear and desolation still clung to her, making it difficult to form coherent thoughts. She wanted to believe him, wanted to believe she had been rescued, but it seemed too good to be true. Something in the back of her mind kept casting doubt on his identity, warning her not to trust him – or anyone else in this place.

The way the man stared at her was heartbreaking. Pity and anger and helplessness mingled in his eyes as he looked down at her disheveled form, the remains of her torn shirt still hanging loosely around her chest. Turning his back to her, he rose from the bed and hastily searched the room.

A moment later, he returned, a wad of green fabric clutched in his hand. He offered it to her wordlessly, but all she could do was stare, clutching her arms around her chest and trying to hold herself together.

Sighing, the guard unfurled the bundle, revealing a large shirt. As gently as he could, he pulled the garment over Burn's head, helping her thread her arms through the baggy sleeves. The cloth hung loosely around her frame, but it covered her exposed skin, concealing what Thestle had laid bare. The smell of him lingered in the fabric, however, and the guard had to stop her from tearing the shirt from her body.

"It's OK, Burn. It's OK," the guard repeated, his hands stroking her arms in reassurance. "I'm here. And I'll make sure no one touches you. I promise. I won't leave you."

Burn looked up at him, trying to find Hale in his eyes, but even those were someone else's, an unfamiliar grayish-blue staring back at her from a foreign face.

"Hale?" she asked again, practically pleading this time. She needed Hale, not whoever this was. She needed his strong arms to take her away from this place, to erase this town and these people from her memory.

"Yes, it's me, Burn," he replied soothingly, taking a seat next to her and moving his hand up to stroke her hair. She flinched at his touch but didn't pull away.

"How?" she asked, her voice sounding small.

Hale sighed, removing his hand and placing it in his lap. He looked at her sadly for a beat before embarking on his story.

"You were right," he said, a cheerless smile on his lips. "Your father did come to Callidus. Apparently he snuck in and began recruiting people to join him on his journey back to Kasis. Except Thestle discovered what he was up to, and your father was forced to flee. He did manage to send a final message to his contacts, though. He told them that once he'd found a way in, he'd return for them, and together they'd make their way home."

He paused, trying to find the words to relay the next part of his story. Burn looked on in confusion, trying to piece together the threads of her father's journey – and what it had to do with Hale's sudden change of appearance.

"He never came back, Burn," he continued solemnly. "They don't know what happened to him. Some think he's still out there, searching for a way back into Kasis. Others assume he perished during his journey."

The thought of her father wandering through the wildlands, lost and alone, touched something in Burn. A pang of sorrow cut through her shock, clearing some of the cobwebs that had settled over her mind. She was on the right track, after all, although something deep inside of her told her that she was rapidly nearing the end.

"What happened?" she whispered, needing him to go on.

"Well, most of the people he recruited are still here, and they still want to find a way back. I told your story to the guards, and one of them knew your father. She was one of the people that had agreed to go with him. She told me what had happened. And she helped me escape."

"Is that why you look…like that?" Burn asked, a hint of her former confidence returning to her voice. They were finally getting somewhere, and the progress restored more of the strength that Thestle had sapped.

"Yes," Hale said quietly. "She can change people – their

face, their body, their voice. She helped me become one of the guards. It was the only way to get in here without a fight."

A sudden moan of pain emanated from the floor beside the bed. Burn and Hale immediately shifted their attention to Thestle, who had begun to regain consciousness and was clutching the spot on his head where Hale had struck him.

Moving with purpose, Hale grabbed Thestle and tossed him into a nearby chair. In the blink of an eye, he'd snatched the strips of fabric from the bed and fastened them around Thestle's arms and legs, securing him tightly to the seat.

Thestle's head lolled against his chest as he tried and failed to sit up. Finally, he managed to right himself, swinging his head around to an upright position.

"Be careful," Burn warned as Hale considered his prey. "If you get too close, he can steal your voice."

Hale's look of pity returned as more pieces of her ordeal fell into place. He spun to face Thestle, his gaze filling with rage. Fearing that he'd do something rash, Burn gingerly leveraged herself off the bed and walked to his side. Putting her hand on his shoulder, she turned him to face her.

"We need him," she said slowly, drawing him back from the edge. "He might know what happened to my father."

"He deserves to die," Hale said, his fists clenching and unclenching as he spoke.

Burn couldn't disagree with that, but right now she needed him alive. After that...well, after that she'd wash her hands of him.

Sighing, she turned to face Thestle, who was fully conscious now. His gaze flicked between his captors, his thin mouth turned down in disgust.

"I won't tell you anything," he said boldly, raising his nose toward the sky. "Do whatever you want, but you'll get nothing from me."

He was so proud of himself, so pleased by his own fortitude. Burn wanted to wipe that smile off his face, to fight his fire with hers. Yet striking him wouldn't help her get the answers she needed; it would only feed into his sick sense of control, confirming that he still had the power to influence her actions.

"Fortunately, I don't need you to talk in order to get answers," Burn replied, plastering on a cocky smile.

The courage may have been an act, but the sentiment behind it was real. All she needed was a single thought, a momentary recollection, or a flash of memory to discover what he knew. Hale seemed to intrinsically understand her plan. Cracking his knuckles, he moved behind Thestle, placing his hands menacingly on the man's shoulders.

"Now," Burn began, pacing slowly in front of Thestle's chair, "we know that you were acquainted with my father, Arvense Alendra. He came here and tried to lure away your people and take them with him to Kasis. You had a problem with that. You wanted him gone. That much we know. What we don't know is what happened to him after he left Callidus." Burn paused, letting her words sink in.

"I think you know what became of him," she continued. She leaned in toward Thestle, scowling as she raked her eyes over his fleshy form. "What did you do to Arvense? Why is it that he never returned to Callidus?"

A small, almost imperceptible smile turned up the corners of Thestle's lips. He stared at her silently, smug in his own defiance. Yet, despite his exterior composure, his thoughts were ablaze with memories.

Burn didn't hesitate. Closing her eyes, she stepped fully into his mind, surrounding herself with his thoughts. His memories were unlike anything she had ever experienced. There was something sinister about them, and they tasted wrong, leaving a tinge of rancid meat lingering on her tongue.

Instead of forming a linear pattern, his past swirled around her like a sandstorm, with bits of it clinging to her skin and others threatening to choke her.

"What did you do to my father?" she repeated, her eyes still closed.

At her question, bits and pieces rose in his memory, and Burn seized them, coaxing them into her mind. Little by little, a story emerged, wrapping its tendrils around her and drawing her into its fold.

A picture of her father appeared before her eyes, so clear that she could almost feel him beside her. He looked different than he had in Kasis, older and more tired. His wild red hair was now complemented by a shaggy beard, and his light skin had darkened in the desert suns. His loose clothing was dirty and torn, but he still had that same gleam in his eyes, the same sharp intelligence that she'd always admired.

Burn watched as her father crept around Callidus, making friends and enemies in one fell swoop. Thestle despised him, that much was clear. He wanted Arvense gone. He considered her father a threat to Callidus and its people, and he would stop at nothing to be rid of him.

But Arvense was smart. He learned of Thestle's plan and escaped from the city just in time. Or so he thought.

Because Thestle knew where he was headed. There was another camp on Arvense's agenda – a place called Aberra. It was the closest colony to Kasis and his best chance at discovering a way back in. Only, he never arrived in Aberra.

A blood-drenched scene filled her mind and threatened her sanity, but she held tight, needing to know the ending. Three guards, covered in blood, made their way into the very tent where Burn now stood. The leader, sporting a gash along one cheek, proudly held something in his outstretched hand. Thestle took it, a euphoric smile stretching across his face, and Burn felt his elation leech through her like a drug.

From behind Thestle's eyes, Burn observed the source of his delight. It was Arvense's head.

Burn disconnected from Thestle's mind. Turning around, she retched onto his bed, spewing up bile and disgust until nothing was left in her stomach. Still, violent convulsions racked her body, sending her to her knees.

She longed to believe that it had been fiction, that Thestle had concocted the scenes to torment her further, but she knew that wasn't the case. He could never have fabricated such detail, such clear and gruesome facts. He had killed her father – she knew it in her bones. Arvense was dead.

The hope that had sustained her vanished, sapping every emotion until only despair remained. She had mourned her father once, but it was nothing compared to this. Seeing the true extent of Thestle's villainy had broken something in her, leaving a hole where mercy used to lie.

She didn't realize Hale was holding her. She didn't realize she was on the ground, curled into a ball. Her scarred heart had been ripped back open, and it took everything she had to hold back the fire so it didn't consume her completely.

It was Thestle's laughter that finally broke her out of her stupor. Burn could read him now, interpreting his thoughts without even trying. He was proud of himself, proud that he'd managed to break her without uttering a single word.

An eerie calm swept over her, and she rose from her place on the ground. She approached him slowly, the wicked gleam in his eyes now mirrored in hers.

"How many people have you killed?" she asked evenly, her body straight and her head held high. "How many have you tortured? How many have you used like you tried to use me?"

She let the thoughts wash over her and through her, adding fuel to her rage. As each face flowed past, she tried to memorize it, acknowledging the sacrifices they'd made. These people deserved to be remembered. They deserved to have their lives and their deaths honored. She could do that much for them. She would carry them with her, away from this place, away from this monster. She would make sure their memories lived on when his did not.

Once again, Hale was by her side. As the images trickled to a stop within her mind, she looked up at him, searching for the man she knew within the stranger's face. Reaching his eyes, she held them for a heartbeat, silently asking for his help. He raised one eyebrow in question, and Burn gave a small nod.

Turning her back, she strode to the mouth of the tent. Behind her, a sharp, quick crack resounded from the direction of Thestle's chair. A moment later, Hale joined her. Together, they left the scene behind and walked into the night.

Chapter 16

The Lunaria's chosen safe house for the evening was a dump. Well, technically the safe house was next to a dump, but Scar still maintained that the house itself could be chucked in with the rubbish and no one would even notice. But that's what they got for securing a safe house near enough to the Corax End that you could still smell it.

As planned, Scar was the first to arrive – and she immediately wanted to leave. Piles of debris carpeted the lane outside, and she was forced to wade through used bottles and bags and the rotten remains of things that had once been food. Even with her mask secured tightly around her face, the smell was so potent that she found herself holding her breath.

The house itself promised a modicum of relief, but, unfortunately, she couldn't enter. She'd promised to meet Kaz outside so she could escort him in – a promise she was now wholeheartedly regretting.

The lights in this part of the city were inconsistent at best, and they flickered overhead, casting her in and out of shadow. More than once, she heard movement around her and turned to find a not-so-small rodent burrowing its way into a nearby trash heap.

When Kaz finally did arrive, Scar nearly mistook him for yet another member of the rodent kingdom. She had taken aim and was fully prepared to throw a shoe at his head when he spoke up from the darkness, confirming his humanity.

"Scar?" he asked tentatively, feeling his way through the gloom. "Scar, are you there?" Scar dropped the shoe back into the pile at her feet, returning it to its rightful home.

"I'm right here," Scar shot back, giving him a target to aim for as he shuffled through the debris. "Remind me to upgrade your goggles with night sight," she murmured as he got closer. "Maybe then you'll actually arrive on time."

Turning to the door, Scar scanned her finger and entered. The house itself was warm and stuffy, and it still retained the distinctly sweet smell of decomposing matter. The floors, however, were clean and tidy and mostly devoid of refuse – save for the few pieces that Kaz tracked in as he tagged along behind her.

The pair made their way down a narrow hallway, passing several locked doors as they traveled deeper into the house. At its end, the hallway opened into a surprisingly large room, which was made all the larger by its lack of any proper furniture. Only a handful of battered aluminum chairs stood around the space, some upright and some knocked askew as if their former inhabitants had left in a hurry.

Getting to work, Scar began to tidy the meeting space,

righting the chairs and organizing them into a shape that resembled a circle. While she worked, she snuck glances at Kaz, who had taken her lead and started work on the other half of the circle.

"Something's different about you," Scar said abruptly, breaking the silence that had lapsed between them.

"Oh, yeah," Kaz stuttered, straightening to rub the back of his neck. "I shaved. And got a haircut. I wanted to make a good impression on the Lunaria."

Scar found that strange. After all, the reason most of the Lunaria didn't like him wasn't because of his too-long hair or his scraggly beard. They didn't like him because he was a member of the very organization they were fighting to overthrow. Unless he had somehow changed that, as well, she didn't see how a haircut would help him.

She didn't say that out loud, though. It was probably best to let him think that he had a chance at changing their opinions. In reality, he was more there as a prop to back up her findings. She didn't need them to like him; she needed them to respect her ability to get him to do what she said.

"It looks nice," she finally managed to respond, the politeness feeling thick and unnatural on her tongue.

Without further conversation, they took their seats in the circle. Just like at the last meeting she'd attended, the Lunaria trickled in steadily, filling up the chairs and spilling onto the floor. Unlike previous sessions, however, there was very little chatter. The mood was subdued, almost despondent, and Scar wondered what she'd missed.

Cali, the woman who had proposed the ventilation scheme, sat to Scar's right. She seemed more downtrodden than most and was consciously avoiding everyone's gaze by looking down at her shoes. Intrigued, Scar waved her hand in front of the woman's face to grab her attention.

"Why is everyone so quiet?" Scar whispered, trying to soften her normally blunt tone. "What's happened?"

Cali's large eyes darted around the room, as if to make sure that no one was eavesdropping. When she was certain that their conversation couldn't be overheard, she leaned toward Scar conspiratorially, her mouth uncomfortably close to Scar's face.

"Things haven't been going well," she began, sounding on the verge of tears. "We've been trying to stall the repairs on the ventilation system, but it hasn't worked. The Peace Force keeps making progress. Nothing we do seems to make a difference. At this rate, the repairs will be completed within a few weeks, and the Lunaria have started to blame me! They think I have something do with it. But I swear I don't! You have to believe me!"

Scar was taken aback by the woman's flood of emotions, and she tried to process everything that Cali had said.

"On top of that," Cali continued, "Raqa's PeaceBots went offline and we haven't been able to re-establish contact. We don't know anything that's happening inside the Peace Force."

Things in the Lunaria were worse than Scar had anticipated. Looking around at her peers, she could now sense the tension thrumming through the room. Some of the members had begun to cast untrusting looks at their fellow rebels, while others hadn't even deigned to show up. The Lunaria was falling apart.

Scar stood suddenly, and all eyes turned toward her. Crossing her arms, she stared back defiantly, daring them to question her authority. When none of them did, she began her speech.

"The Pit doesn't lead to death. It leads outside the city, and I have proof." She drew the papers out of her bag and tossed them into the middle of the circle. No one moved to inspect them. Instead, all eyes remained glued to her.

"Life outside Kasis is possible," she continued. "It might not be pleasant, but it's possible. Which means that, in all likelihood, Burn and Hale are still alive. And it's up to us to save them."

Scar expected someone to fight back. She expected defiance. Yet no one spoke. It felt like the life had gone out of the room – and the fire of resistance along with it. This was going to be more difficult than she had anticipated.

"Your plans clearly haven't worked," she went on, changing tactics. "So now it's time to try something else. It's time to bring back the people who can actually lead. Because without them, we will never see the end of the Peace Force."

"How do we know we can trust you?" Ansel stood up from across the circle, his arms crossed in a position that mirrored her own. "You bring that son of a bitch in here and you expect us to believe anything you have to say?" he asked, purposely omitting Kaz's name and position as if he were a thing instead of a person. "If we were smart, we'd walk out that door right now and never invite you back."

"Well, good thing you're not very smart, then," Scar replied calmly. She heard a few sniggers from around the room but ignored them, continuing, "If he wanted to betray you, don't you think you'd already be in Peace Force custody? He knew the location of your safe house. He knew your names. He'd seen your faces. Yet here you are, free to wander around Kasis spouting your idiotic ideas."

Scar knew that she probably shouldn't be insulting Ansel, but it was hard to resist. With Hale gone, he'd slotted himself in as the de facto head of the Lunaria, adopting a pompous attitude that he hadn't previously possessed. That, paired with his lack of any real leadership ability, made him an easy target.

Despite her insults, however, he seemed satisfied by her response. He grudgingly sat down, leaving the floor to Scar. Caught off guard, she paused to gather her thoughts.

Raqa took advantage of her silence. Standing, he addressed the crowd in his jittery voice.

"If it were possible to live outside Kasis, don't you think we'd know about it? It sounds suspicious. It sounds like a trap."

Scar had been afraid of this – not of someone disagreeing with her, but of Raqa talking. She hated it when he did that. Sighing, she advanced on him, stopping an arm's length from where he stood.

"The Peace Force thrives on secrets. Their entire governing body is kept secret in order to guarantee their safety. What makes you think they wouldn't hide something like this? This is exactly the type of thing they do every day to ensure we remain at their mercy."

A murmur of assent rippled through the Lunaria. Scar could have sworn she saw Raqa's eye twitch, but he wisely backed down, returning to his seat. She breathed a silent sigh of relief at his surrender. Her battle was nearing its end.

Now that she'd bested her opponents, it was time to reveal her plan. Only, she didn't have a plan, at least not one that was fully formed and ready for action. Despite giving herself a day to decipher the city's blueprints, she only understood small portions of the drawings, and none of them got her any closer to discovering a way through the dome.

She needed someone who could read the cryptic grids and codes, someone who was versed in the language of construction. She needed an expert.

Without warning, she turned on her heel to face Cali. The woman looked startled at the attention, her eyes going wide with apprehension.

"You!" Scar let out, clearly frightening her. Bending down, she grabbed the papers she'd thrown into the circle and held them out to Cali. "Can you read these?"

It was a longshot. She knew that Cali worked in the ventilation department, although she'd never cared to discover in what capacity. Still, there was a chance that her role required at least a basic understanding of building schematics, and even that would be enough.

It took Cali a few seconds to get past her shock. When she did, she dove into her bag, fumbling around briefly before coming out with a pair of large glasses. Putting them on, she gingerly accepted the brittle parchment. She leafed through the pages pensively, making thoughtful noises at periodic intervals.

"Most of these are outdated," she began after a few minutes, her eyes still glued to the papers. "A lot of the original city was demolished when it became clear we would have to build upward. But some of the old parts are still standing along the bottom tiers. They didn't want to have to redo everything, especially since they figured no one of importance would ever live there. So some of the nonstructural elements still remain today."

Cali paused, flipping through a few more pages. Then her eyes caught on something. Carefully, she withdrew a particularly yellowed sheet from the stack, smoothing it out on her lap. A look of confusion slowly spread across her face as she studied it, tracing some of the lines with her fingers.

An impatient hush had fallen over the room, but Cali didn't seem to notice. She was completely absorbed in the drawing now, and she'd even begun to murmur to herself, saying things like "it can't be" and "that doesn't make sense." After a few more vague mutterings in that vein, Scar took charge.

"What did you find?" she asked, gentle enough so as not to startle the woman again. "What's on those plans?"

Cali looked up, surprised to find the whole room staring at her in rapt attention. She had been so focused on the pages that she'd forgotten where she was – and who she was with. Some of her timidity returned as she glanced around at the people who had so recently judged and accused her.

Scar understood her reserve, but she also had no time for it. So she drew Cali's attention, making the girl focus on her alone.

"Whatever you've found, it might be the answer I've been searching for. Please, just tell me."

Cali gulped, but she didn't break eye contact. "Well," she began, her voice quiet, "there's something on these plans that

I've never seen before. It's old, very old. They look like...tunnels below the city. Like something they might have used for irrigation or sewage back before our modern systems came into place."

"Tunnels?" Scar inquired, her excitement palpable.

"Yes. I don't know how big they are – or even if they still exist," Cali stated, her eyes returning to the plans. "They might have collapsed. Or been filled in. But once, a long time ago, they led out of the city."

A spark of elation ran through Scar's body at her words. Out of the city. Tunnels that led out of the city. This was exactly what she'd been searching for.

"Is it possible that any of them are still around? Could a person fit through them? Do you know how to find them?" The questions came so fast that Scar could barely get them out in time. She wanted to know everything.

"I don't know," Cali said apologetically, shrugging her shoulders. "These plans don't provide a full overview of the tunnels. Although as long as we have these, we should be able to locate the entrances. Then we can see what kind of state they're in."

Scar wanted to laugh and cry and shout her thanks. Then again, she wasn't the type to do any of those things. So, instead, she settled for a small, genuine smile.

Chapter 17

Burn and Hale trudged through the desert with nearly 20 people trailing in their wake. It was simultaneously thrilling and terrifying. These people had left their lives behind to follow her. They trusted her to lead them to a better life – but she didn't even know if that was possible.

She also didn't know where she was going. That was currently her most pressing problem.

They had departed Callidus just as night was beginning to fall. With Hale still in his guard form, they'd managed to slip out of the city unnoticed, silently disappearing into the falling darkness. Burn had needed to get out, needed to escape from what had happened – and what they'd done. Climbing back over the hills that surrounded the city had felt like breaking out of a prison, the sudden freedom intoxicating.

Burn hadn't even thought about the people they'd left behind, the people who had been waiting in vain for her father to return and take them home. She was so focused on her own escape that she hadn't even paused to consider theirs. At least not until they'd appeared in front of her, melting out from behind rocks and dunes on the outskirts of the city.

There were more than a dozen of them, their scant possessions slung over their shoulders and their eyes bright with hope. Burn had frozen at their appearance, shock and fear spreading through her body and immobilizing her reflexes. Hale, however, had urged her forward, assuring her that these were friends and not foes.

One woman had stood in front of the rest, quiet and poised as she gripped the reins of their horse. Her beautiful face was framed with long black hair that whipped around her in the growing breeze. Hale had introduced her as Eyana, his new face-changing friend and ally, who had transformed him into a guard so he could come to Burn's rescue.

Apparently, as Hale and Burn had dealt with Thestle, Eyana had been gathering the troops, spreading the word throughout the city that Arvense's daughter had come for them. And the people had responded. Some of them had met Burn's father all those years ago and had been waiting patiently for his return. Others only knew the story of Arvense, the legend of the man in search of Kasis. But all of them were looking for a way out, a way home. And, in lieu of Arvense himself, they looked to Burn for salvation.

Since night had been fast approaching, however, Burn knew their search for salvation would have to wait. Their first priority was to flee, putting as much distance between themselves and Callidus as they could before the bitter cold and darkness made it impossible to continue.

With the help of Eyana's navigational knowledge, the newly formed party had departed, heading off on foot in the direction of Aberra. Arvense had believed that the town held clues to finding a way back into Kasis, yet he'd never gotten the chance to prove his hypothesis. Now it was Burn's turn to take up the mantle and finish the journey he'd started.

They'd traveled for hours through the growing darkness, the sand mingling with the sharp night air to grate at their exposed skin and claw at their eyes and throats. When the desert had finally beaten them down, slowing their progress to a crawl, they'd halted, camping for the night in a rocky inlet that provided a modicum of protection from the brutal wind.

As soon as the first sun had peeked out from beyond the horizon, they'd set off once more, their exhaustion barely diminished despite the rest. Their pace had been slow yet steady, and the rocky landscape had gradually thinned and tapered before them. Now, as midday approached, they found themselves surrounded by a sea of sand.

There was nothing around them to mark their progress – no hills or canyons or rock forms. The wind wiped away their tracks as soon as they made them, and if it weren't for the suns acting as their compass, Burn was sure they'd be traveling in circles for an eternity.

"Is this even the right direction?" Burn whispered to Hale, who was trudging beside her a few paces in front of the rest of the group.

Glancing up at him, Burn was again relieved that Eyana had returned Hale to his original body, replacing the unfamiliar guard with the broad, muscled form that she'd come to know so well. Still, she couldn't help but grimace at the memory of his transformation.

She had watched with fear and awe as Hale's arms and legs stretched grotesquely and his skin rippled as muscles grew where none had been before. Hale had remained silent throughout the whole ordeal, yet Burn had heard his pain, the silent screams echoing in her head as if they were her own.

Since then, Burn had given Eyana a wide berth. Burn had known someone like her once, a Lunaria operative who could change his face whenever he wished, but her power was something else entirely. The ability to take away someone's body, their identity, and replace it with another felt sinister somehow, as if enemies could surround her at any moment, hiding within sheep's clothing.

Hale looked down at Burn, his familiar gaze soothing something inside of her. He raised one eyebrow and shrugged at her question.

"Eyana said that Aberra was a day's journey in this direction," he told her, returning his eyes to the desert. "The others seemed to agree. That means we should reach it in a few hours."

"And if we don't? What happens then?" Burn asked quietly, not wanting to be overheard by the people who trusted her to know what she was doing.

Another shrug from Hale. "We set up our own camp?" he said jokingly.

Burn shook her head. Despite her best efforts, a small smile played on her lips at his suggestion, the utter absurdity breaking some of her tension.

Thankfully, though, it didn't come to that. A few hours later, exhausted and drenched in sweat, Burn spotted a minuscule town rising from the horizon. At first she thought she'd imagined it, her mind having played several such tricks on her over the course of their journey. As they drew closer, however, more members of their group began to point and cheer as they spotted the settlement.

Aberra was nothing like Videre. It also bore little resemblance to Callidus. Only the tents looked vaguely familiar, except theirs were spread out, dotting the landscape at irregular intervals rather than being crushed together in a stone valley.

Scattered between the tents were what looked like sheep, although these creatures boasted jet black faces that obscured their eyes and diminutive legs that held them barely above the ground. The small, sandy puff balls meandered around aimlessly, intermixing with the residents as they went about their lives.

Another shocking difference to Callidus was the way they were greeted. Surprisingly, no one accosted them with weapons or appeared from behind rocks to tie them up and drag them into the city. As it happened, hardly anyone noticed them at all. Those that did were unwaveringly friendly, smiling or waving to the newcomers as they passed by.

Burn found the whole thing unnerving. She'd been prepared for a battle, mentally readying herself to face yet another despotic ruler. She'd even formulated a plan with Hale to ensure their swift and secure exit when things naturally got out of hand. All of that appeared unnecessary now.

Glancing around, she saw hints of a simple kind of life. Some of the citizens tended to the sheep, along with the other strange creatures that milled about the town. Others prepared meals on open fires, the smell of bread and game wafting on the breeze. Yet more gathered in groups to wash clothes or shuck corn or simply to share their stories and bond in the midday heat.

Burn heard it all as she passed, soaking in the pleasant conversations and peaceful silence. After her time in Callidus and their harsh journey through the desert, Aberra felt deliciously serene, like a haven amongst the squall.

Yet this wasn't a sightseeing mission. Burn had a job to do and people who were depending on her to do it. They trailed behind her like a flock, pushing her ever onward. Burn scanned the tents, looking for someone who might be able to guide her toward the answers she so desperately sought.

"Excuse me," Burn said gently, approaching a curvy woman surrounded by a small brood of shrieking children. "We've come from some of the neighboring towns. We were hoping to speak to someone regarding an important matter. Is there a leader or chieftain here that we could talk to?"

The woman sized Burn up before glancing at the waiting crowd behind her. Her eyes were kind but cautious as she considered them, taking in their disheveled clothes and their mismatched weapons.

"We don't have a leader," she said, stopping to yell at one of the children before continuing. "We make our decisions together, as a parliament." She paused again to pull one of the younger children away from a nearby fire pit, which gave Burn time to consider her words.

"Is there any way you could convene your parliament today so we could address them? We would be extremely grateful."

To Burn's utter relief, the woman smiled and nodded. "I'll spread the word around. It's not often we get visitors. I'm sure everyone will be eager to meet you."

"Thank you," Burn replied graciously, relief sweeping through her. "How long do you think it'll take to get everyone together?"

The woman sighed loudly, giving Burn a look she couldn't quite read. "Well, most of them won't return until nightfall. Our hunters and gatherers stay out most of the day searching for food, but I'm sure they'll be willing to meet with you later this evening."

The woman tried to sound reassuring, but Burn felt oddly discouraged at her words. Somewhere in the back of her mind, she'd been hoping that this was it, that in a few minutes she'd finally have the answers she'd crossed a desert to find. But no. Yet again she was forced to wait.

Hale moved to Burn's side, breaking away from the group to greet the woman. She was startled by the sheer scale of him and involuntarily took a step back toward her tent, gripping one of the children close to her skirts.

"Thank you for your help, ma'am," Hale said softly, attempting to mitigate his startling appearance. "Is there any place we could wash and rest until then? We've had a long journey and would appreciate any hospitality you're able to provide."

"Of course, of course," the woman said, her voice slightly higher and faster than when she'd spoken to Burn. "Mika!"

she shouted behind her, summoning one of the children.

A scrawny boy of 10 or 11 appeared from behind the tent, peeking his head out to assess the situation before stumbling to the woman's side. He looked at the assembled strangers with unabashed curiosity, craning his neck to better see the group.

"Please show our guests to the well," the woman instructed him. "And be sure to get them some food. We don't want them to think poorly of us, now do we?" She reached out absentmindedly to flatten some of his unruly brown hair before continuing. "Go on now! Off you go!" Turning her back to them, she began to round up the children who had wandered off during their exchange.

Mika bounced off, waving for them to follow. They did as they were bid, setting off farther into the town. After a minute spent bounding in front of them, the energetic boy suddenly appeared by Hale's side, staring up at him as he walked.

"You are very large," he said frankly, causing Burn to snort in amusement. "Are you from Kasis?" he continued, speaking rapidly. "I've never been to Kasis. I was born out here, but my parents are from Kasis!" He said the last part so proudly, puffing out his chest as he spoke. "Do you have a magic power? Most of the people here can't do anything, but I've heard that in Kasis everyone has powers. Is that true?"

Unsure of how to respond, Hale merely grunted. The boy, however, wasn't deterred.

"I'd love to go to Kasis someday," Mika said, smiling and swinging his arms. "My parents told me that I have a family there – a grandma and a grandpa and a half sister! I'd love to have a sister! I hope she likes me."

With that, he made a sharp turn, leading them down a perpendicular pathway. He was silent for a few seconds before turning his attention on Burn.

"Are you two together? You look like you're together. Do you have kids? Who are all those people?" he asked, peeking behind her at the Callidan refugees. "They look sad. Why are they sad? Did you kidnap them? Are you bad guys?" He glanced up at Hale again as he said that, squinting as he considered him.

He was apparently satisfied with whatever he saw, since he led them around another sharp corner before stopping abruptly.

"This is it!" he declared proudly, gesturing to a small well surrounded by an empty swath of land. "Stay here," he commanded, turning around to face them. "I'll find you some food." He promptly ran off into a cluster of tents, disappearing behind the fluttering fabric.

Burn couldn't help it; she laughed. Her exhaustion mingled with the relief of their present safety and the utter absurdity of the boy's questions to tip her over the edge. A high, resounding laugh burst out of her, and she clasped her hand to her mouth to quiet it. After a few seconds, Hale joined in, his deep chuckle blending happily with hers.

After their laughter had run its course, they collapsed on the firm ground, surrounded by the others.

Theirs was a strange group. Despite trekking across the desert with them, Burn and Hale were not quite part of their ranks. The residents of Callidus had known each other for years – decades even. They'd been through the same things, the same torment and hope and disappointment. They'd seen the same atrocities and survived them together.

Burn felt like an impostor in their ranks. She'd spent only a day in their camp and knew only a fraction of their lives. They'd been waiting for her father for years, but they'd settled for her, and she wasn't even sure if she could help them. Yet they were in this together now, whatever happened.

So while they waited, they talked. Burn told them of her father's disappearance, of the Lunaria, of her and Hale's exodus. And of Scar. And they listened. Then it was her turn to listen as they shared their lives, their stories, their reasons for escape. And how they had come to meet her father.

"He snuck in under the cover of darkness. Of course, I thought he was a thief," an older lady named Basha remembered, chuckling to herself. "So, naturally, I went after him with my kettle. Chased him around and around our tent while he tried to explain who he was. I nearly got him, too!"

The group laughed at her story, and others chimed in, adding their own accounts of how charming he was and how sure he was that he could get them back to Kasis.

From the outskirts of the group, a man's voice joined in. "I couldn't tell you about his charm," he said, "but he sure did love his daughters. That's how he convinced me to join him."

Burn turned to him, needing to hear more. "What do you mean?" she asked breathlessly.

"He told me about you. Both of you," the man began, smiling sadly at her. "He said that your sister was clever beyond words. But you – you were brave. Together, he said you had the power to change the world. He just wanted to be there when you did."

Burn tried not to cry, but tears pricked at her eyes. It had been so long since she'd seen her father or heard his voice, but as this man talked, she could almost see him, almost hear him whispering into her ear.

"I had a daughter of my own back in Kasis," he continued. "She must be all grown up now. When I first found myself out here, she was all I could think about. As time went by, though, she began to fade. After a few years, she was only a painful memory. But when your father talked about you, it made me remember my fire, my passion. It made me want to fight to get back to her."

People around the circle nodded in agreement, each adding their own memories to the mix. At some point, food arrived and they ate, but they paid little attention to the meal. Instead, they laughed and cried and traded tales about the things they'd lost and the people they'd loved.

When night finally fell and Mika appeared to inform them that the parliament was ready, they were no longer the strangers they had once been. They were something else, something more. So when they stood before the town, their faces illuminated by firelight, they stood united, a single unit with a single goal.

The townspeople were arranged in a large circle on the outskirts of the city. The parliament, composed of a representative from each family unit, was stationed at one side, with the remaining residents seated around them. Burn and her party stood in the middle, with Burn herself their designated head.

An older woman stepped out from the parliamentary line to address them. "Welcome, guests. We rarely have a chance to visit with those outside of our camp, so it is an honor to meet you. But we know this is not a social call. You have business here – important business. So, please, present your case. I hope that we may be of assistance to you." Her speech finished, she stepped back and disappeared into the sea of faces.

Burn stepped forward, her heart dancing like the flames beside her. Taking a deep breath, she began. "Thank you. You have been so kind to us, and for that we are truly grateful. I've traveled a long way to meet you – all the way from Videre. My friends here joined me in Callidus. Despite our differences, we're united by a singular aim: to return to Kasis."

Burn paused to let her words sink in. Whispers erupted around the circle as people voiced their varied thoughts and opinions on her pronouncement. Undeterred, she continued.

"I know that many people believe it's impossible, but we don't. Since you live closer to the city than any other camp, we hoped that you might be able to aid us in our quest. If you know anything that might help us get back inside, we would be forever in your debt. We come to you as mothers and fathers and sisters and children searching to reclaim our families and our homes. And if any of you would like to join us on our journey, we would be more than happy to have you."

Burn gave a small nod to the parliament before stepping back into the crowd. With a nod of their own, the parliament withdrew to discuss what they'd heard. Unable to help herself, Burn listened in to their debate.

By the time they returned, she already knew what they were going to say. Yet that knowledge didn't make it hurt any less.

"Thank you for your appeal," the same old lady said, her lined face looking older in the flickering light. "Of course, any of our residents are free to join you. Their lives and their decisions belong to them, and we encourage them to consider your offer. However," she paused to draw a breath and gather the courage she needed to continue, "we do not know a way back into Kasis. Our journeys around the city have not revealed anything that would be useful to you. We are truly sorry."

Burn heard the disappointment in the minds of her crew. They felt it so strongly that it sang in her head, crushing her with its force. The optimism she had felt, and the camaraderie of her fellow travelers, seeped away as the words sank in.

The woman continued, "Naturally, you are welcome to stay here while you determine your next move. Whatever you choose, we offer our assistance and our support." She gave them a sad smile before returning to the crowd.

Burn tried to keep her hope alive, telling herself – and the others – that just because they didn't know a way back in, it didn't mean there wasn't one. Outwardly, they agreed. Inwardly, they mourned.

One by one the gathered townsfolk left, breaking off to return to their own homes and their own families. Eventually, their group left as well, supplied with makeshift tents and blankets to keep them warm through the night.

They pitched the tents by the well in silence, each too consumed by their own thoughts to give voice to them. Even Burn and Hale found no reason to speak. The hush that had fallen was heavy, oppressive, and Burn found it difficult to block out the jarring thoughts of those around her.

A small sound suddenly found its way through the silence. Only Burn's ears picked it up – partially because they were highly sensitive and partially because the noise was coming from her own head. Her confusion was quickly followed by a sharp pang of excitement as she realized what the noise was: a message.

Pulling her goggles over her eyes, she hurriedly read the incoming thread, and her broken heart soared.

"We're coming to get you. We think we've discovered a way through. I will find you. – Scar"

Chapter 18

Scar's message had made it through! After weeks of sending and amplifying and sending, it had finally worked. That had to mean that Burn was out there, alive and close by. It also meant that Scar hadn't lost her touch with technology. Both of those were comforting thoughts.

Now she had to make good on her promise. She had to find a way to bring Burn back. And for that, she needed Cali.

Since the Lunaria's meeting, the two women had been poring over the plans of Kasis, marking every possible entrance into the tunnels. There were at least a dozen of them, scattered throughout the lowest level of the city. They didn't know how many were functional – if any – but they planned to leave no stone unturned.

Brilliantly, Scar had once again repurposed her pet PeaceBots to aid them in their search. Now, instead of canvassing the dome for weak spots, they were tasked with tracking down each of the former sewer entrances and relaying the images back to Scar. Without even leaving the house, she could discover which access points had been rendered inoperable and which ones were still feasible.

She'd already ruled out six of the tunnels. A few were now home to buildings, with the sturdy foundations poured directly on top of the entrances. Other sites bore no hint that the shafts had ever existed, having long since been filled with concrete and disguised by the dust and grime of time.

Yet a few were promising. Two, in particular, gave Scar hope. The photos the PeaceBots had sent back were dark, but they appeared to feature in-tact grates that led downward into unblocked tunnels. It wasn't much, but it was a start.

The robots did have their drawbacks, however. Despite the relative ease with which they scoped out the tunnels, they were of little use when it came to exploring them. Since the shafts didn't appear on their internal schematics, the machines didn't even recognize their existence. That meant that in addition to not being able to see them without the exact coordinates, the bots also couldn't travel down them.

So it was up to Scar and Cali to investigate. No one else in the Lunaria had volunteered, save for Raqa. But Scar considered him more of a hindrance than a help, so she had declined his offer. They were on their own now, at least until they found a viable way through to the other side.

That's how the two women found themselves atop a rusty iron grate in a semi-deserted corner of the gritty bottom tier. For her part, Scar was gradually cutting through the solid bars with the help of her laser cutter. Beside her, Cali kept watch, her eyes trained on the dark lanes around them.

The pollution was so thick that the cloud of smoke Scar

created simply rose and blended with the haze. Unlike the grate below her, the fog itself was impenetrable, a solid and unyielding force that coated the world in nightmarish shadows. Chances were, if no one was looking for them, then no one would spot them. Yet it was nice to have a lookout, nonetheless.

Scar was relieved to note that Cali was different outside of the Lunaria's meetings. She'd feared that the woman would retain her nervous, skittery disposition, adding an extra level of anxiety to their criminal endeavors. As it turned out, though, Cali was an intelligent woman with a keen eye for details, and away from the Lunaria's judgmental gaze she was calm and levelheaded. She also made a damn good sentry – mostly because she didn't insist on any kind of small talk.

The bars on the grate were thick, but they were no match for Scar's laser. Within 10 minutes, she'd made a neat, Scar-sized square and pried it up. Glancing into the hole, she could just make out a drop of 6 or 7 feet, which ended in a passageway that stretched out to either side. With a quick nod to Cali, she carefully lowered herself down.

Turning her goggles to night mode, she immediately took stock of her surroundings. To her left, the tunnel traveled a few feet before ending abruptly in a collapsed heap of stone and jagged rebar. To her right, the passage continued into the darkness, where sounds of dripping water and scurrying rodents echoed off the stone walls.

Seeing no other option, she took off to the right. The passage wasn't tall enough for her to walk upright, so she stooped, shuffling along the damp tunnel a few feet at a time.

As she moved, she tried to keep her mind off the thick, lingering smell that clung to her nostrils despite the mask. It was a stench that blended excrement, mold, and decay, and it was made all the worse by the sporadic crunch of small animal bones underfoot. Instead, she focused on her steps, mentally mapping her progress in terms of the streets above her.

She was so fixated on putting one foot in front of the other that she nearly walked headfirst into a hard metal wall. As it was, she stopped a mere foot away, caught off guard by the severe steel monolith blocking her path. Putting her hands to it, she moved them across its smooth, cool surface, searching for a way through. Except there wasn't one. Unlike the rock fall at the other end, this obstruction was deliberate. Someone had placed it there to ensure that people like her never found what they were looking for.

Scar frowned, studying the barrier. If her sense of direction was right, she was nowhere near the edge of the city. Even if she could break through, there was a good chance she'd face even more barricades on her way to the wall. No, this was a dead end. It was time to retreat.

Slowly and carefully, Scar did just that, following the tunnel back the way she had come. As she returned, she spotted a rope dangling from the hole – yet another sign of Cali's usefulness. Grabbing it, she hoisted herself up, careful not to cut herself on the bars' rough edges. Cali offered her hand to help, and Scar gratefully accepted, leveraging herself onto the filthy street. She took a moment to wipe the unidentifiable tunnel residue from her clothing before filling Cali in on her findings.

"It's no good," Scar said simply. "The tunnel's blocked on

both ends. We'll have to try another."

To her great relief, Cali didn't ask for details. She merely began packing up the rope while Scar replaced the grate in its hole, soldering the iron back together so no one would suspect their trespass. Once done, the pair moved on, picking their way across the city to the next tunnel entrance.

This one was a great deal closer to the edge of the city, located amongst the perplexing maze of passageways that led to the outer rim. It was close enough to the sections of the city that Scar had once explored to make the streets feel familiar, and a sense of déjà vu briefly overcame her as she walked.

She'd been so close to it all those weeks ago, so tantalizingly near the thing she'd been searching for, yet she'd walked right over it. That knowledge grated at her, but she pushed it away, forcing it to the back of her mind. She had a job to do, and she couldn't let something as useless as regret stand in her way.

Once they'd located the spot, Scar got to work. Within minutes, she'd carved out an entrance and dropped into the tunnel below. She was relieved to note that this passageway was larger than the last and considerably drier. It still bore the reek of mold and death, but it was at least bearable.

Adjusting her goggles, she realized that this channel split into three distinct paths. Once again, one was already blocked, this time by a heavy wrought-iron gate. The other two, however, appeared clear.

"I think this one might work," she shouted, peering down each of the corridors and mentally mapping them. "One of the passages seems to lead toward the dome. I'll check it out."

Her progress was quicker this time, and her excitement rose as she neared the edge of the city. Here and there, pipes protruded from the walls or cut across the ceiling, threatening to tear at her. Yet each time she managed to avoid them, twisting out of the way just in time.

Some of the pipes spewed gas into the chamber, filling it with puffs of dark, polluted air or scalding steam. More than once she found herself inhaling a foul mixture of fumes and fog that clung to her throat and tried to choke her. Her coughs became more regular the farther she traveled, but she couldn't stop to catch her breath.

Eventually, the smog became so thick that she could barely make out the walls around her. Even her goggles provided little protection from the mist, casting only a dim light into the murky clouds. She held out her hands to feel her way along, her pace slowing to a crawl.

She didn't see the hole in the floor. One second she was walking, the next she was falling, and the next she had landed with a thud in yet another stone tunnel. Except this tunnel was different. This tunnel had only one corridor, one direction she could travel. Rising to her feet, she followed it, her eyes focused on the path ahead.

A minute passed, then two. Still she walked, disappearing deeper into the labyrinth. Then, without warning, it ended. Another steel wall blocked her passage, its smooth surface taunting her with a reflection of her own frustration. This was the way out. She knew it. She could feel it in the way her skin prickled and her hair stood on end. Yet she couldn't see it.

Irritation and exasperation built up inside of her until she could no longer bear it. Curling her hand into a fist, she struck the barrier with all her might, the metal on her hand meeting the metal of the wall to produce a resounding clang. Withdrawing her hand, she saw that she hadn't even managed to leave a mark on the pristine steel surface.

Sighing, she pulled out her tab, unfolded it, and sent a quick message to Cali. "Come down. Bring rope. Watch out for the hole."

She cast one last hate-filled look at the barricade before turning and stalking back the way she had come. She reached the hole quickly, propelled by her annoyance and the whirling thoughts cascading through her head. Taking a seat on the damp ground along the wall, she waited, steaming.

She was so wrapped up in her own deliberations that the sudden appearance of a rope came as quite the shock – as did the entrance of Cali, who proceeded to scramble down the line and land lightly in front of her.

"What'd you find?" she asked breathlessly, straining her neck to see down the length of the tunnel.

"A dead end," Scar replied, grabbing the rope with the intention of climbing back up.

Cali, however, had other plans. With a flash, she took off down the passageway and into the darkness. Mildly curious about her reaction to the blockage, Scar tagged along, barely able to keep up with the small woman.

Nearing the end of the tunnel, Cali froze. Unable to stop her own momentum in time, Scar collided with Cali's immobile form. Steadying herself, she began to apologize, then paused, watching her new friend. Cali was staring at the wall, transfixed, with her mouth open and eyes alight.

"Such an ingenious way of rendering the tunnels inoperable," she muttered to herself, not even aware that Scar was stationed beside her. "Instead of filling them in, which would have required vast amounts of resources, or collapsing them, which would have risked destabilizing the city, they blocked them off while simultaneously reinforcing them."

Cali's wonder irked Scar. She shouldn't find this clever. She should find this infuriating, just like Scar did.

"If I'm right – and I'm usually right – this is the way out," Scar said, trying to pull Cali back from her daze. "If we were able to break through, then we might actually have a way to bring Burn back."

"Then let's break through it," Cali said simply.

"And how do you propose we do that?" Scar asked, with only a hint of cynicism creeping into her voice.

Cali thought for a beat before stepping forward and pressing her body against the steel surface. Scar stared as the woman tapped on the wall and listened, adopting a look of sheer concentration. After a long moment, she withdrew, giving Scar a small smile.

"Well, I propose we blow it up."

Scar scoffed. "Wouldn't that cave in the entire tunnel? And what about the noise? The Peace Force and their bots would definitely hear an explosion."

"As long as the explosion is controlled, the passageway should remain structurally sound," Cali replied, taking into consideration the walls and ceiling of the space. "But you're right. It's hard to mask the sound. It will certainly draw attention."

Something tickled the back of Scar's mind. She cast her thoughts back to Burn's mission all those weeks ago. Based on what she'd pieced together, before everything went sideways their plan had been to detonate each device simultaneously, causing confusion and panic. What if they did the same thing here?

"What if we cause a diversion – or 20?" Scar asked, excitement creeping into her voice. "We plant explosives in out-of-the-way places throughout the city, anywhere that won't be occupied at night. Then we set them off all at once. The Peace Force won't know where to look. They'll focus their attention on the top tiers, like always, leaving us free to rescue Burn and Hale."

Cali thought about it for a second, nodding thoughtfully. "That could work. We'd have to be extremely careful so no one gets hurt, but we might just be able to pull it off."

The two women looked at each other, self-satisfied smiles stretching across their faces. After a second, Scar turned her attention to the metal wall, her previous irritation dissipating. Now all she saw when she looked at it was her sister, smiling as she climbed into the tunnel and back into Kasis.

Whipping out her tab, she began to type. With a tap of her finger, she sent the message. It didn't bounce back.

"We've found a way through. Give us two days. Then come to the south side of the city at nightfall. I'll be waiting to bring you home."

Chapter 19

Burn had two days to travel to Videre and back. People were waiting for her there – people like Nara, who were depending on her to get them back into Kasis. They'd already been disappointed once, when her father hadn't returned for them. She couldn't abandon them again.

She'd started packing shortly after the message had popped up on her goggles. She had tried to respond, tried to ask for more time, but her messages wouldn't send. That left her only one choice.

Hale had demanded to come with her, but it just wasn't possible. They only had one horse, and even with its fortitude, their combined weight would tire it too quickly. If she wanted to reach Videre by sunset, she'd have to travel alone.

Hale had argued. He had offered to go in her place, but she had to do this. This was her mission, and she alone could finish it.

Burn gave Hale her goggles, unlocking them so he could

read any transmissions Scar sent while she was gone. With her away, it was up to him to protect the group. And if she didn't return in time, he would need to lead them back. There would be no time to wait; they would have to return without her.

Laden with food and water from the generous people of Aberra, she set off into the desert at a canter. The glaring afternoon suns beat down on her back as she traveled, but she paid them no mind, focusing only on the path ahead. Twice she stopped to rest and refuel, gulping down water to wash the sand from her mouth, but within no time she was back on the road, her sights set on Videre.

She arrived just after nightfall. To Burn's dismay, the gates had already been shut for the evening, barring her way into the town. In her haste, she hadn't even considered the possibility that she'd find herself locked out of the city.

Unwilling to lose valuable time, she rode back and forth along the wall, searching for a way in. Yet she found nothing. Videre was a fortress. She'd once felt safe within those walls, their strength comforting amidst the unknowns of the wildlands. Now she hated them, and she violently cursed their ability to keep out friend and foe alike.

"You certainly have quite the vocabulary." Burn heard the soft voice as she was pacing in front of the gates and stopped to pinpoint its source. Nara. "I've been waiting for you. I've kept watch every night in case you returned. Glad it wasn't for nothing."

Burn wanted to respond, wanted to tell her that it would, indeed, be for nothing if she didn't find a way in, but she knew Nara would never be able to hear her. Instead, she used her hands to mime the gates opening, hoping Nara would get the message.

"I know, I know," Nara said as she disappeared from view. A few moments later, Burn heard the grinding of the gears as one of the doors lurched forward ever so slightly. Without hesitation, she squeezed inside, barely managing to get her horse's wide flank through the narrow gap. Just as they crossed the threshold, the door closed behind them, sealing them in.

Before they'd even taken five steps, Nara was beside them. "Did you find what you were looking for?" she asked quietly, leading Burn along the edge of the city.

"Yes. I have a way back in. Although we have less than two days to gather everyone together and get back to the dome. Do you think it's possible?"

"Yes," Nara responded calmly. "Since you left, I've been searching for the people who were planning to leave with your father. I think I've discovered most of them, and most of them still want to go."

"It'll take a while to get everyone across the desert on foot. We'll have to leave by dawn if we want to make it in time."

"Then we better get to work," Nara said with a smile.

Tethering the horse to a post where it would have access to food and water, Burn and Nara set off into the town. One by one, they knocked on doors and spread the news. Some of the residents met them with a change of heart, unable or unwilling to leave their current comfort now that the decision was on their doorstep. Others cast their uncertainty like a pall on the mission. But most were overjoyed. They couldn't wait to return to the homes and lives they thought they'd lost for good and the people they'd left behind.

They agreed to leave by first light, which left several hours to pack and rest before their journey. Burn was unable to return to the boarding house for fear of Luce alerting Imber to her presence. Instead, she spent a restless night on the floor of Nara's small home, tossing and turning and envisioning everything that could go wrong.

By dawn, Burn was washed, dressed, and ready to go. She woke Nara, who had been sleeping soundly, and together the two quietly readied themselves for departure. In preparation for any trouble – either within the gates or beyond them – Nara suggested they arm themselves, strapping knives to their waists and ankles, and lashing fighting sticks to their backs.

As Burn had no real belongings, these weapons were the only thing she carried, her sole keepsake from the city. Nara grabbed only a few precious items, chucking them into a small bag and throwing it over her back, where it nestled comfortably between her wooden fighting dowels.

By the time they arrived at the gates, several people were already waiting, their anxious energy palpable. Upon seeing Burn, their faces lit up. This was real, they realized as she entered their midst. They were finally going home.

Over the next quarter of an hour, more and more people joined them, increasing their ranks until they were more than 20 strong. Burn had known most of them from her brief stay in Videre, at least by sight if not by name, but some were strangers to her, and she spent a few minutes getting to know each.

When the first sun finally poked above the horizon, they knew it was time to go. The city would awaken soon, and Burn wanted to be long gone before anyone noticed their absence. Gathering everyone together, she prepared to slip into the wildlands, giving Nara the signal to open the gates.

Yet the gates didn't move. Nara put all her might behind the switch, forcing her body against it, but the doors didn't budge. Confused, she looked down into the medley of gears that controlled the entrance. She raised her head, preparing to shout something to Burn, but she stopped, her wide eyes focused on something behind the group.

Burn didn't need to turn to know they were surrounded. She could hear their approaching footsteps and detect their breath in the cool morning air. People were descending on them from all sides, closing in on her troupe as they backed against the motionless doors. Reluctantly, she turned.

Imber stood in front of a small army, his face blank as he stared at Burn and the group she'd assembled. Burn tried to read him, to detect what was going through his mind, but his thoughts were too rapid to pick out with any certainty. All she could see was that he did not want them to leave.

"Did you think you could sneak out without me knowing?" Imber asked, addressing the question to her. "I know everything that goes on in this town. These people are loyal to me, not you."

"You've led them well," Burn said, taking a few steps toward him. "You've made sure they're fed. You've given them water. You've kept them safe. I understand their loyalty. I'm not trying to turn them against you. I'm simply offering them a chance to go home."

"This is their home. This is their family," he said, casting his eyes over the people behind her. "There's nothing for you back in Kasis. If she can even get you back in, what's to stop them from throwing you right back out? Or killing you on the spot? You were enemies once and you are enemies still."

"These people have made up their minds. They know the risks and they're willing to take them. I didn't force them to come with me. I merely gave them a choice. All I ask is that you allow them the freedom to choose their own path. Let us go in peace. We don't want to fight you."

Imber was silent as he contemplated her words. As the silence stretched on, Burn turned and walked toward the gate. Motioning to the others to join her, she pushed on one of the doors, the locked gears groaning under the pressure. With their combined effort, paired with whatever Nara was doing on top of the wall, the gate gradually began to move, cracking open to reveal a sliver of the world beyond.

Before they could open it further, however, something heavy crashed into Burn's back, throwing her against the wood. She dropped to the sand with a thud, her body drenched from the torrent of water that had hit her. Turning around angrily, she spotted Imber with his hands angled toward her, threatening to unleash another wave.

Burn had no time for this. She needed to get these people out and back to Aberra. They only had a day before Scar put her plan into action, and they needed to get back to the dome in time to meet her. But if it was a fight Imber wanted, then it was a fight he was going to get.

Throwing caution to the wind, Burn charged at him, expertly dodging the icy jets of water that erupted from his hands. Her gift helped; she could sense it each time he prepared to strike, and she'd leap out of the way just in time.

Once she was near enough, she unsheathed one of the fighting sticks from her back and sent a blow to his midsection. She didn't intend to kill him – or even injure him too gravely. She merely wanted his attention. Imber doubled over with a grunt but quickly righted himself, sending a rapid burst of water to her chest. Unable to avoid it, Burn was flung backward onto the packed earth.

Around her, Burn heard sounds of battle. The others had taken her action as a cue to fight, and they were now using their own unique gifts to face off against their friends and neighbors. The violence sent of shiver of guilt through her veins, and she knew she had to finish it before it went too far.

Burn sprang to her feet, facing Imber in a fighting stance. His right hand stretched out in an attack, but this time she managed to sidestep the rush of water. Imber recalculated and moved to strike again, but she took advantage of the pause. Sprinting behind him, she dealt a blow to his spine that sent him to his knees.

"Why are you standing in our way?" Burn asked between heavy breaths. "You say these people are your family, yet you treat them like your subjects. Why can't you let them go?"

Imber spun around on his knees and fired a quick surge of water at her feet, which swept out from under her. Burn landed hard on her shoulder, which sent a shock of pain down her arm and knocked her weapon from her grasp. As they both scrambled to their feet, Burn unsheathed her second stick and aimed a strike at Imber's legs, but the man jumped out of her reach.

"You're taking them to their deaths," he yelled at her from a safe distance. "I can't stand back and watch as you ruin their lives."

Burn rounded on him, closing the gap between them. Once again he tried to knock her off balance with a rush of water to her feet, but this time she was faster. She leapt over the stream and rolled to his side, sweeping his legs out from under him. He landed roughly on his back, and Burn dropped her dowel and jumped atop him, pinning his arms above his head.

"You don't get to decide their fates," she told him, almost pleading. "They have the right to make up their own minds, whatever the outcome. Who knows? Maybe one day they'll come back to you with their families in tow. Think of how powerful Videre will be then. But if you keep them here against their will, you become the enemy, Videre becomes their prison, and they'll never stop trying to escape it."

Imber's struggles faded as he processed her words. Burn could hear him thinking, hear the debate warring inside his mind. He didn't want to lose these people – not because they were valuable, but because they were loved. They were his children, his siblings, his parents. It hurt that they needed to search for a family when he'd built one for them right here.

Yet he also knew that he needed to let them go. When Burn heard that, she loosened her grip on his hands, allowing him to pull his arms free. She still remained on top of him, though, not willing to give up her advantage entirely.

"Look what you're doing to your family," Burn instructed him, glancing around at the fighting. He did as he was told, taking in the violence. Neighbor hitting neighbor.

Blood mingling with water to seep into the dark earth. People screaming.

"Stop!" he yelled into the chaos. "Stop fighting."

All around them, people paused in the midst of their attacks, turning their attention to their leader. Burn relinquished her control, rising from his chest. She offered him her hand and helped him gently up from the sodden ground, allowing him to take the floor.

"This is not how a family behaves," Imber told the rapt audience. "A family should meet differences with acceptance, not violence. I see that now."

Taking a deep breath, he prepared himself for the most difficult part of his speech. "Those of you who want to return to Kasis are free to do so. We will miss you terribly, and Videre will not feel whole without you, but we will not stop you. Maybe one day you'll return to us," he said, sending a small smile to Burn. "But if you don't, I want you to remember us kindly. Remember the people you've met here and the love you've received. We were lucky to have you with us, even for the briefest time."

He gave a sad smile to the people of Videre. One by one, they released each other, picked themselves up, and dusted themselves off. Burn noticed with relief that there were no casualties from their battle. Plenty of people were injured, with gashes and cuts peeking out from beneath torn clothes, but no one was seriously wounded.

Imber turned to her. "I'm sorry," he said truthfully. "I only ever wanted what was best for them."

"I know," Burn replied, accepting his apology.

"I hope you succeed. I truly do."

Burn nodded and was about to leave when he touched her arm lightly. "Oh, and say hi to your *husband* for me." He gave her a wry smile before turning and walking away.

She stood there for a moment, shocked. He'd known the whole time that Hale wasn't her husband – she could read it in his mind. Yet he'd let her stay. He'd seen how Hale had stood up for her, and that had been enough for him. Burn smiled her own small smile as she turned her back on Videre. She was actually going to miss this place.

Chapter 20

The Lunaria were stunned. Or awed. Or upset. Sometimes Scar found it difficult to interpret others' emotions. The main point was that they were quiet, which was a pleasant relief.

She and Cali had just presented their ingenious plan to get Burn and Hale back into the city, and the Lunaria seemed suitably impressed. Or apprehensive. Definitely one of the two.

Scar stood in the center of the circle, studying the members. There were more of them than at the last meeting, no doubt spurred on by the idea of a fresh plan – one that wasn't concocted by Ansel or Raqa and, therefore, doomed to failure. Fresh leadership and fresh ideas, it seemed, were great motivators for action.

But, of course, it wouldn't be a Lunaria meeting if there weren't some spirited objections – particularly from those afraid of losing the limited authority they had accrued in the absence of the group's real leaders. Naturally, Raqa spoke up first.

"We don't even know for sure that they're out there," he said, shooting up from his seat in the corner. "Do we really want to take the risk on the off chance that they'll be there? I don't have to remind you that the last time we set off explosions in the city, it didn't quite go as planned. Who's to say the same thing won't happen again?"

Ansel latched onto Raqa's words and added his own dissenting voice to the mix. "And what if the diversions don't work? What if the Peace Force sees right through them and heads straight for us? We don't have the resources to fight another battle with them. We used up most of our weaponry in the last fight – and lost some good people. Another encounter like that would decimate us."

Scar sighed in frustration. Why did things like this always have to be so difficult? Why couldn't they just accept her genius and move on? That's what they were going to do in the end, after all. Why put it off?

"The Peace Force is full of idiots," Scar started, sounding bored. "They'll do what they're trained to do. If they think they're being attacked on multiple levels, they'll focus their efforts and their resources on the most important – the highest tiers. Then they'll work their way down. Our explosion, the real one, will be so low on their radar that we'll be long gone before they get to it – if they even get to it at all."

Ansel and Raqa did not look convinced. Then again, the decision wasn't up to them. The Lunaria was a democracy. As long as she had everyone else on her side, their scruples wouldn't matter. Looking around, however, she couldn't tell where the others' loyalties lay.

That's when Cali jumped in – literally. She sprang up from her spot on the ground and hopped over people until she arrived at Scar's side, positioning herself next to Scar like a sister in arms.

"Scar's right," Cali said, sounding braver than Scar had ever heard her. "The Peace Force has no interest in what's going on at the bottom of the city. They'll use their resources to protect their own kind, even if it means leaving entire tiers to fend for themselves. We can use that to our advantage."

Scar fed off of Cali's enthusiasm, gaining confidence from her support. "And we won't be going in empty-handed. We'll have you, any of you who are willing to come with us," she said, rotating to meet their upturned eyes. "We are powerful. We have our own kind of weaponry. We've driven them back before and we can do it again."

She turned to Ansel, concentrating her fire on him. "Think about Hale. And Burn. Think about everything they've done for the Lunaria, everything they've suffered for the cause. They deserve our help, and we need theirs if we ever expect to make any real progress against the Peace Force."

"And if it doesn't work?" Ansel asked, sounding tired. "If we do all of this and there's no one on the other side? What then?"

It was the same question that had been lingering in the back of Scar's mind for days, the question she'd been unwilling to answer, even to herself. What would happen if Burn wasn't there? What would she do if her sister and all the others that had been sentenced to the Pit were actually gone for good? She didn't want to consider the possibility, yet it was an ever-present fear. How would she go on once all hope was gone?

"Well, then we'll figure out how to keep fighting. Together." She stared Ansel down, unblinking. An agonizing second passed, then another, and neither moved. Finally, Ansel broke eye contact, relinquishing his control.

Unfortunately, Raqa wasn't so easily vanquished, although his opinion held less sway amongst the group. Still, every time he spoke, Scar could feel the muscles in her jaw tighten.

"You still haven't told us where we'll be doing this. Or when. Shouldn't we know the specifics before we decide whether or not to put our lives in your hands?"

Scar could feel her teeth grating against each other as he spoke, and she had to consciously control her features to stop herself from scowling.

"It's going down tomorrow night in the lower tiers. That's all you need to know for now. We'll release more details when the time comes."

It wasn't that Scar didn't trust the Lunaria. Well, technically she didn't. Then again, she didn't trust anyone completely, other than Burn. It was more a numbers game for her. The more people that knew the plan, the more likely it was to leak out. The Peace Force wasn't above bugging rooms or sending their PeaceBots to listen from the shadows – or administering a few well-honed coercion techniques to pry out juicy tidbits from suspected terrorists. And Scar wasn't willing to take any chances, not with her sister's life.

So until everything was in place, only her and Cali knew the plan in its entirety. Anyone else who wanted to participate would just have to trust them.

And, as it turned out, they did trust her. Not only did they vote almost unanimously in favor of her plan, but she received double the expected interest from people wanting to serve by her side. Even Ansel and Raqa reluctantly raised their hands to volunteer, although Scar would have preferred it if they hadn't. Still, a body was a body, even if she didn't like their personal politics. She'd just have to station them as far away from herself as possible.

With the Lunaria's help secured, Scar felt electrified, as if a surge of pure power had been released under her skin and was now coursing through her veins. She wanted to get to work immediately, to put the plan into motion without delay. But pleasantries stood in her way, and she found herself drawn into an array of meaningless exchanges before she could extricate herself and slip into the night. When she finally did, she found Cali by her side, the now-emboldened woman still eager to help in any way she could.

"Fine," Scar said tersely, unaccustomed to such prolonged company. "You can help me put together the explosives. Just don't blow yourself up." She promptly took off into the streets, with Cali tagging behind her like an enthusiastic puppy.

The pair crept through the darkness back to Symphandra's house, expertly avoiding the patrols. The night was still and quiet, and they arrived at the red-doored dwelling without issue. Yet Scar never dropped her guard – which came in handy when a black-clad form suddenly materialized next to them from somewhere in the shadows.

Without a thought, Scar lunged forward and knocked

the man to the pavement before placing herself on top of him. She was just about to reach for her pen when she realized who it was. Kaz.

"You have to stop doing that," she whispered, not moving from her advantageous perch.

Kaz groaned, reaching up to rub the shoulder that had struck the ground. Scar used the opportunity to take stock of him, noticing that he was wearing his all-black military gear instead of his civilian apparel. He was also armed, although her position astride him made it impossible for him to draw his weapon.

"What do you want?" she asked, getting straight to the point. It didn't look great to have a Peace Officer outside of her house, no matter how friendly the officer.

"Can I come inside?" Kaz finally said, glancing between Scar and Cali in hopes that one of them would take pity on him. "I just want to talk." He held out his empty hands to show that he meant them no harm.

Scar considered him for a tick before relenting and freeing him. She still kept a wary eye on him, however, even as she scanned her finger and opened the door. Together, the trio made their way inside, a new tension thrumming between them.

They spread themselves out in the living room, each settling on a different piece of furniture. Cali and Kaz, whose only interaction thus far had been at the Lunaria's last meeting, sized each other up tentatively.

"So, what do you want?" Scar asked again, louder this time and more insistent. She had a lot of work to do, and the last thing she needed was Kaz slowing her down. He'd already played his part in her plan, and she no longer needed his assistance. As far as she was concerned, his role in this drama was over.

"I want to know what you're planning. I want to help," Kaz almost begged.

"You've already helped," Scar said, dismissing him. "You got us the plans to the city. We can take it from here."

"No." Kaz's sudden sharpness was startling. "That's not enough. I need to do more."

Scar considered him for a minute, finally taking the time to really look at him. The light that she'd noticed in his eyes was still there, but it was now accompanied by a steely resolve that made his face gleam with purpose. He'd had a taste of insurrection, and now he wanted more.

"Why?" Scar posed, curious about his newfound appetite. "Are you doing this for Burn? Once you get her back will you be satisfied? Will you go back to the way things were?"

Kaz paused to process Scar's question, choosing his words carefully. When he finally spoke, his conviction was apparent.

"I don't think I can ever go back to the way things were. Of course I want Burn back. I want to tell her how sorry I am and how I understand why she did what she did. But that's not why I want to help – why I *need* to help."

Scar waited as he took a long breath, preparing himself for his first real step into rebellion. She found it strangely satisfying to see him fight within himself for the courage to question the status quo. He'd been part of the Peace Force for so long that he hadn't even noticed that the world outside was crumbling. And now that he'd seen it, he couldn't look away.

"They've hidden so much from me – and from everyone," he began, referring to his iniquitous employer. "And they've made me an accomplice to their crimes. I thought I was doing what was right – cleaning up the streets, foiling anarchist plots, keeping the citizens safe. But that wasn't what I was doing at all. I was just maintaining the balance of power, keeping control in the hands of the few. It took Burn's disappearance for me to realize it, but it's been happening for years right under my nose. And I can't sit by any longer. I need to act."

"It's dangerous, being on this side of the law," Scar warned. "Even with your gift, your safety will never be guaranteed. Are you really prepared to lose everything?"

Kaz gulped as a flicker of fear passed over his face. But just as quickly as it had appeared, it was gone, replaced by a grim determination.

"I'm starting to realize that I never had much to begin with. Although if it means getting even one step closer to a better world, I'm in."

Scar nodded. She didn't know if, when the time came, he'd be willing to do whatever it took to win. But right now he believed he would – and right now that was enough.

"We need someone on the inside," Scar said, finally relenting to his request to help. "It's going down tomorrow night. We need you to make sure the Peace Force stays away from the bottom tiers. If they even think about heading down, stall. And alert us immediately."

It was Kaz's turn to nod. He seemed elated to be given another chance to prove himself. A small, excited smile played on the corners of his lips.

"Good," Scar barked. "Now please leave. We have a lot of work to do." Her precisely planned schedule had already been set back by his appearance, and she was eager to jump into her extensive to-do list. She got up, attempting to shepherd him toward the door, but he stayed put, glancing around the small house.

"What are you doing? Can I help?" he asked quickly, keen to be of more immediate use to the cause.

"That depends," she said, raising an eyebrow. "How steady are your hands?"

Time was not on Burn's side. They'd already spent a day and a night on the road, camping at sunset and leaving at first light. If she'd been on her own, the trek to Aberra would have been simple, but her progress was slowed by several elderly gentlemen, a brood of young children, and a mother whose leg had been injured during their skirmish in Videre.

Burn couldn't be angry at them; she knew that. However, she could be frustrated – and she was. Walking several paces in front of the group, she silently urged them on.

Even the animals mocked them, passing them one by one as if flaunting their speed. Burn watched with envy as a large-eared furball in a muted shade of orange hopped along beside them, pulling slowly away. In the distance, a catlike creature with curling horns walked parallel to their path, easily overtaking them. Burn resented their progress and the ease with which they moved, bitterly hating her own sluggish pace.

She'd planned to be back in Aberra already, to be back with the Callidans – and with Hale. They needed time to plan their moves, to hash out the possibilities and determine their course. And to rest. Getting back into Kasis wouldn't be easy. They'd need their strength – and their wits – to face whatever the future held.

Nara appeared at her side but remained silent, searching the horizon. To Burn's eyes, the path ahead was littered with dunes and peaks and clusters of small animals, all threatening her progress and impeding her sightline. Nara was different, though; Nara could see.

"Are we close?" Burn asked breathlessly, both impatient and scared to know the answer.

"I can't see it yet," Nara replied, giving her the same answer she'd provided every time Burn had asked. "But there are a lot of things in the way," she continued, trying in vain to bolster Burn's spirits. "We could be closer than we think."

"I have to get to the dome by tonight," Burn whispered, as much to herself as to Nara. "I can't miss this. I don't think we'll have another chance."

Burn felt loathsome for even considering leaving these people, yet the thought kept flashing through her mind. And she knew she wasn't alone. She could hear the same idea surge in and out of the Viderens' thoughts, fueled by their excitement and impatience.

She looked to Nara, her eyes pleading for another option, a way in which all of them could make it. Sighing, Nara refocused her attention on the road ahead.

"Leave it to me," she said, lunging into a run and rapidly

disappearing behind the sandy hills.

Burn glanced back at the crowd behind her. If it was possible, they'd slowed even more while she'd been talking to Nara. They were lagging, and it was slowly killing her, tearing her heart between duty and desire, between helping these people and finally returning home.

They needed something to spur them on, something to aim for and work toward. She'd already given them a rousing speech, trying to light their fires with visions of sweet reunions and glorious homecomings. But their momentary fervor had soon been squashed by the reality of the desert, with the heat and the sand and the slog intermingling to sap their collective drive. It was painful to watch, and Burn turned her gaze away to protect her own faltering optimism.

A sudden movement seen from the corner of her eye made her freeze, cementing her feet in place. She didn't want to look, didn't want to discover yet another obstacle in their path, but curiosity and fear got the better of her. Off to the right, a pile of sand was moving, gently cascading down as a creature rose from beneath it.

Nearby, an array of animals lurked, their eyes glued to the shape in wary intensity. Burn's own eyes went wide, and her veins beat a warning from her stuttering heart. It was a sand bear; she was sure of it. Yet she couldn't move, couldn't convince her feet to carry her away from the threat. Flashes of her previous encounter played before her eyes like a preview of what was to come, filling her vision with violence and terror. She tried to swallow, but her throat had gone dry, as if the fear had sapped her body's moisture along with its strength.

Her eyes were fixed on the pile of sand, yet it had stopped moving. Her heart still hammered as she watched, but the creature made no further attempt to free itself.

Burn didn't know why she did it. There were no rational thoughts in her mind, no clear goals behind her actions, but she found herself changing course, walking with quiet steps toward the creature that could so easily be the death of her. One step, then two. Before she knew it, she'd halved the distance between them. Still the creature didn't stir.

Then Burn saw it: white. But it wasn't the white of hair, the white that had haunted the shadows of her thoughts for days. It was the white of a torn shirt.

With that realization, Burn flung herself forward onto the heap, digging with frantic fingers into the burning desert sand. Before long, her hand brushed skin and she grabbed hold, pulling with all her might on the figure's arm.

Panting, she heaved the torso out of the earth and began to wipe the sand from his eyes and mouth. And his hair – his vibrant red hair.

"Jez?" Burn asked, holding his face in her lap. "Jez, can you hear me?"

A moan came from his prone form, and Burn nearly wept with relief. He was alive. He was injured and clearly in need of food and water, but he was alive. Burn shouted for someone to bring her a canteen, and she poured some of the cool liquid into his open mouth, praying that they weren't too late to save him.

As she worked, the others gathered around her, issuing shocked gasps and worried declarations as they took in Jez's state. Even the animals drew closer, their actions somehow tied to his. Burn shut them out, too focused on the man in her arms to care about what happened around her.

"Jez?" she asked again, gently shaking his beaten body. "Jez, it's me. It's Burn. You're safe now. I'm here."

She was surprised how small the gangly man felt, how breakable his body seemed. She wanted to take care of him, to nurse him back to health – but she also knew that she didn't have the time, not if she wanted to return to Kasis. There were too many lives to protect, and she couldn't possibly help them all.

Just then, Jez's head moved, twisting to the side, and he coughed, dislodging some of the sand and dirt from his throat. Weakly, he opened his eyes, taking in the scene before him.

"Well, hi there," he croaked to the assembled crowd – both human and animal – eliciting a genuine cheer from their ranks. The Viderens' anxiety shifted to relief and joy as they realized that their friend and neighbor was alive – and likely would remain that way. Burn could feel their spirits lift and their thoughts soar as they thanked the gods for his safety.

A crunching of sand underfoot alerted Burn to another presence in their midst, and she quickly turned her head to locate its source. Peering up between bodies and over furry forms, she could just make out Nara in the distance. Within a few minutes, she was upon them, making her way to the center of the crowd.

"What did you find?" Burn asked, still seated on the sand with Jez. Looking up into Nara's eyes, she couldn't tell if the news was good or bad.

Sighing, Nara crouched to Burn's level, letting her gaze sweep over Jez before returning to Burn. "I saw Aberra," she said simply, a small smile playing on her lips. "We're not far now."

Another cheer, this one bolder and louder, flowed like a wave through the people of Videre, and this time Burn joined in. This was just the inspiration she'd been looking for.

Chapter 21

Jez was in love. He kept threatening to steal Aberra's sheep and abscond with them into the night. Based on the fact that he couldn't yet walk without assistance, the Aberrans didn't take his warnings too seriously. They had, however, kindly offered to give him a mating pair in exchange for some of his animal expertise.

Jez wasn't coming with them to Kasis. He'd made that clear, and Burn respected his wishes. Still, she found it more difficult than she'd anticipated to leave him behind. She hadn't realized how much his death had been weighing on her until that weight had been lifted. The sight of him alive and smiling had eased some of her sorrow, and saying goodbye threatened to make the darkness descend once again.

But she knew she had to go. It was no longer a choice to be made, but rather an imperative standing immovable in her path. So she bid Jez adieu.

It was oddly fitting that his was the last face she saw

before setting off back to Kasis. He was, after all, the first person she'd set eyes on in this place. It was only right that his freckled face would be there when she departed, book-ending her adventure in this harshly magical world.

Their company had swelled to over 50 people, with several Aberrans even joining their ranks. Burn was secretly delighted to see that Mika and his parents had chosen to accompany them. The boy was overjoyed to finally be going to Kasis, and he kept listing all the things he'd tell his new-found sister once they'd met.

An anxious excitement buzzed over the crowd as each person envisioned what the coming days might hold. Burn, too, felt a thrill of anticipation at seeing Scar again and returning to the familiar streets of Kasis, but her enthusiasm was tainted with apprehension. She couldn't help feeling that something would go wrong, that fate would require a sacrifice. It was silly, she knew, but the thought nagged at her, tempering her euphoria.

As if sensing her unease, Hale appeared by her side and slid his hand softly into hers. They walked in silence for a few minutes, leading their motley crew across the final few miles to the south side of the dome.

"How do you think they're going to do it? Get us back in, I mean?" she asked in an attempt to break the silence.

Hale shrugged, keeping his fingers interlaced with hers. "You know your sister better than anyone, so you probably have a better idea than I do. But my guess would be something clever. Maybe she'll cut a hole through the glass with a laser disguised as a pair of goggles."

Burn laughed lightly at his suggestion. Hale was

different in the wildlands than he'd been in Kasis. He was freer somehow, more open. She couldn't tell if it was because of her or because of the freedom they'd had away from the Peace Force. Either way, she dreaded losing that part of him when they returned and the pressures of life and rebellion descended once more. She dreaded losing that part of herself, too.

To distract herself from her fears, she asked, "Do you think it'll be dangerous? These people aren't prepared for a fight."

"Yes," he said without hesitation. In response to Burn's questioning look, he continued, "Everything we do is dangerous. It's part of what we signed up for. This won't be any different. Although, knowing your sister, I'm sure she has a plan and a backup plan and backup for the backup plan. Together we can keep these people safe."

It felt like the tables had turned. Where Hale had once been jealous of her certainty, she was now envious of his. Yet his conviction was soothing, and it alleviated some of her anxiety. Looking back at the group they had assembled, she smiled. Maybe everything had happened for a reason – the Pit, Videre, her father. Maybe it was all part of a larger picture, simply a piece of the broader plan. The thought was comforting, and she held onto it, refocusing her eyes on the horizon. She didn't know what was waiting for her out there, but for the first time, she was enjoying the journey.

Traveling through a highly patrolled city while carrying a

pack full of explosives was a somewhat nerve-wracking experience, and Scar wouldn't have recommended it.

She'd felt too conspicuous, too tall, too red, too shiny. Too different to possibly blend in. Yet somehow, she'd managed it. She'd stuck to the shadows, making her way silently upward through the grime and into the light, unobserved by the PeaceBots or their human counterparts.

The top tiers were steadily recovering their brilliance, and the pollution that had been unleashed among them was almost completely controlled, leaving only wisps of noxious air in the otherwise clean streets. It was a pity. The smog suited them.

Once again clothed in some of Symphandra's finest creations, she'd marched through the upper echelons with purpose, as if she owned the world. After all, the people that lived up here did own Kasis, in all its polluted splendor. They owned it and controlled in and ran it into the ground. She was only paying them back in kind.

With quick, precise movements, she'd traveled to the most secluded corners and planted her payback. The bombs weren't large enough to cause serious damage, although they would trigger quite the commotion. It was only a pity that the air intake points were now heavily guarded; she would have enjoyed sending these charlatans back into the dark where they belonged. Instead, she'd have to settle for a different kind of chaos, a slower form of retribution.

Of course, she hadn't been working alone. Kaz and Cali had both volunteered to assist her, and the trio had divided up the city amongst themselves, allocating sectors and quarters like pieces of a pie. She'd taken the top, Cali the middle, and Kaz the bottom.

It wasn't a perfect plan, but it was as close as they could get in two days. The execution, however, left something to be desired. While Kaz and Scar's parts went off without a hitch, Cali wasn't so fortunate.

"There's been a problem," came the message, immediately making Scar pause. She'd been packing her things for the night's magnum opus, placing an arsenal of inspired creations into a mundane cloth sack. But as soon as the message popped up, she froze, the worst-case scenarios running riot through her mind.

"The Peace Force was searching everyone," Cali's next message read. "I couldn't get past them. I had to dump the rest of the explosives."

"How many did you manage to place?" Scar sent back, the wires in her hair sparking in agitation.

"Five. The rest are in a dumpster near the Saffron Quarter. It was the only place I could think to hide them."

Five. Scar had given Cali over a dozen devices to place throughout the mid-level tiers before arming them for the night's event. That meant that more than half of them were currently sitting in a pile of trash, useless.

"Is there any way to retrieve them?" Scar tapped her fingers on the table while she waited for a reply, anxious about this added hurdle. She had precisely timed the evening's order of affairs, and they had no leeway for superfluous errands. If there was even a chance they could salvage the explosives, though, she would have to find the time.

Unfortunately, Cali's next message dashed Scar's meager hopes. "No. The area is crawling with officers. It's like they know something's going down."

Damn, Scar thought angrily, cursing her opponents' diligence. Why had they chosen tonight of all nights to make their presence felt? Had someone tipped off the Peace Force to what they were planning?

Maybe it had nothing to do with them; maybe it was a mere coincidence, a bit of bad luck tossed their way by the vengeful hands of fate. But it felt like a bad omen, a warning of worse things to come.

Still, Scar couldn't dwell on it; she simply didn't have the time. Burn was waiting for her, and she had to believe that they were prepared enough to weather this obstacle – and any others that fate might throw their way.

"It'll be fine. Continue on as planned." Scar shot the brief message back to Cali before tucking the last of the gadgets into her bag and zipping it shut.

This was it. This was what she had been waiting for. This was the night she would finally find Burn. This was the night she would save her.

With that thought, she stepped out from behind the bright red door, closing it with a satisfying thud. Pulling her mask up over her face and her hood down over her hair, she melded with the growing darkness, becoming one with the shadows.

Stealth seemed effortless that night. Scar floated through the streets with ease, aided by the billowing clouds of noxious smog that blanketed the streets, cushioning her footsteps and obscuring her hunched form. Even the Peace Force's presence was light, with few bots and even fewer officers crossing her path. It was still before curfew, so the ones that were out paid her no mind, either not seeing her or not caring to see her as they made their predetermined rounds.

Down she went, sinking deeper and deeper into the city until all that surrounded her were dirt and decay and the harsh faces of those who were forced to live amongst it. She made her way to the tunnel, hiding her destination with evasion and misdirection to further conceal her mission. Yet down here, no one cared who you were or where you were going. So they let her pass unbothered, let her slide out of the city proper and into the dusty wings.

She was the first person to arrive at the scene. Her sentinels were already in place, spread out around the edges of the south side of the dome with their sensors trained on the desert. The PeaceBots were her eyes into the wildlands. Their feeds were synced to her tab, and anything they saw, she saw. They would be the ones to spot Burn and Hale through the night, sending the alert to Scar and setting the events in motion.

So far, all was quiet on the southern front. Earlier that day she'd sent the tunnel's exact coordinates to Burn's goggles, certain her sister could follow them home. Now Scar whipped out her tab to peer into the night, looking for a spark of life. She knew it was too early. Night had not yet completed its takeover of the sky, and Scar could still make out threads of gold peeking from the horizon. Soon, though, it would be time. Soon Burn would appear, and Scar would finally know for certain she was safe.

As if on cue, Cali materialized beside her, looking anxious but eager. "I'm sorry about the explosives…" she started to whisper, but Scar cut her off with a wave.

"It doesn't matter. Everything else is in place. The Peace Force won't have a clue what's going on." Cali didn't look entirely convinced, so Scar gave her a small, close-lipped smile.

It seemed to reassure her, because she nodded and said, "Let's get to work."

Scar turned her attention back to her tab. With a few rapid taps, she delivered her coordinates to the Lunaria, calling them to action. From across the city, they descended, leaving their homes and their families to once again put themselves in danger for the cause.

Of course, not all of the Lunaria would be joining them. Such a large group would have drawn attention. And, when the choice had been put before them, not all of them were willing to partake. That was the danger of a citizen army. Their ideas sparked a passion, a desire to make a change, but not all were made for action. Not everyone could fight.

One by one, the Lunaria emerged from the mist, silently joining this brotherhood of spies. While they gathered, Scar got to work, using her laser to open the passageway into the tunnel. This time it was easier, as if the bars remembered their old injuries and were happy to part at her touch. Within a few minutes, she'd lifted the grate from its frame, revealing the darkness of the tunnel beneath.

In whispers and murmurs around her, the Lunaria divided themselves, splitting the company into saviors and guards. The smaller faction, those chosen to help Burn and Hale back into the city, would go with Scar. The rest would fan out across the area, keeping watch for anything – or anyone – out of place.

This latter crew included Cali. It was also saddled with

Ansel and Raqa, along with more than 20 other gifted citizens. Their job wasn't just to observe; if anything went wrong, they were the front line. It was their duty to protect the others, to guarantee safe passage into the city. Scar hoped, for everyone's sakes, that they'd never be called upon to act.

With a nod to her unit, Scar slipped into the tunnel, leading her troops into the belly of the beast. Behind her, several members rigged a makeshift ladder, allowing for an easy retreat back into the city. Scar paid them no mind, making her way down the central passageway and toward the city's outer edges.

She walked slowly this time, careful to avoid the jagged pipes that threatened to cut her and the steam that threatened to burn her. Toward the end, the tunnel filled with the same blinding haze, but Scar managed to find the hole and affix a light rope ladder to the top before gently lowering herself down. She walked forward, putting her hands on the barrier that stood between her and the outside world, between her and Burn.

Digging into her bag, she withdrew several explosives and placed them around the edges of the steel wall, where metal bit into brick to form an impenetrable seal. Stepping back to consider her work, she smirked in satisfaction. This was going to be good.

Retreating back up the hole and through the tunnel, Scar placed herself a safe distance from the blast site, warning the others to do the same. Seating herself along one of the damp walls, she pulled out her tab and waited.

Scar wasn't a patient person. She wasn't made for sitting still or waiting quietly. She was made for working, for using her hands, for getting things done. If the situation demanded it, however, she could put on a show. She could calm her body and slow her breathing until she eerily resembled the machines that she tinkered with. Yet her mind would never acquiesce to such tranquility.

So in the cool tunnel below the city, she sat, her eyes trained on her tab while her brain pummeled her with questions. Where was Burn? Was she out there? Would she make it in time? Would this work?

All around her, the Lunaria lingered, waiting on her for their signal to move. Outside, night had fallen in earnest, stealing the last of the suns' rays and thrusting a deep blue across the large expanse of sky. The silence in the tunnel itched with anxious energy, and all eyes fell on Scar, watching for any hint of movement, any trace of a reaction.

Staring through the eyes of her PeaceBots, Scar saw nothing, save for the wind blowing across the dunes. Its claws were fierce tonight, tearing chunks of sand from their beds and vaulting it into swirling eddies that lingered like ghosts in the air. More than once, Scar thought she'd detected movement only to find herself staring at columns of sand so solid that she was certain they could never be moved. Yet in the next instant they'd be gone, swept back into the desert like a sea reclaiming its waves.

As the minutes ticked by, she could feel the rising doubt pressing down on her from all sides. The Lunaria's expressions steadily morphed from anxious to worried to doubtful, and Scar didn't know how much longer they'd wait silently for allies that might never show. Those prepared for action, she was finding, were not inclined to remain still for long.

Another column of sand blew across the wildlands, and Scar watched as it dissipated into the night. Except this time it didn't. Instead of ebbing, the sand grew, drawing closer and closer to the dome. Scar sat up straighter, and the movement sent a stir of energy through the tunnel. Something was happening. Something was coming.

With a few taps of her fingers, Scar instructed her PeaceBots to focus in on the spot, giving her a multi-camera view of the approaching squall. Her eyes flicked between the scenes, willing the sand to resolve into a figure, willing forth a picture of Burn.

And then, as if called into life by her need, a person appeared. Then another. And on and on and on until a small army was marching toward them. Out in front, leading the troops home, was the small brunette form that Scar knew so well. It was Burn.

"They're coming," she said through the comms, the satisfaction and righteous glee apparent in her voice. "And they've brought some company. Stand by for action."

Although no one dared to break the silence of the tunnel – or the streets above it – she could sense their surprise and astonishment. They had doubted her, questioned her ability to back up her claims. That was one mistake they wouldn't be making again.

Scar watched as her sister strode toward them, recognizing the quiet confidence in her gait as she escorted her charges back home. Burn had never looked more like a leader than she did in that moment, with the sand swirling at her ankles and her head held high as she marched through the wildlands.

Hale was at Burn's side, the same hard determination plastered on his face as the last time she'd seen him. Scar was somewhat dismayed, having half hoped that Hale would have succumbed to the wildlands – or, conversely, made a home within it and decided to stay. But even his presence couldn't keep her down for long, not when her sister was finally within view.

Scar scanned the crowd behind the pair, combing it for other familiar faces. She secretly yearned to catch a glimpse of red hair amongst the throng, the same red hair that curled in wiry tendrils around her own fair face, but the darkness ate away at their features, and no matter how much she strained she couldn't see her father within the pack.

Coming back to herself, Scar measured the distance from them to the dome's edge. She couldn't set off the explosives too soon, or else the Peace Force would have too much time to investigate the source. She couldn't set them off too late, either, as it would put Burn and her crew inside the blast radius. She had to time it just right.

"Hold for my mark," Scar commanded through the comms, readying her troops. She briefly relished the feel of having so many people hanging on to her every word, waiting with bated breath to obey her commands. Shaking herself, she refocused her attention on the wildlands, assessing Burn's pace and internally calculating the time until detonation. Three, two, one…

"Take cover," Scar said, drawing the detonator from her bag. Taking a deep breath, she pressed her thumb firmly on the button. A silent second passed before the world exploded around her.

Scar could feel the tunnel rumble, shaking dirt and rot loose and showering it down on her shoulders. She waited as the tremors subsided, then dashed back down the passageway. The pipes erupting from the walls tore at her clothes as she ran, but she didn't care. Her mind was on Burn and only Burn, and she craved the sight of her like a plant craves light.

She just managed to catch herself from falling through the hole. Ignoring the ladder, she vaulted over the edge and landed hard on the stone floor. Breaking into a run, she propelled herself toward the tunnel's end.

Dust and debris still lingered in the air from the explosion, but Scar could feel the cool breeze of the wildlands licking at her skin. It had worked. Inching forward through the rubble of stone and steel, she caught her first real glimpse of the night sky, its inky surface so clear without the barrier of the dome. Scar kicked aside torn-apart bricks and mangled metal as she made her way to the edge of the world and looked down.

The sheer drop made her head spin, and she clung to the side of the tunnel as she peered into the night. Clouds of stone particles wafted around her, drifting into the desert air and obscuring her view of the wildlands, but she could just make out the sandy floor several stories below. And there, standing upon its banks, was Burn.

The sisters' eyes met, and they smiled, each drinking in the view of the other. Burn looked healthy and strong and something else Scar couldn't quite name. It was as if the wildlands had bestowed some of their wildness upon her. She was dressed in warm woven clothes, the kind that still bore hints of the plants and animals used in their creation, and she was armed with a colorful assortment of weaponry.

While the two considered each other, more members of the Lunaria took their places, dropping into the tunnel behind her and making their way to her side. One of the women unfurled a long rope ladder and tossed it over the side, lowering it until its rungs just grazed the ground. Beside her, two men lashed the ladder's end to the tunnel, utilizing piles they'd driven into the stone. Their job complete, they nodded to Scar, giving her the go-ahead.

Scar, in turn, nodded to Burn, beckoning her back into Kasis. "Come on in," she said, knowing her sister could hear her.

Burn turned, momentarily consulting with Hale and her crew before stepping up to the ladder and beginning her climb. Her progress was swift and efficient, her lithe body making quick work of the ascent. Within minutes, her hand was reaching over the edge, searching for purchase amongst the rubble.

Scar reached out, taking her sister's cool hand in hers and pulling her up the final few feet. Then Burn was there, standing before her like she'd imagined a thousand times.

"I've missed you," Burn said, not letting go of her sister's hand. Without warning, she moved forward and draped her arms around Scar, wrapping her in a tight embrace that smelled like sand and sweat and home. And, for the first time in a long time, Scar hugged her back, giving in to the warmth and returning it.

"I've missed you, too," she whispered.

Chapter 22

Burn felt like she was on top of the world. Literally. From her vantage point, she could see out across the desert, tracing the path they had taken to get to this point. It didn't hurt that her sister was there beside her, the hard metal of her collarbone poking into her skin as they hugged.

Their tender reunion was cut short, however, by the appearance of a small hand stretching up from the ladder beside them. Reluctantly letting go of her sister, Burn reached over the edge and clasped the hand, drawing Mika up and into the tunnel.

"I'm in Kasis!" the little boy shouted, turning around to locate his parents on the ground. Spying them near the front of the line, he began jumping and waving to get their attention. "Look at me! I'm finally in Kasis!"

Burn laughed at the boy's antics, pushing him lightly to the back of the tunnel to make room for the next person. Several members of the Lunaria were waiting there to escort him up into yet another tunnel and back into the city. Burn paused to marvel at the smooth operation before a new hand reached up from the ladder to pull her attention away.

Together, the sisters helped another citizen back into Kasis, forming an impromptu welcoming committee for their fair city. One by one, Burn and Scar pulled each person up from the wildlands. It was slow going, especially for those whose frailty or youth required additional assistance, but it was worth it to see the smiles on their faces when they finally crested the peak and set foot in Kasis once more.

Nara was within the first dozen to make her way into the tunnel. Hale was facilitating the progression from the ground and would be the final member of their crew to make his way into the city, but Nara was eager to once again stand on Kasian soil, and she'd sweet-talked her way to the front of the line. Or she'd merely flashed her weapons. Burn wouldn't have been surprised at either.

Yet, despite Nara's excitement, once she reached the top she couldn't help but turn back and look out across the desert. Her eyes scanned the swirling swaths of sand as if she wanted to memorize the landscape and every creature within it.

"I think I'm actually going to miss it out there," she said quietly to Burn – and to herself. Tearing her eyes away from the scene, she noticed Scar for the first time and smiled. "You must be Scar. I've heard a lot about you. I can't wait to pick your brain about weaponry." She waggled her eyebrows at Scar, who cocked her head at the stranger.

"And you are...?" Scar queried in her usual blunt tone.

"Oh, of course. I'm Nara." She stuck out her hand, but

Scar merely stared at it, her tolerance for human contact already exceeded for the day. Realizing her faux pas, Nara retracted her hand and gave Scar a smile instead. "I guess I'll see you later," she said, waving awkwardly to the sisters before making her way down the tunnel.

"I see you've made some new friends," Scar said to Burn, her voice inscrutable.

Burn chuckled, glad to see that her sister hadn't changed in her absence. "I think you're going to like them," she retorted, smiling.

To Burn's utter astonishment, Scar started to chuckle in return. Then she laughed. Her sharp, metallic giggles rang through the tunnel for a few seconds, biting into the stillness of the stone. It was eerie, almost wrong to hear such mirth coming from her sister's mouth.

Then Burn remembered the time that she, too, had been overcome with misplaced merriment. The chemicals in the air must be getting to Scar, she realized belatedly.

Burn had long since grown used to the strange air, but the people in the tunnels would begin to feel it within minutes, especially those on the front lines. And she didn't need them going gaga – or worse, developing paralyzing headaches and passing out – while her people were climbing back into the city. So she took action, ushering Scar and the other Kasians up the ladder and putting several strong members of her party in charge.

Following Scar into the higher tunnel, Burn's ears naturally tuned to the sounds of the city above her. It was strange, being back in this place. The noises from the streets – the coughs and carts and footsteps on dirt paths – were both familiar and foreign, like an echo from a long-ago dream. Yet they were also comforting, and Burn took a minute to let the sounds wash over her, bathing her in their staccato melody.

It was Scar's sniggering that snapped her out of her daze, pulling her back to the present. Shaking her head, Burn continued pulling her sister along the tunnel, their progress slowed by the soupy smog that hung in curtains around them. That was one part of Kasis Burn hadn't missed, and she pulled her mask tight around her mouth to keep the vile air from entering her system. Up ahead, she could just make out other figures feeling their way through the mist, and she followed in their footsteps, using her ears as her compass.

Then something made her freeze, a move so sudden that Scar tumbled out of her arms. Burn lunged forward to catch her sister, helping her to her feet while scanning the world for the anomaly that had disturbed her. Something wasn't right. She could hear it – and *feel* it. People were angry, vengeful, and bent on destruction.

Burn closed her eyes, trying to locate the source of the fury. It wasn't coming from directly above them, but rather further into the city. Yet it was rapidly approaching their position.

"The Peace Force is on their way!" Burn shouted to her sister, attempting to tear her from her stupor, but Scar only blinked, confusion and pain dulling her normally bright eyes. Sighing, Burn grabbed the comms unit from Scar's ear and placed it in her own, effectively taking command of Scar's crew.

"This is Burn. We have a problem. A Peace Force unit is approaching from the west. There are at least 50 of them, and more might be coming. I'm making my way up now."

Placing her sister gently on the floor, she took off toward the entrance. If they really were facing the Peace Force, Scar was safer here. But Burn could fight – and she would.

Skirting other figures, she made her way down the narrow passage, scanning for Nara as she went. If a battle was indeed on the horizon, Burn wanted the woman by her side – or watching her back. While she searched, she conscripted what fighters she could from amongst her crew, warning the others to stay in the safety of the tunnels until the battle had passed.

She had to hope it would end in their favor, had to believe they would win. Otherwise she had torn these people from their homes only for them to die in this godforsaken city. She couldn't stomach the idea, so she pushed it aside, focusing on finding her friend.

She eventually spotted Nara near the tunnel's entrance, and she quickly caught her up on their predicament.

"They'll be here any minute," Burn finished breathlessly, unsheathing one of the knives from her belt.

She could have sworn that Nara's eyes lit up at the prospect of a fight, but it was too dim in the tunnel to say for certain. Either way, she followed Burn's lead, taking out a knife of her own and twirling it around in her hand.

"Let's do this," she said with a smile, her confidence on full display.

Burn, on the other hand, didn't feel nearly as prepared. The Peace Force, she reminded herself, had guns. And bombs. And years of training. They had...knives and sticks. This was going to be an uphill battle.

Burn took a deep breath, ignoring the putrid air, before heaving herself up the final ladder and into the city. The grime of this place never ceased to amaze her. It hung in the air and clung to the buildings, seeping into every crack and crevice. It was like a disease, crawling through the depths of the city in search of new victims to plague.

The sound of approaching footsteps spurred her to action. There was no doubt now that the Peace Force was coming for them. Despite the distance, their thoughts sang to her, humming poignant melodies of intruders and death. They were coming for blood, and they were certain they'd get it.

"They're almost here," she whispered through the comms, making sure everyone was in place.

Her mind filled with an anxious energy, and she couldn't tell if it was her emotion or theirs. Either way, it clawed at her, constricting her chest and quickening her heartbeat. Despite the fact that she'd trained for weeks by Nara's side, real battle still shook her, and she strained to find a hint of clarity in the chaos.

Tucked into a corner of the twisting maze, the Lunaria did have a small kind of advantage. The narrow streets and passages provided the protection of a funnel, which would stem the flow of officers from a wave to a trickle. So instead of facing an advancing horde, they'd have the chance to tackle their enemies as they came, evening out the odds. Maybe it would be enough. Maybe they could win.

One second passed, then two. Then, in an instant, the Peace Force was there, their guns drawn and their shouts breaking the stillness of the scene. The Lunaria, backed by their new comrades, jumped, striking the officers before they had a chance to fire. Makeshift weaponry met steel gun barrels in a clang that filled the street, ricocheting off the walls and bouncing back in jagged echoes.

The small square they occupied quickly filled to capacity as more and more soldiers filed in. The battle, which had rapidly devolved from a coordinated attack to one-on-one skirmishes, spread like lava into the adjoining streets as each pair sought the space and freedom to fight.

Burn herself leapt forward into the melee, using the wooden dowel in her right hand to disarm an officer, and the knife in her left to slash cleanly across his chest. She paid no mind to the blood. She couldn't, even though it slicked her arms and her chest, falling to the ground in quiet splashes.

Burn had to focus, had to fight. There was no room for remorse, no space for sorrow. That would come later. Now she had to move. She took off down a narrow lane in search of someone else to challenge, her brain consumed by the combat. Dodging wild blows and entangled foes, she inched through the disjointed battlefield with her weapons at the ready.

Turning a sharp corner, she suddenly found herself situated behind an unoccupied officer, whose attention was focused on something in front of him. Burn seized the opportunity, sweeping his legs from beneath him and thrusting her knife into his chest. He grabbed at the weapon weakly, but the life drained from his body, leaving him limp on the pavement. Burn tugged at the knife, but it was embedded in his armor, wedged between the plates that had failed to protect him.

As Burn struggled to free her blade, something struck her from behind, sending her sprawling on top of the body. She quickly scrambled off the man and spun to face her attacker, just making out the form of a burly Peace Officer before his gun struck her sharply on the side of the head.

As she lay on the pavement, stars danced in her vision, threatening to steal her consciousness and force her into oblivion. Yet she held on, shoving her arm out in front of her. The wooden staff she clutched protected her from a third blow, giving her enough time to leverage herself off the ground and into a fighting position. Her head spun from the movement, and she had to grasp the wall next to her for support.

With her vision compromised, her hearing kicked in. Even with her eyes shut, she could see the man's movements, feel where he planned to strike next. Her body reacted instinctively, ducking to the side and spinning out of his reach. Her free hand grabbed another knife from her belt and threw, lodging the weapon firmly in her opponent's throat. He let out a gurgle of protest before dropping to the dirt, his cries lost in the commotion.

By then, Burn had regained her bearings, and the world cleared in front of her eyes. The street before her was its own miniature battlefield, with blood and dirt mingling to cover the scene. She cast her senses through the nearby lanes, listening as the city filled with screams. The Lunaria were outnumbered, even with the troops from the wildlands. It would take a miracle for them to win.

Without warning, another black-clad form appeared from around the corner, his weapon raised. Burn had just enough time to throw her hands in front of her before he fired, the bullet whizzing toward her chest. Time slowed to a crawl as she tried to react, tried to move, but she was too slow.

Her eyes went wide as she realized what had happened, and she waited for the pain to overtake her. She was sure it was going to hurt. Dying, after all, must involve some amount of agony. But as she waited, the pain never came. Maybe she was already dead, she thought, and simply hadn't realized it yet.

As she watched, the officer who had shot her approached, taking his time to investigate his kill. He was a stone's throw away, then an arm's length, then upon her. Then he was past her, kneeling to the ground behind her.

Burn turned mutely, and the pieces came crashing into place – but the pieces were wrong. Because lying on the ground, bleeding out onto the street, was another officer. This man had shot one of his own, killed his comrade in arms. Burn backed away warily, confusion clouding her thoughts. She was safe, at least for the moment, but she couldn't understand why.

As she retreated, her body still angled toward the bent figure, a third Peace Officer entered the lane, taking in the scene. But the man on the ground didn't stir, too occupied by the life he had just claimed. Reaching behind her, Burn pulled her final knife from her belt and let it fly. Her aim was true, and the man sank to his knees before tumbling into the dust.

Only then did her dark angel look up, seeming to notice her for the first time. Burn froze. She had no more knives to throw. The only weapon left in her arsenal was a single wooden fighting stick, which was of little use at this distance. She braced herself for an attack, listening for anything that might assist her, but what she heard brought her mind to a grinding halt.

"Auburn," the man whispered, a combination of surprise and joy coloring the words.

Burn knew that voice. She knew it, but she didn't believe it. Only when the man reached up and removed his helmet did his identity truly sink in. It was Kaz.

The shock robbed her of her wits, and it took a few seconds for her to process his sudden appearance. And the fact that he had saved her. He had shot one of his own to protect her. They looked at each other for a beat, neither sure what to say.

They were saved the trouble of saying anything by Nara, who rounded the corner like a terror, her fury focused on Kaz. She was about to bring her fighting stick down on Kaz's head when Burn held out a hand and yelled "stop!"

Her sudden exclamation did, indeed, stop Nara in her tracks. With the stick poised above her head, she stiffened, momentarily resembling a stone statue of some ancient warrior. Burn knew she wouldn't stay still for long, so she scrambled over to the pair, placing herself between them.

"He's on our side," she breathed, her hands held up before her in a gesture of surrender. "Don't hurt him."

Nara considered her for a second, clearly assessing her sanity. Judging her to be rational enough to tell friend from foe, she grudgingly lowered her weapon, holding it at her side. Relief washed through Burn as she turned, offering her hand to help Kaz to his feet. He took it gratefully, rising to look at her.

"I didn't think I'd ever see you again," he said, emotion straining his voice. Burn could see it in his head, feel the regret and desolation and relief behind his words, and it stunned her.

But they didn't have time for that, not now. Burn brought herself back to the present, back to the battlefield before her. This was no time for tearful reunions. So instead of acknowledging his words, she quickly got down to business.

"How can we stop them?" she asked Kaz, her voice tight with repressed emotion. "What can we do to drive them back?"

"We need to get everyone out of the tunnels," Nara chimed in, briefing him like an officer in the field. "We don't need to win. We just need to get them to safety. But right now they're surrounded, and more officers are closing in."

Kaz nodded curtly, taking in her words. "Their plan was to come at you from all sides and pick you off one by one. I tried to warn you, tried to tell you that the Peace Force was coming, but I couldn't get through. It's like they knew what Scar was planning and had a strategy in place to stop it."

It made sense – but it didn't do them any good now. That was something they could deal with later. Right now they needed a plan.

"What if we create a distraction?" Burn posed, scrambling for ideas. "We lure them away from the tunnels, giving everyone enough time to get out and back to safety."

"It's a good idea," said Nara, who was now using her gift to scan the area for threats. "But what do we have to distract them with? We're not exactly flush with supplies."

Nara was right. Burn took stock of her own depleted arsenal and grimaced. Even taking into consideration Kaz's gun, along with those of the downed officers, they would still be vastly outmatched.

She was certain there was something she was missing, but she couldn't seem to think. The madness raging around her blended with the thoughts of countless frightened people to make her head spin. She was no longer used to this level of chaos, and the onslaught made it nearly impossible to focus.

Then Kaz's head snapped up, a new light in his eyes. "Scar's PeaceBots!" he exclaimed, as if that was supposed to mean something to them. Instead, the proclamation only served to confuse Burn further.

"What?" she demanded, rubbing her temples in an attempt to rid her mind of its fog.

"Scar took control of a small army of PeaceBots, and she stationed them nearby, along the edges of the dome," he rushed to explain. "If we can get them here and use them to fire on the Peace Force, it could draw their attention away from the tunnel, giving your people time to get out."

Once Burn got over the fact that, in her absence, Scar had apparently created an army of robotic minions, she considered Kaz's plan. It could work. If all of her people had made their way up into the tunnels from the wildlands, then they'd only need a few minutes to escape. She didn't know how long PeaceBots could hold up under fire, but it might just be long enough for everyone to get to safety.

"But wasn't Scar affected by the air out there?" Nara

ventured, doubt clouding her voice. "Are you sure she can do this?"

Burn let out a short, blunt burst of laughter. "I'm sure. As long as she's still conscious, she can make those bots do anything she wants."

Burn silently prayed that her sister was, indeed, still conscious. She was about to radio over when she realized with a start that she'd taken her sister's comms unit. She cursed herself for her stupidity, wishing she'd had the foresight to take someone else's instead. Yet how could she have known it would come to this?

"Anyone who's still down in the tunnels, I need you to find Scar. Find Scar and give her your comms unit stat!" she demanded, holding her breath.

Silence met her ears, hollow in its emptiness. Burn briefly considered making a break for it and attempting to return to the tunnel on her own when a familiar voice crackled through her headset.

"Burn?" Scar croaked, her voice still muddled from the atmosphere's effects on her brain. But Burn didn't have time for her to come around, so she pressed on.

"Scar. I need you to listen and not ask questions, OK?" Not waiting for a reply, she continued, "Tell your PeaceBots to make their way toward your square – but not too close. When they're just within range, have them fire at the force and then retreat. We need them to lead the officers away so the people in the tunnels can escape."

"Everyone else," she said, shifting her attention to the other soldiers on the line, "do what you can to keep the other officers away from the shaft. If you're near the main square, you may have to help lure away the remaining troops after the bots attack. A few of you will need to stay behind to take everyone to safety. I'll try to get there to help you, but I can't promise I'll make it. Protect them with your lives. They're counting on us."

A few seconds of silence passed, seconds that felt like an eternity, where Burn wasn't sure if they'd heard – or if they'd even be willing to follow her into battle. She was an impromptu leader, a proxy general, and they had no obligation to obey her. Yet one by one they consented, handing over their lives into her hands.

Even Hale's voice crackled through the comms, simultaneously giving her strength and making her heart ring with tension. "We're with you, Burn," his deep voice rumbled, adding a sparkling gem of conviction to the wretched uncertainty of battle.

She didn't know how he'd gotten his hands on a comms unit, but he'd managed it, and now he was willing to submit to her command, risking everything simply because she had asked. Burn swallowed down a lump that had formed in her throat, reminding herself where she was and what she was about to do.

"The PeaceBots are headed toward the square," Scar stated, sounding stronger than she had just moments before. "They'll be here any minute."

That was Burn's cue. She relayed Scar's words to Kaz and Nara, and the group paused to grab the guns and knives off the officers they'd downed. Kaz replaced his helmet, hiding once more behind the visage of their enemy, before they took off toward the tunnel.

The trio moved as a single unit, each protecting the others' backs. An officer sprang out from behind a stone wall, and Kaz shot, felling the man with a single blow. It was Burn's turn next. As they rounded a corner, she raised her weapon reflexively, finding a target in an instant and firing before he could even take a second step.

Nara had her own way of dealing with enemies. As they came upon a figure preparing to finish off one of their allies, Nara sprang into action. She leapt into a roll, which took her straight to the man's side. Once there, she drew two knives in fluid succession, using one of the blades to slash at the tendon behind his knee. As he crumpled to the ground in pain, Nara seized his body, a primal, animalistic fire overtaking her. With her other blade, she ripped into the officer's throat, sending dark splashes of blood raining down over the scene.

Satisfied, Nara resheathed her weapons and stood, making her way back to the group. Neither Kaz nor Burn spoke, but they instinctively let Nara take the lead as they embarked on the final stretch to the tunnel.

It wasn't far now. They could see the opening – and the crowd of officers bearing down on it. If they did nothing, the defenseless people below would soon find themselves trapped, sentenced to a brutal end in the very passageway they thought would be their salvation.

Raising her stolen weapon, Burn took aim at one of the nearest officers. She took a breath, steadying her hands, but a sound from behind her gave her pause. She focused her attention on the alley at her back and, as she stared, the familiar form of a PeaceBot came whirling around the corner.

Burn grabbed Kaz and Nara and pulled them against

the wall. A split second later, the PeaceBot fired, aiming at the officers. Shots echoed around her as yet more bots rained gunfire on the troops from the surrounding streets.

The Peace Officers shifted their attention, turning from the tunnel to face the bots. Burn could feel the confusion emanating from their minds as they wondered why their own machines were attacking them. That confusion rapidly turned to rage as another volley of shots headed in their direction. Some of the officers dropped as the bullets hit their targets, but more survived, turning their fury onto the machines.

Burn and her friends ducked out of the way as a storm of officers came crashing through the lane, intent on making the PeaceBots pay. Not all of the troops took the bait, however. Many remained near the tunnel, their efforts unhindered by the commotion.

That's when the Lunaria turned the tables. Popping out from behind corners, they struck, enticing the officers to leave their posts and follow them through the maze. This time the officers bit, spreading themselves out through the alleys and lanes in search of their attackers.

Only a few officers remained, their sights trained on the hole in the ground. Almost gleefully, they lunged forward, believing the coast was clear. They were wrong.

Burn, Kaz, and Nara darted onto the field, joined by several more of the Lunaria who had been hiding in the shadows, waiting for their turn. A sudden blazing inferno engulfed the area in front of them, a localized fire that raged just for them. As it receded, leaving prone officers in its wake, Burn spotted Ansel nearby, his hands outstretched as he reclaimed the flames.

Glancing around, Burn noticed Crete, the healer, who was on his knees tending to one of the injured. She also spotted Dormaline and Lore, and their familiar presence reassured her somehow, centering her in the here and now.

With the immediate threat neutralized, Burn dashed to the tunnel's entrance, dropping to her knees to peer into the hole. The barrels of several guns greeted her, and she had to quickly proclaim her identity before the guards would lower their weapons.

"You have to hurry. We only have a few minutes. Get everyone up and out. Now!"

Her command kicked off a flurry of movement, and suddenly hands and arms and torsos were thrust in her face as people rushed up the ladder and into the city. She reached out a hand to help them, while behind her the others kept watch for any errant officers who might come to their senses and double back.

One by one, the people emerged from their underground bunker, their eyes wide and their bodies shaking. Scar was the last to surface, her now-clear eyes meeting Burn's in a familiar look. Even without words, Burn knew the meaning: You did good. I'm proud. Now let's finish this.

Hoisting her sister up, Burn turned to look at the group before her. She instructed the Lunaria to assist her, holding up the frail and carrying the young. Together, the remaining rebels formed bookends to their ragged lineup, offering protection on all sides. With everyone in place, they set off, snaking through the city's narrow streets in a tentative, halting trot.

While Kaz and Nara took up the rear, Burn ran in front, directing the ragtag parade. She sent her thoughts out across the streets, searching for the corridors that promised safety amidst the anarchy. Around her, guns fired, people screamed, and the remnants of violence remained, but she ignored them, pouring all of herself into her mission.

They were moving. Slowly but surely, they were finding their way through the city, inching closer and closer to safety. The main thoroughfare was in sight now, and beyond it the stairs to the next level. Burn could almost taste the relief as they forged their way forward, leaving the misery of battle behind.

But escaping couldn't be that easy. The hands that had trapped them wouldn't release them without a fight.

Burn stopped in her tracks as a sound registered from the tier above. Without a thought, she retreated into the lane, pushing her charges back into the safety of the enclosed stone passage. She closed her eyes, breathing through the fear, and sent out her senses to hunt for the threat. Her stomach dropped through her body like lead as the sounds came into focus.

A fresh battalion of troops was descending on them from above, blocking their path to freedom. At least 20 men marched in unison toward them, their thoughts bent on destruction.

Burn briefly considered retreating. She knew they could wind their way back through the maze, finding another route with the promise of escape. But the troops above weren't the only ones that had caught their scent. As Burn listened, she detected a smaller faction closing in on them from behind, trapping them where they stood.

"We're surrounded," she whispered, half to those clustered around her and half to the troops on the other side of the comms. "Hale, if you can hear me, we need you," she added, sending out the personal plea through the airwaves in hopes that he'd come.

Almost as if they'd rehearsed it, the Lunaria members and gifted expats made their way to the edges, placing themselves on the front lines to protect their kin. It was a poignant display of camaraderie with a single missive for the world: We stand together, and we protect our own.

A handful of heartbeats was all that stood between their adversaries and them. Before Burn knew it, the Peace Force was there, closing in on them from both sides.

Burn faced their fury out front, trading shot for shot until her ammo ran dry. Tossing aside her weapon, she reached for a knife. Before she could free it, however, a bullet bit into her leg, dragging her to the ground.

The pain tore at her like fire, sending her into a momentary blackness before she resurfaced, clinging to the light. As she lay in the dirt, trying to find the strength to stand, she took in the terror around her.

The Peace Force had pushed their way past the Lunaria's guards, converging on the helpless souls within. Screams of panic and pain pierced her ears, threatening to drive her mad. And on the ground beside her, covered in blood, was Mika, his dead eyes staring sightlessly at the city he'd wanted so badly to see.

Chapter 23

Scar was frozen, anchored in place by shock and indecision and the people pressing down on her from all sides. Her back was up against a wall – literally – and she felt pinned in place, as if any attempt to move forward would only result in her being shoved deeper into the confines of the brick.

She couldn't understand how things had gone so wrong so fast. One second they were free, with her PeaceBots creating the perfect diversion, and the next they were trapped, with Burn on the ground bleeding and the Peace Force closing in.

But Scar was not helpless. She was far too proud to ever be a damsel in distress. While she might not have the same combat expertise as Burn, she did possess her own bag of tricks.

First things first: She had to stop any more of the Peace Force from joining them. They were already outnumbered as it was, and they couldn't afford for the odds to tilt further against them. With deft fingers, she removed the comms jammer from her bag, tuning it to the Peace Force's frequency. Pressing the button with fervor, she sent a powerful signal across the channel, disrupting their communications and making it impossible for them to coordinate.

Of course, she still had the problem of the Peace Officers who were already on the scene. They wouldn't be so easy to disrupt. Yet it wouldn't be impossible. At least that's what she was choosing to believe.

Grabbing her tab, she got to work, getting a lay of the land through the eyes of her PeaceBots. Their cameras were still on and still connected to her device, allowing her to survey the action taking place across the battlefield. And it wasn't good.

Three of her bots had already suffered too much damage to continue, flashing error messages alongside fuzzy pictures of the ground where they lay. A fourth was barely holding on, its systems going critical amidst a hail of gunfire. The fifth and final bot, however, stood strong, its systems stable with no pursuers in sight.

Scar wasted no time, rerouting the bot to their location and giving it a new core imperative: to take down as many officers as it could. In between keystrokes, Scar glanced up at her sister through the cluster of bodies, making sure she was alright. But Burn was strong. Despite the bullet in her leg, she wasn't giving up. In fact, the injury seemed to spur her on, fueling her strikes and lending fire to her blows.

As Scar watched, Burn pulled herself up, balancing on her uninjured leg with the support of the wall beside her. She grimaced, the move clearly paining her, but she didn't back down. Instead, she unsheathed a wooden stick that she'd lashed to her back. Taking aim, she brought it down on an unsuspecting officer, ripping the gun from his hands. The weapon clattered to the ground, and Burn lunged for it, letting out a grunt as her shattered leg slammed against the dirt road.

Yet she didn't allow the discomfort to slow her down. Her fingers closed around the weapon and she turned, rolling onto her back to aim at her disarmed foe. The man realized her intention and moved to kick the gun from her grasp, but she was quicker. As Scar watched, Burn let two bullets fly, striking the man in the shoulder and the gut. He fell, toppling onto Burn as his momentum carried him downward.

Burn shoved the man off her battered body, dealing an extra blow to his head to ensure that he no longer posed a threat. She pushed herself up against the wall and sought another target, her face determined. It was clear she could take care of herself.

With her sister's safety secure, Scar returned her attention to her own efforts. The PeaceBot was on its way, winding toward her through the narrow streets, but Scar knew it would take more than a single droid to save them. So she dove back into her bag, searching for a weapon.

Her hand grazed the cool metal of several coins, which had fallen loosely to the bottom of her pack. A small smile crept onto her lips as she grabbed them, yanking them out into the dim light. Despite their diminutive size, the faux currency felt strangely powerful in her hand, and a shiver of eager anticipation ran through her.

Pushing off the wall, she snaked through the sea of

frightened people, winding her way toward the rear flank. Her progress was slow, with scared families and refugees huddled together in shivering clumps, trying desperately to sink into the shadows. Those that could were using their gifts to fend off the enemy's advances. They filled the space with sudden gusts of wind or cyclones of fire or bright bangs of light so fierce they blinded both friend and foe for seconds at a time.

It was bedlam, madness, a hellscape of fire and blood. Shots punctuated the night as officers fired blindly into the unarmed crowd, and screams echoed through the streets as the bullets tore apart flesh and sanity in equal measure.

Finally, Scar reached the tail end of the battle, placing herself just inside the safety of the pack. Shouting a warning to her own troops to take cover, she let loose her barrage of coins, aiming her fury at the clusters of officers bearing down on them. Scar watched as the coins sailed through the air between them, landing with unheard clinks at the soldiers' feet.

A heartbeat later, a shudder shook the street as the coins exploded, sending the men flying. Some collided sickly with walls before sliding limply to the ground. Others met each other in the air, bodies crashing in wet thuds of flesh against flesh, armor against armor. Some were merely swept off their feet, thrown to the ground in violent crashes that were strong enough to stun.

Even Scar found herself staring up at the tier's dark ceiling, her legs brushed from beneath her in the sudden wave of pressure. Her ears rang from the blast, making the world feel disjointed around her. Yet as she leveraged herself up, the scene came into focus.

The Lunaria – and her final tenacious bot – had pounced amidst the confusion, leaping to ambush the downed officers while they lay stunned in the dirt.

Then, through the comms, a growling voice burst through. "The front is clear. Get ready to move," said Hale, panting. "And make sure we're not followed," he commanded, almost as an afterthought.

Hoisting herself up, Scar craned her neck to see toward the front line, but she could only catch glimpses of movement through the mass of figures. Trusting the others to guard the rear, she took a step toward her sister, only then realizing that a sharp sliver of steel debris had embedded itself into her left thigh. She attempted to yank the shard free, but it wouldn't budge. Tearing at her pants, she saw that the chunk had fused with the metal of her leg to form one unbreakable piece, adding yet more steel to her cold metallic skin.

Sighing, she gave up on her attempts to dislodge the fragment and instead twisted her way back through the crowd, careful not to cut her comrades with her newly weaponized leg. Alongside her, the group also started to move, first inching along the lane, then quickening to a soft run. Scar continued her push forward, dodging the sections of street still smoldering with flames and sidestepping the downed officers that littered the ground.

Eventually, Scar emerged at the front. She noticed with some degree of bewilderment that Hale had swept Burn up into his arms and was carrying her through the street, cradling her injured form like a child who was too weak to run. It seemed out of character – both for Hale and her sister – and Scar wondered for the first time what had happened out in the wildlands.

Shaking her head, she decided that was a question for a later time. Now they needed to get to safety, and she knew just where that was. Drawing alongside Hale, she spared one curious glance at Burn before taking the lead, resuming her place as captain of the crew.

"Follow me," she said over her shoulder to Hale, imbuing her voice with authority. "There's a safe house nearby we can use."

This hadn't been the plan. The plan had been to whisk Burn and Hale up through the city, ferrying them to a more secure site to regroup, but this would have to do. Plans were, after all, made to be broken.

With Hale and Burn and the rest of their motley group in tow, Scar raced through the main thoroughfare and up to the next level before darting once again into the maze of side streets. She made her way up one more tier, pausing briefly to ensure everyone was still accounted for before taking off toward the outskirts of the city.

Their Corax End safe house glowed like a beacon in the night. After making sure they hadn't been followed, Scar scanned her finger and held the door open for the ragged procession. More than 30 people filtered in, followed by a weary-looking Nara and a disheveled Kaz.

The relief that came from closing the door behind her was acute. Removing her mask, Scar drew in her first full breath in what felt like hours. Her head pounded in the sudden silence, and she watched as all around her figures collapsed onto the cool floor.

They were in rough shape. Burns and cuts and bullet

wounds marred exposed flesh, and blood tinged the air with its metallic scent. Some cried, some shook, some stared blankly at the walls. Others held the bodies of those they'd lost, while more mourned for those they'd left behind.

The stimuli was a lot for Scar, and she battled against her body's instincts to shut down or run away or withdraw into the confines of her own mind. She knew that she couldn't disappear, no matter how much she might crave the safety of solitude. For once she needed to stay – and that fact frightened her more than all of the Peace Force's weapons combined.

There was a sudden sound from beyond the door, and Scar turned, a sharp terror rushing through her at the thought that they'd been followed. As she looked through the peep hole, though, she realized it was yet more of the Lunaria, beaten and bruised, seeking shelter from the storm.

She rapidly opened the door, granting access to the wounded battalion. They filed in one by one, each looking grimmer than the last, until all the troops were nestled safely inside. Scar hurriedly shut the door behind them before turning back to the now-crowded space.

Someone had unlocked the doors on each side of the hallway, and people spilled into the adjoining rooms, strewn over floors and moth-eaten couches. Scar gingerly stalked forward, her eyes set on the large room in which they'd met only several nights before. In the blink of an eye, it had transitioned to a makeshift infirmary, with the sounds of tearing cloth and murmured pleas drifting through the hall.

Scar wanted to find Burn. Her sister would know what to do – or at least have some idea of their next steps forward.

But when she caught sight of Cali, all other thoughts rushed from her mind.

The woman was white as a sheet, seated against a wall and barely conscious. Her right hand was clasped tightly over her left shoulder, but it wasn't enough to stem the flow of blood that was coursing down her arm and onto the floor.

Kneeling, Scar gently peeled Cali's hand from the wound and ripped away the tatters of her shirt, exposing her torn flesh. What she saw made her blanch, and she had to fight back the nausea that sprang to life in her gut.

A bullet had torn through Cali's shoulder, piercing skin and muscle, and exposing bone. With shaking hands, Scar gently tilted the woman away from the wall to peer at her back, and Cali moaned in pain. The sound of her friend's agony sent a guilty stutter through Scar's body, but she tamped it down, taking a deep breath to steady herself.

"You're going to be OK," she told Cali in her best attempt at a comforting tone. "The bullet went straight through. As long as we can control the bleeding, you'll be fine. I'm sure Crete will be able to fix you up in no time."

She hoped she sounded more certain than she felt. As softly as she could, she positioned the woman back against the wall, leaning her on her side to avoid aggravating the exit wound. She glanced around, searching for Crete, but the healer was nowhere to be seen. Scar prayed he was just off tending to the others – or recovering from the toll his gift took. She couldn't bring herself to imagine the worst: that he'd been claimed by the battlefield, yet another soul lost to the vagaries of war.

Not knowing what else to do, Scar shrugged out of her

cloak and held it to Cali's wound, hoping to stem the bleeding. Some of the light had returned to Cali's eyes by then, and she gave a weak smile before pushing Scar's hands away.

"I can take it from here," she whispered, her voice hoarse yet resolute. "You should be with your sister."

Scar gave her a questioning look, and Cali responded with a small nod. Rising to her feet, she spared one more glimpse at her friend before turning her attention to the room.

Looking out at the injured and broken, the wounded and dying, something potent rose up within her. It wasn't guilt or pity or contrition. It was anger, hot and bright, and it pulsed through her in rapid bursts. Something that had been lingering at the edges of her mind finally clicked into place, and she stepped into the middle of the room, scanning the sea of desolate faces.

"We have a traitor in our midst," she shouted, drawing all eyes to her with her sudden declaration. "This attack wasn't random. It was deliberate. The Peace Force knew where we were going to be. They knew about the decoy explosions and our plans to break through the dome. They had it all figured out."

Those that were able stared back at her with shocked expressions, eyes wide and mouths agape as they took in her words. As Scar turned to meet their gazes, more details fell into place, fueling her rage.

"And it wasn't just tonight!" she cried, as much to herself as to the crowd before her. "I couldn't figure out how Burn had gotten caught during her mission, even with a buffoon as a partner. But now I see. The Peace Force knew that they were coming. They knew the whole plan all along, and they were waiting for them!"

Scar could almost see the cogs turning as the Lunaria's expressions evolved from confusion to disbelief to anger. They knew she was right. They knew they were harboring a spy. Some people shifted uncomfortably on the ground, while others openly glared around them, as if they could suss out the traitor with a glance.

"Someone even thwarted our efforts to stall the airflow repairs!" she continued, gaining momentum. "This person sold us out, telegraphing our every move to our enemies. I bet the Peace Force knows everything! Our names, our ideas, our plans to bring them down. They've weaseled their way into the Lunaria, and they'll use their spy to make sure we pay."

A wave of unease passed over the room as the group realized the precarious hand they'd been dealt. They weren't safe. They weren't free. They had been betrayed.

Scar was about to continue her tirade when another voice chimed in from behind her.

"You're right," said Burn, her voice calm despite the chaos. "The traitor is here in this room."

Scar twisted her head to face her sister, a questioning look in her eyes. "How do you know?" she asked, squinting down at Burn. "You haven't been here. How could you possibly know?" She didn't mean it as an accusation, merely a statement of fact.

"Because I can read it in their thoughts," Burn said simply, as if it was something one did every day.

Scar stared at her sister, truly seeing her for the first time since she'd come back into the city. Burn was on the ground, her injured leg held gently in Hale's large hands. Not only was Burn fine with that, but she actually appeared content. She was also leaner than she had been before, with curved muscles apparent beneath her shirt and a new hardness to her face. And, apparently, she could read minds.

Scar wondered again what had happened in the wildlands. What had Burn gone through to change her so drastically? What had she faced that took that kind of toll? She opened her mouth to ask, but Burn beat her to the punch, drawing the attention of the room as she spoke.

"He's scared. He knows there's nowhere to run," she said, closing her eyes for a brief moment as if listening to something only she could hear. Opening them once more, she turned her head slowly, scanning the room until she locked on her target: Raqa.

Chapter 24

Everything was so clear inside Raqa's head. He was terrified, which made Burn's job easy. It felt like he was projecting his thoughts directly to her, giving her access to everything he'd done.

He'd been working with the Peace Force for months. After he'd joined the Lunaria, he'd approached them with an offer. In return for his service, they'd promised to pay him handsomely, rewarding his espionage with a house and a job and a comfortable life on a respectable tier. The decision to betray the Lunaria had been simple.

At first it had been small things. He wasn't privy to everything the Lunaria did, but as time passed and he gained their trust, he'd been able to feed their enemies more and more. The location of a safe house here, the identity of an operative there. Piece by piece, he'd meticulously undermined their entire operation, all while giving nothing away to the operatives inside.

His big break had come when they'd agreed to sabotage the ventilation system. The Peace Force had salivated over that intel, all but throwing money his way. Yet, despite the information, they hadn't been able to thwart the Lunaria's efforts completely. They'd blamed that on Raqa. A spy, after all, was a convenient scapegoat.

After that, they'd put the pressure on him to bring down the Lunaria once and for all. And he'd tried. He'd fed them every tidbit he could learn about the Lunaria's efforts to keep the airflow systems offline. He'd dismantled his own Peace-Bots to gain their trust. And he'd cast doubt upon Scar's theories about the wildlands, discouraging any plans to look into things the Peace Force wanted hidden.

Of course, Scar's desire for secrecy – and her tendency to work alone – had put a wrench in his plans. He'd wanted to know what she was up to, wanted to learn what she knew, but until recently she hadn't been willing to share. When he'd finally learned of Scar's plan to bring people back into the city, he'd tried to sidetrack that, as well, before realizing that he could use it to his advantage.

The Peace Force had latched onto the plan like leeches desperate for blood. Raqa's lack of specifics, however, had been more than a little frustrating. So they'd given him an ultimatum: Help the Peace Force take down the Lunaria and any refugees from the wildlands, and he'd finally be free to live a life of luxury. So as soon as he'd received the coordinates, he had relayed them to the Peace Force, and they'd attacked.

Coming back to herself, Burn processed what she'd seen. Raqa had been responsible for everything – her getting thrown into the Pit, the attack on the Lunaria, the death of her friends. A picture of Mika, pale and still and covered in blood, flashed before her eyes, and she tried to lunge at the man. Her claws met with empty air, however, as her wounded leg gave way beneath her and she fell, landing with a thud on the wooden floor.

"He's been betraying us all along," she gritted through barred teeth, letting more able-bodied members restrain him as he tried uselessly to flee. Ansel and Coal each took hold of a shoulder, forcefully encouraging him to stay where he was. He struggled but eventually saw the futility and went limp, resigning himself to his fate.

Burn watched as her sister absorbed the information, her expression shifting from confusion to understanding to rage. With a small nod to Burn, Scar turned to face Raqa. In three long strides, she was across the room. Before anyone knew what was happening, she'd punched the man squarely in the jaw, sending his head flying back with a painful snap.

A small cheer went up around the room, and she smiled, evidently proud of herself. To be honest, Burn was proud of her, too.

Burn was exhausted. It had been a trying few days, sapping her energy both physically and mentally until she felt like a shell of herself.

Following the battle, they'd relocated to one of the safe houses that had been exempt from Raqa's espionage. There, they'd been able to regroup, gaining strength and willpower and securing some desperately needed rest.

Her leg was healing slowly, aided by the careful administrations of the healer, Crete, who had blessedly made it through the battle in one piece. After they'd removed the bullet from her leg, he'd been able to close the wound enough to stop the bleeding and start her on the path to recovery. It still hurt like hell, and she couldn't walk without the support of a rather ugly old cane, but it would heal. She just had to give it time.

Others hadn't been so lucky.

Altogether, the Lunaria and the refugees had lost roughly a quarter of their ranks. Like Mika and his mother. And the man who had wanted so badly to see his daughter. And so many others who had counted on Burn to bring them home. Many more had survived, reuniting with their families and finding their way back home. Some had even stayed on, pledging their loyalty and their fealty to the group that had saved them.

Still, the losses weighed on Burn. She felt like she should have done more to protect them, or else never have convinced them to join her in the first place. Nara told her that that way of thinking would get her nowhere, that those people had known the risk they were taking. Yet she didn't feel like she'd ever truly forgive herself for their deaths.

She was coming to see that this was the true burden of leadership. People put their lives into her hands and, no matter how hard she tried, she could never hold onto them all. Some of them were bound to slip through her fingers, and it was up to her to make sure that their deaths weren't in vain.

Burn had spent the hours and days since the battle

putting her gift to use in hopes of salvaging the Lunaria's mission. One by one, she'd screened the members, sifting through their thoughts in search of any acts of defiance, any hints of treachery. But it appeared that Raqa had been acting alone, a sole insurgent in a society of rebels.

Yet even a man acting alone can do an untold amount of damage. Most of the members' identities were compromised, as were many of their safe houses and undercover missions. They'd been crippled, brought to their knees by one man and forced into the darkness.

Then again, the darkness wasn't always a bad place to be. Under the threat of discovery, the Lunaria had been forced together, pushed to re-examine their priorities and their problems, and pressed into finding new ways to resolve them.

Burn wanted to be part of that solution. In fact, she'd begged to help, needing to surround herself with ideas and immerse herself in change. Yet her gift made her useful in other ways.

No one was certain how long their souped-up powers would last. Without direct exposure to the planet's harsh atmosphere, Burn's mind-reading could start to dwindle in a matter of days. It wasn't a situation anyone had ever experienced before, and no one was quite sure how it worked, but they weren't going to let the opportunity pass them by.

That was how Burn had ended up in a tiny cell, staring into Raqa's mind. It wasn't a pleasant task. She didn't want to see behind his eyes, to witness the treachery he'd taken part in, but she was the only one who could manage it. So she sat there, hour after hour, combing through his thoughts.

After two days, she knew Raqa better than he knew

himself. His childhood, his family, his gift. Burn had once thought he resembled Scar, that their minds functioned in similar ways, but she had been wrong. Raqa's thoughts were dark, and his gift was fueled by the creation of discord rather than the creation of beauty. He wanted to see others suffer. He wanted to be part of it.

Burn tore herself away from his mind, relishing the absence of his poisonous thoughts. Rubbing her eyes, she got unsteadily to her feet, her leg protesting the sudden change in position.

Raqa sat in front of her, chained to the wall. He looked gaunt and hollow, with dark circles under his eyes and a deep purple bruise climbing his jawline. Over the last several days, Burn had shoved her consciousness into him, tearing him inside out as she'd sifted through his memories. She wasn't sorry for the toll it had taken. He deserved it – along with so much more. Thankfully, Burn had an idea of how the Lunaria could repay him.

Turning, Burn knocked on the door to the makeshift cell, beckoning the guard to let her out. But before he could get there, Raqa spoke, yanking Burn's attention back to him.

"You'll never win," he croaked, shaking his head in disdain.

Burn was half surprised that he had enough strength left to speak – and enough gall left to bait her so blatantly. Instead of reacting, however, she merely stared at him, a blank expression plastered on her face. Behind her, the door opened as the guard finally reached it, but she didn't move, focusing her attention on the traitor at her feet.

"They are stronger and smarter and more coordinated

than you will ever be. They will always be a step ahead," he spat, daring her to fight back.

Burn didn't respond. It helped that she could see the words before he spoke them, see them forming in his head, filled with malice and disdain. Yet she let him get them out, let him speak, let him believe he had power.

"I'm not sorry for siding with them," he continued, proud of himself for his small display of courage. "I bet on the right horse. One day soon, they will crush you. And you will have nothing to show for your actions – nothing but blood and pain and carnage. They will rip you to shreds, and I'll be there to see it all, watching as they tear you limb from limb."

"No one is coming for you," Burn said evenly, the corners of her mouth twitching upward in a satisfied smirk.

"Of course they are," Raqa shot back, clearly agitated. "I've been indispensable to the Peace Force. Once they notice I'm gone, they'll know you've taken me, and they won't stop searching until they find you."

Burn bent down to Raqa's level, her eyes boring into his. "They don't care about you. They don't care about anyone. All that matters to them is power." She could see that Raqa wanted to fight back, but she raised her hand to silence him.

"I can guarantee you that no one will notice you're gone. You will rot in this cell, and no one will care – not your family or your friends or your precious Peace Force. Because we are stronger than you know, and we won't let anyone stand in our way."

She got to her feet, the movement sending a shock of pain through her leg. She swallowed the cry that rose to her lips and strode out the door, refusing to show weakness.

Once she was clear of the cell, she breathed a sigh of relief, closing her eyes and enjoying the luxury of silence. After a long moment, she roused herself and began her climb to the upper floor, leaning heavily on her cane for support. Cresting the top of the stairs, she took a second to recover before following the sound of conversation to the front of the house.

Turning the corner into the main room, Burn could see that congress was in session. The committee that had been convened to find a solution to their current woes sat in a circle, debating their next move. Debating, but not deciding.

Burn stepped into the circle, interrupting a man who was proposing that they storm the Peace Station in hopes that the element of surprise would grant them success. Scar sat on the opposite side of the circle, showering silent censure on the man and his idiotic plan. Burn gave her sister a brief smile before looking around at the rest of the circle.

Meera, Cali, Hale, and Ansel were also present, along with Nara and a few delegates from the wildlands. The rest of the circle was comprised of tenured Lunaria operatives, who considered her carefully.

"We can't turn Raqa on the Peace Force," she began, getting straight to the point – a tactic she knew Scar would appreciate. "And he would never agree to being a triple agent, even if we thought we could trust him. But the good thing is, we don't have to turn him in order to use him."

The group stared at her, their tired minds not following her train of thought. So she connected the dots for them.

"Have any of you met Eyana?" She glanced around the circle, seeing several members nod. Others merely looked at her in confusion, unsure what this new topic had to do with the last.

"Eyana can transform anyone into anyone else," she clarified. "Eyana can turn someone into Raqa. So instead of a double agent serving the Peace Force, we have a double agent serving the Lunaria. We feed them lies, misdirects, half-truths. We place them right where we want them."

Nara smiled at her encouragingly, seeing where she was going. Others, however, weren't so certain.

"But changing someone's face won't convince them," Ansel piped up, always ready to take the dissenting role. "This person would have to live Raqa's life, do his job, go home to his family. They'd have to be convincing on every level."

Burn tilted her head and smirked, prepared for this particular argument. "Good thing I know everything there is to know about him. Anyone we send in can be briefed on his entire life."

"It's an interesting idea," Meera chimed in, adding her voice to the mix. "But it'll still be risky. You can never fully prepare someone for a role like this. Even if you think you know everything about him, there will still be hurdles. Whoever takes up this position will be in great danger. Any missteps could spell disaster – or even death."

Burn thought about that for a beat, her excitement tempered by Meera's wise words.

"The risks are significant," she acknowledged, nodding slowly. "But this could be the opportunity we've been waiting for. The Peace Force trusts Raqa. He's provided them good intel. They'll listen to what he has to say. And they might even reveal their own plans against us in hopes that Raqa will help the force facilitate them. We could learn more than we have in a year. Who knows? Maybe we could even get enough intel to take them down."

The room went quiet as the group considered her speech. Glancing around at her colleagues and friends, she willed them to accept her words, to see the possibilities beyond the perils.

After a minute of silent debate, Meera slowly rose from her chair and plodded to Burn's side. The move was oddly reassuring, and Burn found herself gulping down a lump in her throat.

"I think Burn's plan is a good one," her friend stated, smiling grimly at the group. "We've been put in difficult circumstances. Our numbers are diminished, our identities compromised, our friends and families endangered. If one man was able to do all of that *to* us, just think what he could do *for* us. This could finally tip the odds in our favor. This could be the beginning of the end."

Murmurs of conversation swept across the space as people considered their options. On the one hand, they could do nothing, lying in wait for the Peace Force to find them and finish the job. On the other, they could act, seizing their chance to secure a spy in the ranks of their enemies. For Burn, the decision was simple.

When she sensed the deliberations were nearing their end, Burn called for a vote. "All in favor, please raise your hands," she declared, casting a glance around the room.

The mood was tentative at first, but it quickly transformed into resolution. One by one, hands went up around the circle until nearly all of them were raised. Burn nodded in acceptance.

"Motion passed," she said, a sliver of gratification thrumming through her. "Now we just have to decide who to send in."

It was a simple statement, yet it sent the room back into a cold silence. No one wanted to be the one to give up their identity for his, to forfeit the safety of the shadows for the danger of the front lines. Burn let her eyes drift once more around the room, seeking a delegate, an envoy, a spy. Yet all hands had mysteriously dropped as the once-brave soldiers shied away from the role.

Then a voice behind her broke the silence and stole her breath in one fell swoop.

"I'll do it," said Hale, rising to enforce his offer.

Burn didn't want to turn, didn't want to face him. She knew it was selfish, but she didn't want it to be Hale. Yet the others were already nodding their agreement, voicing their praise for his sacrifice. They knew he was a good fit, and they made their approval clear.

Reluctantly she turned, raising her head to look at him. The eyes that met hers were soft yet resolute. He had made up his mind, and there was no changing it. She could see that clearly.

Still, she had to fight against the urge to bite back, to deny him his chance to change the tides of war. She almost regretted proposing the motion, having not foreseen this conclusion – or the toll it would take on her.

Finding herself unable to speak, Burn simply gave a tight-lipped smile, devoid of cheer, and nodded. It was resignation more than approval, an understanding rather than acceptance. This was his choice, and it wasn't her place to stop him.

There was no need to vote on Hale's appointment to the role. Since he was the only candidate, his offer was taken as fact, and the meeting quickly tapered, devolving into a string of well-wishes and hopes for his safe return. Then one by one the crowd thinned, each member seeking solitude to contemplate their near escape. Because their identities were safe; their lives would continue. The same could not be said for Hale.

Before Burn knew it, they were alone, surrounded by nothing but silence and empty chairs.

"Burn, I..." Hale began, but she shook her head to stop him.

"You don't need to explain," she said, staring up at his rough face and trying to memorize its curves. "I know why you did it. I can see it in your mind."

"But I want to tell you. I want to explain," he responded, seeking approval in her eyes.

Burn shrugged as a wave of exhaustion rolled over her. Suddenly, standing required too much effort, so she made her way to the curve of chairs and collapsed, the metal groaning under her sudden weight. Hale sat gently on the seat next to her, angling his body toward hers with his hands in his lap.

"I love you," he said simply, his eyes locked steadfastly to hers.

Even though Burn had heard it in his mind, out loud those words had a power, a presence that beckoned to her and begged her to respond. She resisted their call, however, unwilling to be sidetracked by their lure.

"So that means you have to leave?" she asked, sounding tired and worn.

"It means I want to be better. A better man, a better leader. And to do that I can't let someone else risk their life for us – not when I could do the job just as well, if not better. I've been in someone else's body. I know what that's like, and I know how to handle it. And I'll still have my strength. If anything goes wrong, I am the best suited to get out of there alive."

Burn knew what he said was true, but that didn't make his choice any easier.

"Don't you see?" he continued, as if begging her to understand. "I'm finally certain of something. I know what I need to do. And that is all thanks to you. You gave me the strength to be the kind of leader the Lunaria need. You gave me a reason to fight."

"I don't want you to leave," Burn responded, itching to reach out and clasp his hands in hers. "I need you."

Hale let out a light chuckle, and this time the low rumble made Burn's heart tighten, as if it were trying to hold onto the sound.

"You don't need anyone," he said, shaking his head as he smiled.

Burn and Scar sat in silence on the cool ground. They didn't need to talk, despite the fact that each had so much to say. In that moment, none of it seemed important.

What mattered was that they were there. Together. The

rest would fall into place in time.

For now, words seemed too mundane, too thin, too empty to describe their fullness. It was as if, in each other's company, order had been restored and balance regained amidst the howling storm.

That's not to say they felt no sadness. They mourned in their own ways, each grieving the people they'd been and the parts of themselves they'd lost along the way. Yet they rejoiced in what they'd found.

After an eternity of stillness, Burn was the first to speak.

"Dad...didn't make it," she began, barely managing to speak the words before their power overcame her.

Scar simply nodded, speaking volumes despite her silence.

"He was trying to get back to us," she continued, as much for her own benefit as for Scar's. Out in the wildlands, she hadn't had the chance to fully process the loss, to give in to the anguish and drown in the despair. Now it stared at her, willing her to look, to feel.

Again, Scar nodded, taking solace in the silence.

"He told them about us, though – the people of the wildlands. He said that I was brave, and you were clever. And together we'd change the world."

Scar finally chose that moment to speak. "He was wrong," she said plainly.

"What do you mean?" Burn countered, confused. "You don't think we can change the world?"

Despite being able to see flashes of her sister's thoughts, she was no closer to understanding Scar. Most of the time that was fine, but now her comment stung, as if she had no faith in their mission, no confidence in the cause.

"It's not that," Scar clarified, giving her sister a wry smile. "But my cleverness – it's a part of my gift. It's like saying that you're a great listener. It's an accident of birth."

It was Burn's turn to be silent. She understood what Scar was saying, but she couldn't tell where she was going. So she did what she did best: She listened.

"You, on the other hand, found a way to survive in the wildlands. You made friends, found love, learned how to fight. You inspired those people to follow you. You found your way home. That's true cleverness."

Scar wasn't saying these things to flatter Burn. She was stating a fact, at least as she saw it. Yet Burn was flattered, nonetheless.

"And what about you?" Burn asked, turning the tables on her sister. "You captured PeaceBots, explored the outer reaches of the dome, crafted an army and led them into battle. I think you might be the bravest person I know."

Scar just snorted, rolling her eyes at the sentiment, but Burn could tell by the small upturn of her sister's lips that she was pleased – both with the compliment and with herself.

"And what about changing the world?" Burn asked. "Do you think we're up for it?"

Scar scoffed. "Look around you," she commanded, pointing at the families they'd reconnected and the rebels they'd inspired. "I think we already have."

AUTHOR'S NOTE
& Acknowledgments

This whole process has been a whirlwind. Writing *Burn this City* and founding Glass Fish Publishing was basically akin to jumping out of a plane (which is something I've actually done, thank you very much). It was nerve-wracking and exhilarating and scary as hell, and I had no idea what I was getting myself into.

With *Burned and Scarred*, I was still finding my way through the metaphorical maze, but I was also able to take a step back and enjoy the process. The simple fact is that I love to write. To me, words are beautiful and powerful and evocative. They draw you in. They entertain you. They move you. They make you want to be better.

Like Maya Angelou said, there is no greater agony than bearing an untold story inside you. And, to me, there is no greater joy than putting that story down on paper and setting it free. I am delighted that I have been able to do that not once, but twice. And, hopefully, I'll be able to continue for many years to come.

That's not to say that this whole process has been pure bliss. It's been a struggle each day, trying to find the courage to be creative and the confidence to put my words out there – especially these days. COVID ransacked my life. Like Burn, I understand the pain of being deemed unessential. I understand the uncertainty and the loneliness and the desperate ache for things to return to the way they once were. Yet I also understand the beauty in change and the freedom in having one's life turned upside down.

Burned and Scarred is about loneliness, change, and finding your way through a strange and unfamiliar world. That theme is universal. It's something all of us have struggled with – not only during COVID, but throughout our lives. But this story is also about adventure and love and surrounding yourself with people that you trust. Because those are the things that quell the loneliness and help you find your way through the darkness.

So thank you to the people who have helped make this book – and this journey – such an incredible adventure. Thank you to my husband, Robert, who put up with me through months of quarantine. Thank you to my friends, who have acted as editors and beta readers and cheerleaders. (Particular thanks to Kinnon Schreiber, Kayla Suhm, Robert Herlache, and Greg Poppy.) And thank you to my family, who have supported me by enthusiastically telling everyone they've ever met about my books.

Thank you, also, to my online family – my #bookstagram crowd, my advanced readers, and those who have taken the time to write such amazing reviews.

As an indie author, it's hard to gain traction in a world run by the Big Five publishers. Even the smallest bit of support goes a long way. If you've enjoyed this book, please consider leaving a review on Amazon.

If you want to do more, you can follow Glass Fish Publishing on Instagram, like us on Facebook, or join our mailing list at *glassfishpublishing.com.*

Thank you for your support! And stay tuned for news on the final installment of the *Burn this City* trilogy!

ABOUT THE AUTHOR

Brenda Poppy has spent more than a decade writing and editing for publications across the country, as well as lending her writing and graphic design talents to companies to help them craft their brands. With a degree in journalism and sociology from Marquette University, she loves to seek out unique stories and capture them for others to enjoy. When not writing, the Milwaukee native can be found acting in local theater, spending time with her adorable corgi, Darcy, or traveling around the world with her husband in search of craft cocktails, good food, and inspiration for her next novel.

Connect with Glass Fish Publishing on Facebook and Instagram, or join our mailing list at *glassfishpublishing.com*!

Made in the USA
Las Vegas, NV
02 April 2021